THE FIREBIRD'S FEATHER

THE FIREBIRD'S FEATHER

Marjorie Eccles

This first world edition published 2014
in Great Britain and the USA by
SEVERN HOUSE PUBLISHERS LTD of
19 Cedar Road, Sutton, Surrey, England, SM2 5DA.
Trade paperback edition
first published in Great Britain and the USA 2015 by
SEVERN HOUSE PUBLISHERS LTD.

British Library Cataloguing in Publication Data

Eccles, Marjorie author
    The firebird's feather.
    1. Murder–Investigation–Fiction. 2. Aristocracy (Social
    class)–Fiction. 3. Family secrets–Fiction. 4. Great
    Britain–History–George V, 1910-1936–Fiction.
    5. Russia–History–1904-1914–Fiction. 6. Detective and
    mystery stories.
    I. Title
    823.9'14-dc23

ISBN-13: 978-07278-8426-8 (cased)
ISBN-13: 978-1-84751-534-6 (trade paper)
ISBN-13: 978-1-78010-578-9 (e-book)

Except where actual historical events and characters are being
described for the storyline of this novel, all situations in this
publication are fictitious and any resemblance to living persons
is purely coincidental.

Typeset by Palimpsest Book Pro‹
Falkirk, Stirlingshire, Scotland.

Prologue

Frosty winter evenings, patterns of ice forming on the window panes outside, fresh coal piled on the red embers, and the fire spurting sulphurous flames of blue and green. Then it seemed to Kitty as though magic was happening inside the warm cave of the nursery. It didn't matter that it was so cold outside, or that the leaping flames threw frightening, goblin shadows on to the ceiling, because she was curled up on Mama's lap before being tucked up in bed, mesmerised by the stories she told. The same stories *her* father, Nikolai, had told her, of how the two of them had fled Russia, wrapped warm as toast in furs and long felt boots, speeding across the miles of frozen wastes in a sleigh drawn by three horses kicking up clouds of snow, the sleigh-bells ringing and the driver's shouts of 'Hey, Hey, Hey!' echoing to the great dark forests that stretched forever on either side. Wolves lived in the forests, and bears, but none came out to attack them: they flew too fast, owing to the speed of their horses, which went like the wind.

Other, kinder creatures than wolves and bears might live in the forest, too, said Lydia, if you knew where to look: magical creatures like the great black horse with strength beyond imagining, the dove that told of peace and the delicate white animal with shining silver hooves, a horn on its head and magical powers, whose name was the unicorn. But you would need help from others along the journey to search for the secret, elusive firebird, a magnificent, fiery creature with the greatest of all magical powers, who lived far, far away. If you were lucky enough to find even one of his golden feathers it would lead you to the far-off, secret place where the great bird nested, and perhaps you would be granted your heart's desire, though sometimes the firebird could be malevolent, a bringer of doom, and your heart's desire might not come in the form you hoped for.

'Wishes are sometimes liars. They hold out too much hope, so always be careful what you wish for, little Katyusha,' said Mama, stroking Kitty's hair.

Sometimes she would take out one of her treasures, a black lacquer box with a marvellous likeness of the firebird applied to the lid, a glorious creature with a long, sweeping tail like a peacock's. Kitty, a little afraid, would cautiously stroke the feathers on its back, worked in gold wire and studded with tiny, winking rubies. Its breast was a blaze of yellow and golden-brown polished amber stones with more in red amber; its eyes were ruby and the crest on its head was surmounted by yet more rubies. The box looked as though it must hold exciting secrets but when you lifted the lid it was disappointingly empty and its interior was only cheap, plain wood, rather than fine polished cedar or some other beautiful lining you might have expected. Mama explained: Nikolai Kasparov had always said the contrast was deliberate; it was what he called a metaphor for the state of Mother Russia – splendour and luxury and heedless extravagance on the surface, while at its empty heart was poverty and cruel deprivation. Although the point would have been made more forcefully, Nikolai had added, if the interior of the box had revealed images of writhing snakes to demonstrate the seething discontent of the Russian people against the unimaginable suffering inflicted by their country's oppressive Tsarist regime. Revenge that was boiling up under the surface and would one day surely erupt.

Kitty hadn't understood then all of what she heard but she had always wished she had known her grandfather, who sounded so splendid. He had died before she was born and there was sadness in Mama whenever she spoke of him. The same passion that had driven Nikolai Sergeivitch Kasparov from the Motherland he loved so deeply, and had caused him to work ceaselessly and self-lessly to bring about a state where serfdom was banished and people could live in freedom, had seriously undermined his health. He had died in Britain, exiled, poor and penniless.

Kitty never questioned anything Lydia told her, not then. Her trust in her mother was complete.

One

May, 1911.

Summer arrived early that year, as if it couldn't wait to offer its own contribution to all the excitement of what was to happen in London.

Sunday. A shining May morning, everything suddenly burgeoning and green, promising yet another day of cloudless skies and unseasonably hot and summery weather. A day so lovely Kitty could hardly bear to be indoors. The cool shade of the private gardens beyond the railings in the square beckoned; even here in the drawing room you could smell the heady scent of the white and purple lilacs planted among the shrubs and the plane trees. She longed to be outdoors but she'd made a promise to herself not to leave the house, not even to cross the square; she was honour-bound not to, having fibbed her way out of going either to church or out horse riding with her mother, for reasons that wouldn't bear much scrutiny.

It was too quiet, even for Sunday. Bridget had consented to go to morning service with her own mother, Aunt Ursula, and Hester Drax was presumably singing hymns with the Methodists. Papa was out too, most likely at his club, certainly not at church – he didn't trouble himself with religion and only ever went under sufferance, for christenings, wedding and funerals, and there hadn't been any of those in the Challoner family for some considerable time. As for Mama, Lydia . . . well, Kitty didn't believe the Russian Orthodox Church had seen much of her lately, either. Today she was out riding in the Park with Marcus Villiers. Apart from the servants below stairs, Kitty had the house to herself.

Since that day, she had often wondered whether the major turning points of our lives are not pre-ordained. We believe we are making our own decisions, whether random or considered, that sometimes set us on courses which change our lives and possibly the lives of others. We think there is always choice, this way or that. But is it choice, an act of free will, or pre-destiny? Would it have made any difference, for instance, if she hadn't that day decided she'd had enough of everyone fussing around her and telling her what she must and must not do, enough of hearing about all the new rules she must henceforth observe as a young woman on the brink of a new life? If she hadn't felt, too, that she was being kept in the dark and needed to stifle her suspicions once and for all? Would it in some unforeseen way have prevented the appalling thing that happened?

Even if the chief reason she had stayed at home had been because she simply refused to be an unwanted third.

She had escaped both church and riding by saying she had a little headache. Lydia had looked at her – pink-cheeked, clear-eyed and perfectly healthy – and raised a sceptical eyebrow. Then her face cleared. 'Oh, I see! Poor Kitty! I'll get them to bring you a hot water bottle and you can lie down, darling,' she whispered, patting her cheek and making her cringe in case Marcus Villiers had overheard. But thankful as well that Mama seemed preoccupied today, otherwise she would have made a drama of the situation.

'I dare say you've been concentrating too much on our game, Miss Kitty,' was all Marcus said, however, while Kitty gathered up the cribbage board, cards and pegs. As usual there had been time and enough for a game between them while waiting for Lydia.

'I still didn't beat you.'

'Since I'm invited back for lunch you can look forward to claiming your revenge this afternoon. I hope your headache will have gone by then.'

Kitty had watched them go, Lydia looking wonderful as usual in her midnight blue, tailored riding habit with a white stock, her bowler hat set precisely straight on her brow, her glorious hair firmly pinned up beneath it, smiling at Marcus, tall and handsome, always ready to provide her with an escort. Not that you could truthfully call Marcus Villiers handsome. Lean and very dark, an intelligent face with watchful, grey eyes under black, heavy brows that came together rather too easily. Thick, long eyelashes, the sort a girl might envy. A firm jawline that hinted at stubbornness, and a humour that had a sardonic tinge. Getting a real smile from him was like getting blood from a stone. Kitty found both him and his interest in her mama – not to say her encouragement of him – an enigma. He was not at all like the usual sort of languid young man who found it fashionable to hang around older married women in a way Bridget said was not always platonic. But Kitty wouldn't let herself believe he was anything more to her mother than someone who was useful whenever she needed him to amuse her and pay her compliments, or simply to dance attendance on her in a general way. Except that he didn't pay compliments, pretty or otherwise; nor did he go out of his way to amuse. He was a sober young man of few words. As for Lydia . . . well, perhaps it was no stranger than other things around her mama lately.

One of her more maddening traits was that she was invariably late for everything, and she had lately sent Kitty to keep Marcus company until she was ready to put in an appearance, often as much as half an hour or more later. Patience was not something one automatically associated with Marcus Villiers, but he'd learnt enough by now to come prepared with a book, and to do him justice he put it aside readily enough when he saw Kitty. He was hardly a person she warmed to easily – and she wondered at her mother for not seeing this and almost forcing her to entertain him – but talking to him served its purpose; it helped her to polish her social manners, and if the conversation she practised on him fell somewhat short of the required wit and sparkle he was too polite to show that he noticed. This art of being agreeable – and above all amusing – it was constantly impressed upon Kitty, was an asset she would need when she officially 'came out', to entertain whomsoever she was placed next to at the dinner table, whether it be one of her papa's business acquaintances, an elderly family friend or one of the eligible young bachelors who were even now being lined up as 'possibles' for her, carefully selected by Aunt Ursula, Papa's sister, in her element with that sort of thing.

It was to be a summer of celebration. The time of mourning was over for genial, urbane King Edward, loved by all despite (or perhaps because of) his all-too-human frailties while he'd been Prince of Wales and later, king – and perhaps because his reign had been such a refreshing antidote to that of his strait-laced mother, Queen Victoria. He had been popular abroad too, his furthering of good relations with other European countries having earned him the name of Peacemaker. But he was now gone and preparations for the coronation in late June of the new King George and Queen Mary were in full swing. The knocking of hammers was audible the day long as spectator stands were being erected to line the royal processional route from Buckingham Palace to Westminster, along Whitehall and outside the Abbey. The flowerbeds in the royal parks and gardens were already ablaze with thousands of eye-catching bedding plants, public buildings had been smartened up and festooned with bunting, and iron railings painted and gilded. London was in the mood for celebration. So much so that even the women Papa called 'that bunch of pesky viragos' – those brave women who were daring to demand the vote for women, as well as men – seemed to be calling a truce on their window-breaking and other violent protests, and agreeing only to protest peaceably, at any rate for the time being.

The general excitement was infectious and she was caught up in it but even more important than the coronation was what would be happening to her, Ekaterina Challoner, this year.

Now that she was a young lady of eighteen, the preparations for her coming out were going ahead full steam. She was already wearing her hair up in a simple knot, the black ribbon bow to tie it up and her black stockings had gone forever, and she was trying hard to accustom herself to the detestable stays she must apparently be laced into henceforth in order to attain a graceful outline. Her schoolgirl blouses and skirts and white muslin party frocks had been replaced with delicious rows of new clothes hanging in the wardrobe – especially the ravishing dress destined for her own big dance. (Two hundred guests. Goodness knows how many cases of champagne. A grander house than their own being rented from Lady Dunstable for the occasion. Papa regularly declaring it was all going to bankrupt him!) The dress would be her first ball dress, in the newer, narrower fashion, with a high Empire waistline and a long trail of silk roses curving down the length of the skirt – still white, but supple satin, and shot through with shadows of the palest blue, and sometimes amethyst, in the folds. Everything was being arranged by Aunt Ursula, Lady

Devenish, who was to bring Kitty out and act as her chaperone, her position in society giving her the entrée for this. Because of it, she and Bridget had come up from the country at Christmas and were to stay until the end of her first Season.

So many preparations meant that Kitty was at the moment the centre of everyone's attention, which made her more impatient than she should have been. But at the same time she was looking forward – well, what young woman who liked pretty clothes and fun wouldn't be? – to the prospect of all the parties, dances, theatre visits and so on that were to come, everything that was to be her introduction into Society. Despite her total agreement with Bridget that these shenanigans, as Bridget called them, were nothing more than a marriage market which she herself, three years older than Kitty, had been forced to endure through two previous Seasons.

'Endure? What nonsense you talk, Bridget!' said Aunt Ursula, tracking them both down into Bridget's bedroom. It was a token protest. She must have been well used to these sort of remarks from her daughter by now but she couldn't let it pass. 'Of course you'll meet young men, Kitty, and someone who'll want to marry you. And what's wrong with that, pray? You don't want to be like my tiresome daughter here! And not for want of offers, either, to make matters worse!'

Bridget had merely smiled and said nothing. Of course she'd had offers – she was very good-looking, with smooth, dark wings of hair and a clear, pale complexion. She was also awfully clever and there was a place reserved for her in the autumn at Newnham College, Cambridge. As a woman she would be allowed to attend lectures and be granted a certificate, though not permitted to take a degree – but at least it was the first step into a male-dominated world, although she didn't express it quite like that to her mama. Her aim was higher education first of all, perhaps a career later, and if marriage came into it somewhere along the line, well and good. By which time it would be much too late, despaired her mother, incredulous that any young woman should voluntarily espouse spinsterhood, deliberately throw away her chances in life by choosing to do such an outlandish thing as going to a university. But Ursula was a widow, without a husband's backing against their wayward children. What had she done to deserve two such offspring, she was always asking. Not only Bridget but also Jon, who had been sent down from Cambridge for giving more attention to socialist politics than to his studies and was, if you please, presently editing some subversive newspaper and stubbornly refusing to use the title he had inherited from his father, Sir Alfred. She was no match for either, when they wanted their own way.

'I've rather let the side down, Mother, haven't I?' was Bridget's answer to Ursula's last remark. She didn't sound at all contrite and added, 'But don't try and avoid my horrid example, Kitty, by panicking and accepting the first one who proposes simply in order not to be left on the shelf.'

'Bridget, how can you *say* such – good gracious me, so this is what you are proposing to wear for the coronation? How extraordinary!'

Until then Ursula had been too busy talking to notice anything unusual. Now she was momentarily sidetracked as her eye alighted on the enormous, white hat, its crown frivolously covered in ruched chiffon and trimmed with velvet parma violets, delivered by the milliner and now lying on Bridget's bed with the white raw silk dress spread out beside it. There was nothing extraordinary about either dress or hat. In fact when Bridget had tried them on, Kitty had thought them both extremely smart, the dress narrow and modishly short enough to show an inch or two above the ankles. It was presumably the wide satin sash Aunt Ursula was referring to, in bands of purple and green, which Kitty suspected Bridget intended to wear, not around her waist, but crosswise over her bosom. It didn't seem to have occurred to her mother that the colours of the outfit – purple, green and white – were those chosen as their own by the Votes for Women campaigners. And that wearing them on that particular day would be an act of defiance, not to mention disrespect – the suffragettes, as the women who wanted universal suffrage were disparagingly called, being held in such abhorrence by the new king. Though it might possibly be repeated by many other daring women.

The dress was subjected to a closer inspection and eventually received a nod of approval at the cut and the way the seams were sewn. Ursula loved fashionable clothes, despite her own inability, unlike Lydia, to wear them with any sort of panache, and Bridget's dress allowance was generous. But her satisfied comments on the new outfit not having elicited any appreciable response, she switched her attention back to the previous conversation as if she'd never been deflected from it. 'I hope, Bridget,' she said severely, 'you won't let your uncle and aunt hear you speak like that. Left on the shelf, indeed!'

Kitty suspected her mother would simply laugh; it was the sort of thing she might have said herself. Papa, however . . .

They were not very much alike, Kitty's parents. Where Lydia was exuberant, unpredictable and extrovert, her father, Louis Challoner, was an amiable, unhurried and indeed rather indolent man who was taken to his offices in Bishopsgate each morning, made a lot of money and wanted nothing more than an untroubled existence along with his wife and daughter. He adored Lydia and she – well, he was a decade older than she was; he liked his creature comforts and was already settled well into middle age, set in his ways. Neither of them would expect Kitty to marry a man she didn't love but they did expect her to marry *someone* and were not encouraging when she asked what she should do if she didn't find the right man, Papa because he was a fuddy-duddy old thing who still thought women should adhere to the Victorian ideal of wifehood and motherhood, and Lydia because she no doubt knew where dangerous ideas could lead.

'Besides,' Aunt Ursula went on, 'dear Kitty was born too sensible, thank goodness, to do anything so rash as make an unsuitable choice.' She smiled approvingly.

She was correct, in one way. Too many of the young men considered eligible would be those Kitty had known as spotty, unprepossessing boys – her friends' brothers, or boys who had galumphed around with her at dancing classes – and there was no danger of her choosing any of *them*, however suitable a match! Sooner would she die an old maid. But afterwards, after the excitement of her first entry into adult life had subsided, what would there be to occupy her time, even if she were to be married? The tedium she had felt throughout the last impatient years, waiting to grow up, would simply continue in a different form. Idle days filled with shopping for new clothes and other luxuries, a succession of parties, dinners, balls, Saturdays-to-Mondays at country houses, and other pointless occasions.

Becoming a society hostess if she should be lucky to catch someone
ambitious and moneyed enough to want such a wife, and giving
him children, providing him with heirs?

When all the time she wished – how passionately she wished
– for a different life, one with meaning and purpose to it.

Other women never seemed to find those sort of routines
boring, even Lydia, but then, Papa allowed her freedom to arrange
her life as she chose. In addition to the usual trivial pursuits, she
had her passion for bridge (sometimes gambling rather reckless
sums, the only one of her activities Louis ever objected to), and
riding and exercising her horse – not to mention the hours she
spent working in her room with Hester Drax.

That thought took Kitty abruptly back yet again to something
she had witnessed a day or two previously: Lydia and Miss Drax
leaving the house together for some unspecified destination,
walking and not taking a hansom, even though it was raining
quite hard; Hester wearing a dismal mackintosh and her usual
sour expression, holding the umbrella over herself and Mama,
who had tucked her arm inside Hester's as they hurried away,
talking earnestly together. Nothing wrong in that – except that
a lady and her maid didn't normally walk arm in arm, even if
you were Lydia and it was only for the comfortable convenience
of sharing an umbrella.

The Challoner house was brick built, tall and dignified, situated
in Egremont Gardens, a large, quiet square not far from Hyde
Park. Street noises were muffled by thick doors and heavy, luxurious window drapes and today, now that Mr Findlater from
two doors away had managed to get his motor car started and
had driven his dust-coated and motor-veiled passengers away in
clouds of smoke and a great deal of noise, the square was left to
its usual Sunday morning silence, undisturbed save for the distant
traffic sounds, church bells, the boom of clocks from Westminster,
the occasional clop of hooves as a carriage or a hansom drove
round the square or the yap of No. 22's fat pug as their footman
took it for its daily trot around the railed gardens. Indoors, too,
there were no sounds apart from the monotonous ticks of the
clocks Papa endlessly fussed with. The thick carpets hushed her
footsteps as Kitty trailed around; and she distinctly heard the soft

plop of falling rose petals from one of Lydia's lavish flower arrangements as they scattered, ruby red on to the wavy, richly banded deep green of polished malachite. Louis's generosity with money meant that Lydia, who worshipped anything beautiful and Russian that kept alive her origins, had filled the house with many similar, ornate pieces of furniture and ornaments. With enviable flair she had set them against fashionably pale walls, creating an effect that was much admired. Kitty carefully scooped the scattered rose petals together and threw them into a waste-paper basket, using her handkerchief to remove any traces they might have left on the semi-precious polished stone.

It was still not yet midday.

Tempting smells of Sunday lunch were escaping from behind the green baize door to the kitchen quarters. Half an hour and then everyone would be back home, and she had already frittered away nearly all the precious time she'd wangled, but still she couldn't nerve herself to do what she'd intended. Inside the house it was dark and cool with the blinds prissily drawn by Mrs Thorpe to prevent any fading of the upholstery and carpets. It seemed perverse to keep out the sun and she went from room to room, sending them shooting up again, opening the windows wider to let in more of the scent of the lilacs, not caring about the housekeeper's pursed lips. Finally, she made herself go upstairs.

But when her hand was on the knob of Lydia's door, she stopped. It wasn't forbidden to go into her mother's room when she wasn't there, but it was understood. She hesitated, went in, then closed the door behind her and leant back against the panels, feeling like the interloper she was.

Facing her was the icon on its stand in the corner that Mama called the *krasny ugol*, the beautiful corner. She professed to have given up on religion and there was no Bible or cross, no vigil lamp or other holy object to share the corner. Kitty had often wondered: was the icon a vestige of the faith she had been brought up to and in spite of what she said was reluctant to abandon, or was it superstition that made her keep it? Or even perhaps simply for decoration? It was very beautiful. The Madonna's gentle, sorrowing face under her unadorned veil was dim but haloed in gold leaf and the icon was elaborately decorated with precious stones.

She deliberately avoided looking at the writing desk and wandered to the dressing table where her mother sat in her red silk peignoir while Hester Drax brushed her hair or fixed it into its elaborate wide puffs and rolls. It came past her waist when it was down, thick, beautiful hair like pulled toffee, with golden, and sometimes red lights through it. Not like Kitty's – thick, that was true, but just uninterestingly fair. She had been told she had a regular profile and she knew she had good teeth; she was tall and had a slim figure, which admittedly gained interesting curves when she could be persuaded into the detested boning and lacing; but she was afraid that was as far as it went for her.

Restless and unsettled, she picked up the heavily chased silver hand mirror to view that regular profile but it seemed just the same as anyone else's. (The very mirror in which she'd caught Lydia several times lately studying her face as if seeing it for the first time, or seeing it in a different light. Smiling. Sometimes she also spent minutes staring out of the window at nothing.) Disappointed with her own reflection, as usual, Kitty sniffed at the various bottles and creams, stole a dab of Chypre to put on her wrist and then idly opened the inlaid, velvet-lined trinket box where Lydia kept her ambers. This she wouldn't mind: as a child Kitty had always been allowed to play with them as long as she was careful – her more valuable jewels, and the diamonds and the pearls Papa had given her were locked up in the safe in his study, and the lacquered firebird box was kept hidden in a drawer. The greatest value of these lay in their sentiment, because they had belonged to Lydia's own mother. Kitty had heard the story so often she could have recited it in her sleep . . .

Her Russian grandfather, Nikolai Kasparov, had been an intellectual, a young university professor who was foolish enough to encourage and support the left-wing revolutionary activity gathering momentum like a rising tide amongst his students. He was the son of a military officer of aristocratic lineage but he, too, had come to be sickened at the enforced feudal dependency of the working people by his homeland's ruling elite, and their cruel subjugation of the peasants. It came to the point where he could no longer shut his eyes and he didn't hesitate to show his sympathies with those who rebelled. In consequence of this he had fallen foul of the authorities and had narrowly escaped imprisonment by fleeing to find sanctuary and permanent exile in England, crossing the snowbound miles to Finland from St Petersburg in a horse-drawn troika with his baby daughter Lydia wrapped in furs, her dead mother's jewellery in a chamois bag around his neck.

Kitty let them run through her fingers, her grandmother's bracelets, rings and brooches, pieces in different shapes and colours, though all of it was amber, mostly set in old, worked silver. A necklace of cherry amber beads; another as milky and opaque as butterscotch; a bracelet studded with shining cognac amber cabochons and a heavy ring set with an amber that was an unusual dark, bitter green. Best of all was a pendant piece suspended on a silver chain, clear and golden as honey, embedded in which was a minuscule, black insect, scarcely more than a speck, and a tiny sprig of delicate fern. When she was very young she used to cry for the poor little baby insect, simply alighting all unaware on a fern leaf when the tree resin that formed the amber had dropped stickily on to him, hardening and imprisoning both for all eternity.

Lydia sometimes shared her tears. She cried as easily as she laughed. She was a mercurial, quicksilver creature, a delight to be with when she was happy, possessed of a great sense of fun and humour, the sort of person who lit up every room she entered. On the other hand, there was no one more dismal than she when the moods of deep, Russian melancholy descended on her, bewildering easygoing Louis, who had never had a temperament in his life and was at a loss to comfort her when she was weighed down with a despair quite unknown to him. He waited patiently until it was all over. Although she had been spirited away from her homeland at less than two years old and lived all the rest of her life among the phlegmatic British, he recognised that every day had to be full of drama; it was as necessary to her as breathing. Russian angst was deep in her soul, after all. These volatile moods, which usually ended as suddenly as they had begun, were marked by the presentation of a huge beribboned box of chocolate bon-bons, flowers or some other treat he knew she loved, handed over with a wry smile and a look in his eyes Kitty could never quite make out.

But where was the cross? The silver, traditional Orthodox,

three-barred cross with ornately worked trefoil motifs, embellished with a single, black amber cabochon, threaded on a chain and designed to be worn as a pendant? It was heavy, masculine in style and not the most attractive piece, and although Lydia treasured it, she never wore it. Certainly not with her riding outfit. She had probably decided to keep it elsewhere, but to make sure it wasn't in the box Kitty tipped everything on to the polished top of the dressing table. The heavy ring with the dark green stone slid off and rolled across the room, where it came to rest between the connecting door to her father's bedroom and the bookcase next to Lydia's desk. Was it a sign? She scooped the rest of the jewellery back into the box and retrieved the ring and as she straightened, let her glance rest on the book standing resplendently alone between two weighty, carved soapstone elephants that were used as bookends.

The lower bookshelves were crammed with Lydia's preferred reading: Russian novels, of course – Tolstoy, Dostoevsky, Turgenev, Chekhov, as well as books by English authors and a collection of tracts in Russian. The one standing on top between the elephants, red with gilt lettering on the spine, *Deborah's Fortune,* was a romantic novel – written by Lydia herself. Not as Lydia Challoner, or even her maiden name of Lydia Kasparov, but under the pen name of Marie Bartholemew.

Unlike many of her other interests, quickly taken up and as quickly abandoned, this one had survived, though she insisted her authorship was a secret kept within the family, for what reason Kitty could never imagine: enough people had liked and bought the book for the publisher to want more. Maybe she thought everyone, like Ursula, would suspect anything written by her must be too trivial to read. Kitty could see the point – Lydia, her *mother*! It was difficult to imagine her having enough perseverance and concentration, enough staying power, to write a whole book, much less another in the process of being typed for the publisher.

There was only a single drawer in the desk, and though as far as Kitty knew she only kept in there the exercise books with marbled covers in which the rough drafts were written, her hand went towards it. Stopped. For a moment she was shaken with doubts. There was a word for what she was doing, and it wasn't nice: snooping. Even snooping because she was worried. She had no idea what she was looking for. Something to convince her she must be mistaken? But *here*, among her personal things? That was ridiculous, yet she needed somehow to find reassurance that in spite of everything there would be an innocent explanation for what she had lately seen and suspected. She hated herself for thinking the worst.

What stopped her was the sight of one of the exercise books lying on the desk. This, labelled with a large number three, must be for the next projected work. Lydia was adamant about not letting anyone, not even Kitty, see work in progress. It was easy to see why when she opened it, the guilty impulse to read it being too strong to ignore. There were only a few pages already written, covered with her distinctive handwriting, so wildly erratic that after a cursory glance Kitty abandoned all thoughts of attempting to decipher it. Written in green ink, in huge, loopy letters with many blots, misspellings and scratchings-out, scribbled at speed, it would later be transcribed by Miss Drax into a neat manuscript for her publisher. It was this heroic feat that made Hester Drax so indispensable, and all credit for it was given to her by Mama. 'I simply couldn't do it without Hester!' she declared. To which Hester replied dryly that of course that was very true, the manuscripts would have been unacceptable without her help.

'Plain-speaking will be the downfall of her one day,' Louis sometimes said. 'She has no sense of her place in the scheme of things, that woman.'

'But that's why we get on so well, darling,' smiled Lydia, who was nothing if not plain-spoken herself. 'She doesn't mean to be unpleasant.'

'Well, if you get on with her I suppose that's all that matters.'

Hester Drax occupied what would surely be a unique position in any household. She was ostensibly employed as lady's maid, but Mama, although scrupulously turned out day and night, despised the sort of woman who never lifted a finger to help herself, and this left Miss Drax free to make herself useful in other ways. For this purpose, she had a small room equipped as an office, complete with typewriter. It was an odd arrangement that seemed to work for both of them. They always had their heads together. And it was obviously true what Lydia said. She would have been the first to admit that she had not been well taught. Nikolai Kasparov had been too busy over the injustices being perpetrated thousands of miles away to see what was going on under his own nose, his own daughter growing up steeped in the terrible history of their people but basically uneducated in the formal sense. Through the offices and financial assistance of a good friend, she had in the end been sent to a fashionable school where she learnt little more than to be a young English lady, but where she also made friends who later introduced her to Louis, thus enabling her to make the sort of advantageous marriage that would otherwise not have been possible for her.

Well, she might not have received a formal education, but she still had a wonderful way with a story. Even if Kitty couldn't read her rough notes.

She closed the exercise book just as from behind her she heard someone say, 'What are you doing here, Kitty? I thought you were out riding with your mama.'

Kitty jumped. The only person she knew who could move without making a sound, Hester Drax had entered the room, tall and thin in her chapel-going clothes, determinedly unattractive, in a grey, three-quarter-length coat-and-skirt, her large, droopy, brown hat skewered to her bun with a hatpin. She was myopic and viewed the world through a pair of severe, steel-rimmed glasses, which at the moment were fixed directly on Kitty.

Mortified by being caught in the act, but determined not to feel guilty, Kitty said carelessly, 'I had a little headache and Mama thought I could be excused. It's quite gone now, thank you,' she added, though Miss Drax hadn't expressed any concern. 'I was just hoping to sneak a preview of the next book – but I can't make head nor tail of Mama's handwriting. It's almost as though you have a secret code.'

She smiled but Miss Drax was not amused. 'Which is why she doesn't like people to see it at that stage,' she replied sharply. Kitty pretended not to notice the rudeness. The woman had a high spot of colour on both cheeks. The Methodist preacher's sermon must have been very stimulating.

'Is your mother not home yet?'

'No. She's awfully late. She should be changing by now. And

Papa's not home, either.' Kitty crossed the room and put the ring she was still holding back into the trinket box.

She knew Miss Drax had already noted the open lid but she made no comment, other than to say, 'I suppose I had better go and ask them to put luncheon back.'

'I'll do it.'

'I think not. It will come better from me,' Hester Drax said, with the martyred air of one whose fate it was to impart unpleasant news.

Two

The tedious service at last came to an end and Bridget and her mother were finally able to leave church after shaking hands with the vicar. Ursula had politely complimented him on his sermon but Bridget could not bring herself to do likewise. Nothing short of hypocrisy, that would have been. He was a dry and humourless man, which had translated itself to the sermon.

Impatient and cramped from sitting in the pew, she longed to stretch her legs but of necessity she had to accommodate her stride to her mother's much shorter one. She was unusually silent, frantic with calculations about whether she would be able to get away this afternoon without attracting attention. Although she was naturally devious she wasn't sanguine about achieving this. Sunday luncheon, to please Uncle Louis who liked to keep up tradition, was always a family occasion, a big, heavy meal compensated for with something light in the evening, a reversal of the usual daily proceedings. Everyone was expected to be present and it went on for ever. No question of avoiding it entirely – she and her mother were, after all, guests in the house – or of trying to slip away before the pudding and cheese, though she might possibly dodge the coffee. The meeting was scheduled to begin at three thirty and she was on pins to hear the result of what had happened that morning. Always presuming, she thought, her heart beating faster, that she had not heard anything before she got to the meeting.

Shortly before Christmas, Lady Devenish had decided she must take charge of bringing Kitty out. (No use relying on her sister-in-law for that, she would be hopeless! Nor had she the right connections. Whereas Ursula knew *Debrett's Peerage* from A to Z and saw it as a failure on her part that Bridget had emerged through two Seasons without catching a suitable future husband from those listed within its pages, one she did not intend to be repeated with Kitty.) Since Lydia had thanked her gracefully, no doubt glad to be rid of the obligations, she and Bridget had moved into the Challoner house in Egremont Gardens, where they were to stay until Kitty was safely launched, and had completed her first Season.

Early in the New Year, Bridget had been working in the little room at the back of the house that was known as the book room because Lydia thought that to call such a small room with only a moderate amount of books in it a library was too pretentious. It was cosy and quiet, and people rarely came in to disturb Bridget as she worked, preparing for her first term in Cambridge. She looked up as a tap on the door announced the arrival of mid-morning coffee.

Emma, the parlour maid who had now also been detailed to maid Kitty if and when she needed it, which was not yet very often, came in with the coffee and put it on the table Bridget was using as a desk. Absorbed in her work, she murmured her thanks absently and went on writing. After a moment she was aware the girl hadn't left the room but was still standing by her side, her eyes fixed on the banner headlines of the newspaper lying across the corner of the table. The big story of the East End siege a few days ago, when hundreds of police had surrounded a house where a trio of armed criminals, said to be Russian anarchists, had been holed up, and which had ended only when the house caught fire and two of the three had been burnt to death, was still eclipsing even the news of the forthcoming coronation. 'Too dreadful, isn't it?' Bridget remarked, though she was surprised that the girl hadn't been careful enough to conceal her interest. Servants were expected to keep their thoughts to themselves. 'Let's hope they catch the one who escaped very soon.'

'Oh, I don't know,' Emma replied surprisingly. 'They're only fighting for what they think is right.'

'What? But they've deliberately killed several policemen!' And they had been Russian revolutionaries, too, originally disturbed in the act of armed robbery, breaking into a jeweller's shop. Supposedly to enable them to send funds back to Russia.

'Well, I don't say that's right, but you don't get what you want without a fight, do you?'

Bridget looked at her in astonishment and Emma flushed. 'I'm sorry, Miss Bridget. It's not my place to have said anything.' She bobbed and went to the door.

'No, wait, Emma. What did you mean by that – having to fight?'

Emma stood with her hand on the door-knob. Bridget had been living in this house since Christmas but if she'd been asked before that moment to describe Emma she couldn't have done so. She was simply one of the servants. She'd never noticed before what a good-looking girl she was, with a fresh complexion and thick, curly brown hair, and she had certainly never considered that she might be a person with opinions of her own. 'Come on, sit down and explain. You intrigue me.'

'I should be getting on.'

'Another minute or two won't hurt.'

Emma looked at her steadily, then came back and sat stiffly on the chair Bridget indicated. She waited, and after a minute Emma said, 'I would have thought you would have known about all that more than most, Miss Bridget, you going to a university and that. But I'll bet you've had to struggle for it, haven't you? Being a woman.'

Bridget laid down her pen. She wasn't ignorant of the fact that the servants in any house were bound to know a great deal more about the people for whom they worked than those people liked to admit, but she was a little taken aback to find her own affairs such an open book. The hours she spent here, absorbed in her books, had obviously revealed the extent of her obsession. 'I hadn't taken you for a women's rights supporter, Emma. Are you a suffragette?'

'I haven't got the time for that, Miss. And if you'll excuse me, I'll have to be getting on, or I'll have Mrs Thorpe after me.'

'Of course, I mustn't keep you, Emma. But we must have another chat when you have more time. I think you and I might have something in common.'

'I don't think so, Miss Bridget, best leave it. I've already said too much.' Emma bobbed again and left the room.

But they did meet again, and they talked. The meetings were necessarily brief encounters, snatched by Bridget whenever she could catch Emma between duties. She hadn't realised how long the girl's hours were, how hard she worked. But she was physically strong, a willing worker and possessed of a great deal of common sense. Bridget learnt that she had been employed by the Challoners since leaving school. Before that she had lived in the East End where she had been born and brought up, which explained her sympathy with those who lived there, in particular the women whose lives were so hard. She had not been entirely truthful about her involvement with the women's movement. As an uneducated working girl, her time and input was severely limited but since every pair of hands was needed, anyone with enthusiasm was welcomed into the suffragette fold.

Until Bridget went to that first meeting with Emma, purely out of interest, her sympathies with the women's movement had been theoretical, absorbed in her studies as she was. She had read terrible stories of arrest, imprisonment and, lately, hunger striking, and had been horrified – but at a distance. Now she had met women who had experienced all three, not once, but several times. Some of the hunger strikers had even suffered forcible feeding, an intolerable practice permitted through the non-intervention policy of Prime Minister Asquith's Liberal government. At last medical objections, backed up by outraged public opinion at the highly dangerous and inhumane practice, was prompting the government to question whether it had become too politically embarrassing to allow it to be continued.

Even so, not all the population by any means – not even most women – were inclined to support the suffrage movement, a situation that deterred neither their leader Mrs Pankhurst, her daughters, nor their followers from their intentions to press forward. Bridget's eyes had been opened. She had not known such passion and commitment existed: the barbarous treatment some of those women had received had not diminished their fervour for the Cause by one iota. The health of many of them had been permanently damaged, but it had not broken their spirit.

However, at the moment, due to the Conciliation Bill (designed to allow some women, though not all, the vote) which was going through Parliament, an air of hope was stirring and in return, Bridget learnt, some of them had agreed for the duration of this time of celebration to suspend plans for such violent protests as smashing windows, setting fire to pillar boxes, pouring corrosive acid over golf courses and any other form of guerrilla warfare they could think of.

Absorbed in her own thoughts as she and Ursula walked along, Bridget became aware that her mother had been speaking to her and had to ask her to repeat what she had said. 'I asked what it was that seemed to be amusing you during the sermon, Bridget.' Ursula had to turn her head so that she could look from under the brim of the enormous chiffon-and-flower-bedecked hat she wore, a fashion that was not kind to women of her stature.

Bridget had forgotten how observant, under that vague exterior, her mother could be. She assumed vagueness herself. 'Oh, was I amused? I don't recollect. It couldn't have been the Reverend Philpott making a joke, at any rate.'

Ursula smiled slightly. 'I don't suppose it could. Well, never mind. We must hurry. Your aunt is bringing Mr Villiers home for lunch. Shall we cut through the public gardens? I hear the tulips are spectacular this year.'

In fact, Bridget knew only too well what had amused her. A bizarre but tension-relieving intrusion into the turmoil that was churning her insides, consumed as she was by a febrile excitement, knowing what might happen today. Frightened, too, and struggling with her conscience. Should she, or should she not? And yet, in the midst of all that, she had suddenly wondered during that tedious sermon what would happen if she were to emulate one of the women she had met at that first suffrage meeting, who claimed she had the previous week jumped up in church and stood on the seat of her pew, shouting 'Votes for Women!' The same thing would have happened to her, Bridget, she supposed, if she had dared to do it. A few moments of frozen disbelief, then men in the congregation rushing to manhandle the woman from the church, and the vicar himself quoting the scriptures on the lines of it being shameful for women to speak in church. ('Or to speak at all!' someone at the meeting had added, to much laughter.) Remembering that, Bridget had had to suppress a giggle during the sermon.

She had expected amusement from her Aunt Lydia, too, one of her infectious laughs when she had recounted the incident. But it didn't raise so much as a smile. For all her enthusiastic espousal of various good causes, Lydia refused to have anything to do with the women's struggle, or even to listen to the arguments Bridget put forward.

'Take my advice, Bridget, and keep away from those women.' It was so out of character that at first Bridget hadn't believed she was serious. Lydia was usually all too ready to fight for the underdog. But then she went on, 'You're not the first to approach me, you know. But my dear, that sort of thing always leads to trouble, believe me.'

'You don't have to be a militant,' Bridget had retorted. 'I for one am not.'

'I should hope not.'

'There are other ways of showing your sympathy.'

But Lydia was not to be swayed. She had always held herself adamantly aloof from politics. It was politics that had caused her father's exile from his beloved homeland, Russia.

Not quite a quarrel, but nearly so, it was causing a tight-lipped constraint between Bridget and the aunt she loved and admired.

'Yes, Mother, you were right, the tulips are magnificent,' she said as they entered the public gardens, ordering herself to dismiss that particular problem from her mind, only for it to be taken up with that other, more pressing apprehension.

Although he was so easygoing, the axiom that punctuality was the politeness of princes had been drilled into Louis Challoner by his nanny until it was almost as much a way of life to him as the concept of keeping time was unknown to his wife. It was especially unusual for him to be late for a meal. On the other hand, although no one was ever entirely surprised when Lydia failed to put in an appearance by the right time, on this occasion one imagined she would have made an effort to be there by one o'clock, since Marcus Villiers was invited to lunch with them.

Louis in fact arrived home just after one in a motor-cab, looking unusually hot and bothered, and quite upset, giving the explanation that he had been held up by one of the club bores, who had then, poor old fellow, collapsed in front of his eyes with what looked like a heart attack. A doctor who was lunching at the club had been found and fortunately the attack was thought to be nothing more than severe indigestion. Louis had managed to slip away during all the subsequent fuss, but it had been almost impossible to get a cab. All the world, it seemed, was out gawping at the preparations for the coronation. Foreign visitors for the event were already arriving in the capital, adding to the crowds thronging the streets, and families were out too, making a day of it, taking advantage of the fine weather, picnicking in Green Park and elsewhere. Horse-drawn traffic was becoming more of a problem every day, holding everything up, Louis declared. Maybe it was time to think about buying a motor-car, instead of the hansom detailed to take him to the City each day.

Ursula, annoyed with Lydia but anxious to stave off crisis in the kitchen, said crisply, 'Well, maybe it hasn't come to that just yet. Meanwhile, Cook's becoming worried about her roast.' It was a prime rib of beef, and the master liked it rare.

'Oh, very well, we'll eat at once. It's no use waiting for Lydia. There's no telling with her, is there?' For a moment, an unfathomable look crossed Louis's face. 'Give me five minutes to tidy myself. She may be back by then.'

Three

It hadn't really happened. It was a bad dream, a nightmare, it had to be. She would wake up to see Mama walking through the door, tossing her hat aside, breathless, smiling and accompanied by Marcus, full of apologies – so sorry we're late, darlings, please forgive!

The detectives were mistaken – it was some other person who had been shot at while trotting down Rotten Row.

That's what Kitty longed to be true, but she knew it wasn't. The plain, unvarnished truth was that in Hyde Park this morning someone fired a gun, the bullet had hit her mother, Lydia Challoner, and she was dead.

A couple of plain-clothes detectives had come to break the news. Detective Sergeant Inskip, who stated baldly that he was afraid he was the bearer of bad news, told them what it was and seemed to think that was that. With him was another man, a more nondescript, quieter person but who turned out to be his superior, Detective Chief Inspector Gaines. Gaines said very little at first, apart from adding the condolences the sergeant had omitted. He wore a luxuriant, old-fashioned moustache which made him look mournful. Or perhaps he really was sorry, unlike Inskip, who seemed to parrot out the words mechanically, as if they were something he had learned by rote to bring out when the occasion demanded.

Kitty had known that she wasn't being either fair or reasonable. However much they were accustomed to it, she could not truly believe that even the police would relish having to deliver this sort of news. Perhaps it really had upset that Sergeant Inskip, and keeping it so impersonal was his way of dealing with it. Chief Inspector Gaines had a similarly stern face but his eyes were kinder. Inskip's eyes were sharp and shiny, like black boot buttons, the sort that missed nothing. Other than that, he was handsome, and looked as if he knew it. Dark, flat curls like a Grecian statue. His skin was tanned and he looked athletic, tight-packed into his clothes, wearing a check suit that was too loud.

Several hours had elapsed since then, and Kitty knew she ought not to keep dwelling on those first electrified few minutes. Or telling herself it hadn't happened. But neither could she shut it out, the scene playing itself round and round in her head, like a needle stuck in the groove of a gramophone record. Aunt Ursula, collapsed on to the sofa . . . Bridget white as a ghost . . . Gaines, the shorter of the two men, standing aside and looking almost detached, and Inskip in his flashy suit . . .

His sort especially didn't make mistakes.

'No, sir, no mistake, I'm afraid, sir,' he'd said stoically when Papa seemed, like the rest of them, absolutely unable to take in what they had just been told. He had almost staggered, as if he'd been dealt a physical blow. 'There's no doubt the lady who was shot is Mrs Challoner.'

'That, I am not disputing.' Louis's colour had become high and a pulse was beating in his temple. 'A mistake on the part of the gunman was what I meant. A mistake, or downright carelessness – his target being something or someone else, which he missed.'

'Quite possibly, sir,' Inskip said woodenly, looking as though he didn't believe that for a minute.

'Who is this maniac? Why haven't you caught him?'

'He made his escape from the scene, sir, before anyone could reach him. Mr Villiers tried, as you know, but he was too late.'

He had already told them this, and everything else they had found out about the accident, which hadn't taken long because there was virtually nothing to tell. Kitty could only think it was this helpless feeling of being unable to comprehend how or why it had happened – especially *why* – that was making her father so angry; mild-mannered Papa who never lost his temper and was always polite to everyone. Perhaps it was because, like the rest of them, he just couldn't accept something that simply didn't make any sense at all. That Mama should have left the house this morning, happy, smiling and at ease, and that she, out of all those others riding near her, had had her life ended because of a care-less shot by some unknown, cowardly person who ran away when he saw what he had done. Kitty didn't believe the real hurt, the pain, had got through to her father by then, any more than it had to her. The pain would come later, when the possibility that such a calamity might actually be true began to sink in. Though even yet there was still the sense that it was all play-acting, that suddenly the curtain would fall and they would all come back into the real world where such things couldn't possibly happen.

'Are you ever *likely* to catch him?' Papa had demanded, less heated but still in a sarcastic sort of voice that wasn't his at all.

'Our investigations have only just started, Mr Challoner,' the other policeman, Gaines, intervened to remind him. Whereas Inskip had an Irish accent overlaid with Cockney, and that aggressive manner, Gaines was better spoken, even if not quite what Aunt Ursula would call 'one of us'. He had so far kept mostly in the background, despite his seniority.

'That hadn't escaped my notice,' Papa said, 'any more than the fact of irresponsible persons being allowed to run around loose with guns, causing accidents. In a public place like Hyde Park, if you please, amongst women and children!'

'Allowed? Hardly that, sir.'

Inskip cut in impatiently, 'Was it a regular thing for your wife to go riding in the Park, Mr Challoner?'

'Yes. It's not easy to find places to ride in London, so that was where she usually went.'

'You didn't accompany her, sir?'

'I don't ride nowadays. I had a hunting accident some years ago which has left me with a troublesome back – and a certain antipathy towards horses.' It was his stock reply, usually delivered with a smile, but he was a long way from smiling then.

He had never seen any necessity for owning a private carriage, except on occasions like this morning, when he'd been held up coming home from his club and had spoken of buying a motor car. Lydia's chestnut mare, Persephone, and the little filly, Dulcinea, bought for Kitty when she became eighteen, were kept at livery, the only arrangement possible, considering where they lived. Mama rode, as often as possible, but although Dulcinea was a pretty, sweet-natured animal, and Kitty really loved her, she had lately been reluctant to accompany her mother, and got out of it as she had this morning, as well as she could without giving the impression that she had little interest in the generous present she had been given.

'I see,' was Inskip's reply. 'So it was Mr Villiers who usually escorted her?'

'As a rule, yes.' It had been an arrangement perfectly suited to Louis's own lazy inclinations.

'Do you own a gun, sir?' Inskip asked abruptly.

Kitty could see the sudden question was disconcerting, coming on top of the testy remarks Louis himself had made about the heedlessness of people with firearms, but after a moment he admitted that he did. 'Of course I have a gun. It's a sad reflection on our society that no one feels it wise to go out anywhere at night without one. But I'm not in the habit of taking indiscriminate pot-shots in a crowded place like Hyde Park.'

His protests were beginning to sound pompous, a little forced, even to Kitty, but neither policeman made any further comment. They must have been more familiar than he was with all the arguments gentlemen put forward for carrying a small pocket pistol around with them, and perhaps even saw the sense in it: people emerging into the London streets late in the evening after dining out in restaurants or private houses, or visiting theatres, especially if they looked prosperous, were easy targets for thieves and pickpockets taking the chance to assault and rob. It was only common sense to be equipped with a weapon as self-defence, the threat of which was enough to serve as a deterrent to any would-be criminal. You could buy them almost anywhere, over the counter. She knew her father had bought the gun only last month, because he had showed it to them when he brought it home, and explained its workings, while stressing the importance of it being kept unloaded and locked up. He had even urged Mama to have one, too, to carry in her handbag. Many ladies were doing so, he said, since the terrific scare created not two or three months ago, when that sensational gun battle and siege, something unheard of in England before that, had taken place and rocked the nation.

'But that was between the police and criminals in the East End,' Mama had smiled. 'No, Louis, I would rather face being attacked than carry such a lethal weapon about my person.'

He had told her she was being foolish but he hadn't pressed the point.

'May we see your gun, Mr Challoner?' Gaines was enquiring quietly now.

'Certainly,' he said stiffly. It took some moments before the strangeness of the request struck home, and not only to Louis. 'But why?'

The scent of the lilacs that had smelt so delicious that morning wafting into the room from the square garden felt all at once quite sickly and overpowering. Small wonder that Ursula, sitting on the very edge of a sofa, indomitable Aunt Ursula, suddenly gave a little moan and sank back in a swoon. Bridget dropped to the floor beside the sofa, holding her hand, and as she struggled to sit up, pressed her back, wafting a smelling bottle under her nose, bringing tears to her eyes with its ammoniac vapours. 'Lie still for a few moments, Mother, and you'll be all right.' Though Bridget herself looked far from all right, almost ready to copy her mother and faint away.

'Mr Challoner?' Gaines extended his hand towards the door.

'Very well, if you must.' Louis threw a glance at his sister but the smelling salts were reviving her. He had no option but to lead the way into his study.

Kitty followed before anyone could forbid it. Her father didn't notice until they were actually at the study doorway. When he saw her he blinked, as if he had momentarily forgotten he had ever had a daughter, and for a moment it seemed as if he were about to send her away. 'Please, Papa!' The thought of her father, too, going out of her sight even for a few moments gave Kitty a sick, lost feeling.

'Perhaps you might be better staying with your aunt, Miss Challoner,' Gaines advised, not unkindly.

'Kitty shall stay here, if she wishes.'

Inskip looked about to protest but Gaines said, 'Very well.' To Inskip, he gave a small shake of the head.

They all went into the study. Kitty perched uneasily on the edge of a chair, but Louis stood stock still in the middle of the room, looking around as if he suddenly found himself in a strange place.

'The gun, if you please,' Inskip reminded him.

The watch and chain draped across the mound of his pin-striped waistcoat held his gold half-hunter suspended in one pocket, his keys in the other. His hands were steady as he selected a key and unlocked the safe. He stood for so long looking into it with his back to everyone that Kitty began to fear something was wrong. Then without turning round, he said, in a flat, dead sort of voice, 'Well, it's not here.' He began to shuffle things in the safe around. Finally, he faced the room again. 'It's not there.'

'When did you last see it?' Inskip asked sharply, exchanging glances with Gaines.

Louis rubbed his forehead. 'Last week? Yes, it must have been last week. I don't have occasion to open the safe much.'

'Is there anything else missing?'

'No,' he said, after a moment. 'Her pearls, her other jewellery, everything is still there.'

'Who else has access to the safe?'

'No one. There is only one key and it stays here, on my watch chain, always.' He frowned. 'The safe must have been tampered with. There can be no other explanation.'

'And who do you suggest might have done that?'

That was an argument which even Kitty could see had no answer. After a moment, Louis spread his hands helplessly.

While Kitty . . . An image of the missing pendant-cross from her mother's jewellery box had flown instantly into her mind. But even in the highly unlikely event of a burglar getting into the house, creeping around undetected and somehow opening the safe and stealing the gun, it was beyond all logic that he would also steal such an old-fashioned and relatively worthless piece as the cross, while leaving behind jewellery worth thousands of pounds. Even supposing he had known where it was to be found. It had never been kept in the safe. The obvious explanation for it not being with the other ambers was certainly that Mama had simply decided to put it somewhere else and forgotten about it. She was often careless with her possessions and chronically absent-minded.

'If you haven't opened the safe for some time, Mr Challoner, I assume you don't always take the gun out with you?' Gaines asked.

'Not in broad daylight!'

For a moment or two there was silence, and then Inskip asked where he had been that morning. They listened without saying anything as he explained about being at his club and why he'd been late home for lunch because of the man who'd been taken ill.

'Your club is in St James's?'

'Yes.'

The sergeant wrote something down and then as Gaines stood up, he followed suit. Kitty thought it was all over, until Gaines said, 'Perhaps, Miss Challoner, you should return to be with your aunt now. Mr Challoner, I must ask you to come down to the Yard with us. To complete the formalities, you understand.'

Four

Britannia Voice was a young, small, independent newspaper, one of the many publications which saw themselves as a weapon in the class war. Strongly anti-capitalist, it was dedicated to raising the consciousness of the British working people, encouraging strikes for better pay and working conditions, for shorter hours. To a certain extent, like most of the other radical newspapers which abounded, it was modelled on the thriving and popular anarchist paper, *Freedom*. Jonathan Devenish had been the editor of – and so far the main contributor to – the *Voice* from its inception, which had coincided with the time he had been sent down from Cambridge and was kicking around, looking for something to occupy his restless mind that would fit in with his political beliefs.

He was working in the office, even though it was Sunday, on a knotty article that wouldn't come right, when the telephone rang. He answered absently, words and phrases still buzzing around in his head, and found it difficult to make sense of the jumbled, hiccuping sounds issuing from the telephone. 'Mother, I can't understand what you're saying. Are you crying?' *His mother, crying?*

She started again, but even so it was difficult to get a coherent statement from her – Ursula was never the most collected of persons at the best of times – but at last he more or less understood what she was telling him, though he wondered if he might temporarily have taken leave of his wits and simply imagined she had said that Lydia – his Aunt *Lydia*, had been *killed*, in an accident, but Marcus was all right and so were the horses and—

'I'm coming right over.'

'Oh, Jon, darling, I knew you would. We're all at sixes and sevens here. I'll expect you within half an hour – don't walk,' she said, finding firmness. If possible, he was even more vague about time than Lydia, and it was his passion to walk everywhere, covering miles with his long legs, getting to know the streets, nooks and corners of the capital as well as he knew those of

Cambridge and the Kentish lanes and byways round their home, Southfields.

'I'll take a taxi-cab, Mother. I'll be there as soon as possible.'

When he arrived at Egremont Gardens the bell had scarcely finished ringing before the door was thrown open – not by a servant, but by his mother. This in itself was evidence of her distress; she had clearly been sitting there in the hall, right beside the door, waiting for him. 'I wanted to tell you what happened before you saw Kitty,' she explained hurriedly. 'The poor child doesn't need to hear it all over again. Thank God, thank God you're here, Jon!'

He put his arms round her and held her soft, plump body close. She was trembling, and raised a tearstained face that was wretched with shock and fear. 'Oh, Jon, they've taken Louis!'

'Who has? Who's taken Uncle Louis?'

'The police.'

'What?' He stared at her. 'You don't mean they've arrested him?'

'Do keep your voice down, darling!' she whispered, looking over her shoulder, her own voice agitated. 'No, I don't think that's what they've done but . . . to tell the truth, I don't *know* why they asked him to go with them, I simply don't know. My dear, it's so good you're here.' She touched his cheek, white with a shock that mirrored hers. 'One so needs a man in the family at times like this – and I didn't know who else!'

While not flattered by the implication that he had been called in as a last resort, Jon understood what she meant. She and his Uncle Louis, separated in age by only a couple of years, alike in many ways – conventional, with a similar outlook on life – had always been close, especially since Jon's own father died. Now, suddenly, Louis was not there. There were two other Challoner brothers: Barnabus, who had taken himself off to Australia and ran a sheep farm there; and their eldest brother Henry, who farmed in the wilds of Shropshire, a big, bluff man with three equally big, bluff sons, none of whom had any conversation whatsoever – unless it happened to be about horses, and the owning, riding, hunting, racing or breeding thereof. Henry had never been to Ursula what Louis was, and in any case, Ludlow was a hundred and fifty miles away. All the same, she must have been desperate to call on Jon. He felt even more helpless and inadequate now than he usually did when faced with family situations.

'Mother, I think you had better try and tell me exactly what happened, don't you?'

'I wish I could,' she answered distractedly, 'but it's all such a dreadful muddle. It must have been a mistake, but no one seems to know exactly . . . not even Marcus.' She looked over her shoulder again. It was a large, roomy hall, cool in summer, warm in winter, with comfortable seats in corners where one could hold a private conversation, but she still seemed wary of being overheard. 'Come into the dining room, it's the only place where we can be private.'

'Where's Kitty?'

'In the drawing room. With Bridget and Miss Drax.'

'Hester Drax? Oh, Lord.'

'She's being very sensible, Jon.'

'No doubt.' All the same, he thought Miss Drax the last person Kitty would want around her at a time like this. She was so attached to Lydia she was quite likely to be almost as upset as Kitty herself. But at least Kitty had Bridget with her and Bridget, cool and not the sort to stand any nonsense, could be relied upon to fend off anything inappropriate Miss Drax might say or do.

Ursula drew him into the dining room, where it was cool and dark, where the blinds had been lowered against the sun. There were cut-glass decanters of spirits and sherry, and some red wine left over from lunch on the sideboard. Jon decided it wouldn't be amiss to help himself to a glass of his uncle's brandy. 'You'd better have one, too, Mother,' he said as he poured it, but she shook her head.

They sat opposite each other across the expanse of polished mahogany. 'Oh dear, to think that we were all sitting here at this table, chatting, eating Cook's delicious apple pie, though we couldn't think what was keeping them, when all the time—' Ursula's voice broke as she recalled the slight strain in the atmosphere, the frisson of uneasiness – and especially when she remembered her own annoyance with Lydia – that grew as the clock moved on and she still didn't appear. 'We'd decided to go ahead, you see, and have

lunch. Not very well mannered, especially when she was to bring
Marcus, but . . . time was going on and . . . well, we all know
how little time matters to her, don't we? Though it was unusual
even for her to be so *very* late.'

'This Marcus. Who is he?'

'Darling, you know Marcus Villiers! He escorts her everywhere.'
She tightened her lips. She had always known this – friendship
– of Lydia's with Marcus Villiers was unwise, although it was she
herself who had been responsible for introducing them. She blamed
herself for it. People had made assumptions. Wrongly, Ursula was
sure, knowing her sister-in-law. Lydia had evidently been pleased
that a young man was taking an interest in her, but in an amused,
teasing sort of way, almost but not quite flirting. Although that,
too, was dangerous. 'She was out riding with him in the Row
. . . you do know him, poor boy . . .'

'Oh, that Marcus! Of course I do. We've known each other
since we were knee-high.'

Though 'been acquainted' would have been more strictly
correct. Loddhurst, the Villiers estate, marched with Southfields
and the two young men had occasionally met as children, though
Marcus had lived abroad with his father from an early age. They
had both been at Cambridge, but Marcus was a year or two
older than Jon and they had never come into close contact there,
Jon's political leanings having taken him in an entirely different
direction. In fact, he couldn't recall encountering him except
in a crowd, with other people present, and that only rarely. He
had never had a conversation with him alone and now he thought
about it, it was evident he really knew nothing much about
him at all, though at the back of his mind something – rumour?
. . . gossip? – was stirring. What was he doing, squiring Lydia
around?

It was no news to anyone that it was '*de rigueur*' in certain
circles for married women to take a young man as lover, a recip-
rocal arrangement which suited both since, being already married,
such a woman was no threat to the marriage prospects of the
young blood in question, but Jon found the idea of that sort of
fellow and his aunt in this context both repugnant and unbelievable. Lydia was not an open book, not by any means, as he had
good reason to know. She had a varied circle of friends and

acquaintances of whom he knew very little, but if nothing else, what he did know of her made nonsense of such an idea.

Still, Villiers. It was an odd, if not disturbing situation . . .

He forced himself to listen patiently, holding her hand, while Ursula haltingly told him what little there was to be told, a confused mixture of what she had been able to gather from the police and what she *thought* might have happened. Even so, he easily built up a vivid picture in his mind.

On such a beautiful sunny Sunday morning, Hyde Park would have been thronged, the orators at Speakers' Corner in full flow on their soap boxes, crowds of people lining Rotten Row to watch the riders – beautiful horses and lovely women . . .

The number of riders had thinned out a little by midday, as the time for luncheon approached. Along the red sandy strip, the few left were moving at a sedate trot when suddenly eight or nine women ran on to the track in front of them and stood in a line across it, with arms stretched and hands linked. Faced with the choice of stopping or running them down, the riders came to an untidy halt, while the women began to shout their rallying call: 'Votes for Women!' The watching crowds surged further towards the railings in the hope of excitement and policemen began thrusting their way through – which the women had known would happen. The number of people surging into London, thronging the city and taking advantage of the fine weather to sight-see the coronation preparations unfortunately provided opportunities for pickpockets and the like too, and the police had made it known that they were taking steps to make their presence felt and to be extra vigilant in public places. The protesting women expected to be forcibly removed, they actually wanted it; they did their best whenever the police appeared on the scene to make it happen, even if they were dragged away by their hair, as they so often were: the more violence that was shown against them, the more opportunity they had of gaining public sympathy.

The horses were already in a state of agitation caused by the commotion when suddenly a sharp detonation, sounding like a gunshot, caused several of them to shy, throwing the rest into momentary panic, starting off a small mêlée of confusion as the animals nudged together, throwing up their heads as the riders

struggled to steady them. Marcus, riding abreast of Lydia, occupied
in the same struggle, failed to notice that she had been thrown
until he looked for her after he had managed to quieten his own
horse somewhat. She was lying on the ground, one foot caught
in the stirrup; her hat had fallen off, and fearing she might be
concussed he leaped from the saddle. Kneeling beside her,
attempting to raise her, he was aghast to see blood seeping through
her habit, smearing his own sleeve as he held her. He felt for her
pulse, but there was none.

For a moment he thought she must have been harmed by the
feet of the agitated horses, but for a split second only: his mind
had already flown back to the sound of the detonation. Other
riders had by then dismounted, among them a man and a woman,
strangers to him, who were also kneeling beside Lydia. More
policemen who had been patrolling the park were arriving at a
run. Standing up and looking in the direction from which he
thought the shot had come, Marcus said curtly to the couple,
'Look after her.' Thrusting his own reins at someone else, darting
between restive and titupping horses, their nostrils flared and eyes
rolling at the smell of blood, he had vaulted the fence lining the
track and, pushing his way through the panicking crowds, raced
across the grass towards a figure in the distance. After a hundred
yards or so, he came to a panting halt. He had lost his quarry.
The marksman, if that was who the fleeing figure had been, had
already disappeared.

The whole incident had occurred in no more than a few
minutes.

And the suffragette demonstration had fallen flat, in view of
the infinitely more sensational event that had eclipsed it.

Five

It wouldn't take long, the police had said, but after two hours, when Louis still hadn't come back, Kitty had a sinking feeling that they might not be going to let him go at all. She was fighting off the tightness in her chest that was making her feel as though she couldn't breathe, a problem she used to have when she became upset as a child, which she was supposed to have outgrown. Aunt Ursula had abruptly left her and Bridget alone with Hester Drax in the drawing room after Papa and the police had left and they could find little to say. In the end Bridget had silently taken out the cribbage board. At least it might be some distraction. They had done little more than set the pegs up when Ursula returned, with Jon. Kitty wasn't quite sure that it was a good idea to have sent for him, except that he was fiercely opposed to injustice of any kind as a general concept – and taking Papa away like that undoubtedly fell into that category. His social conscience was why he lived and worked in the slums and was devoting his life to that radical newspaper he edited. He always had about him a sort of amiable vagueness which masked the fact that he took life extremely seriously. He believed political freedom could change the world and Kitty knew he worked himself into the ground, not sparing any effort to further any cause he felt worthwhile. The trouble was, the problems of the individual seemed to flummox him, compared to the larger ones of the underprivileged masses. All the same, she suddenly felt very glad to have him there. He was still Jon, tall, lanky, absent-minded Jon who had always been very dear to her, the big brother she had always wished she'd had.

In fact, she had never seen Jon quite so upset. He looked stunned, but that really wasn't surprising. He and Mama had always got on so well; Jon was almost like a surrogate son to her. Whenever he visited they could spend hours talking, often about her writing, or so Kitty believed. She used to say that although Jon freely confessed the sort of novels she wrote were not his cup of tea, his frank comments were invaluable. Kitty had often wondered exactly what Hester Drax thought of that in view of how fiercely protective of Mama's work she was. She didn't think Hester cared for Jon very much. His unexpected arrival was a signal to her to depart. She had been quite silent for some time, twisting her handkerchief round and round, but now, abruptly, she stood up. With a set face, she made her excuses and disappeared, along with her disapproval of what she seemed to see as Ursula's inability to pull herself together. It had been Hester who had found supplies of clean handkerchiefs and ordered the endless cups of tea they had been drinking. Poor Hester! No doubt she couldn't help the conviction she was born with, that she was the only one capable of directing any sort of action, especially in this house – which might have been acceptable if only she did not always generate such an air of righteousness. 'If you need anything else, you know where I am,' she said. The door closed behind her.

'Oh dear,' said Ursula. After a moment she added, 'Well, I dare say she is finding it very difficult.'

Of course that was true, and where else, it suddenly occurred to Kitty, was she going to find a situation comparable to the one she held here? She was, however, not the only one who faced difficulty in what was bound to lie ahead, and hardly the only one who had loved Mama. Even Aunt Ursula, who had not always seen eye to eye with her, it had to be said, was considerably upset – although she had never permitted their differences to amount to much. She regarded family disagreements as vulgar. And Bridget, too, sitting with her head bent, her hands so tightly clenched together that her knuckles showed white, seemed overcome, in a way that wasn't at all like her. She and Lydia evidently had been on less than friendly terms for the last week or two, though Kitty didn't know what the disagreement had been about. Was it guilt that was eating her up – that she and Lydia had last parted before they were able to make peace with each other? She hoped she was wrong, poor Bridget.

In the silence following Ursula's remark came the sound of the front door closing, and through the window Kitty saw someone hurrying, almost running, along the pavement. It was Miss Drax. She watched the grey figure in the woeful brown

straw hat disappear and wondered what sudden urge had come
upon her to send her scurrying out like that. To some friend to
whom she could pour out all that had happened? Or just the
need for some fresh air? Either would be understandable, after
the last hour or so.

The door opened and Emma came into the room, bearing a
tea tray. It was her afternoon off, so she must have come back
early for some reason. Kitty couldn't remember anyone ordering
yet more tea, and her last cup still stood cold and untasted where
she'd left it on the window sill beside her, but as if more tea was
the most welcome sight in the world, Bridget sprang up and
made way for it on a small table. She and Emma exchanged a
few, whispered words, Emma nodded and went out. Bridget let
a moment or two pass, then murmured some hurried excuse
about needing some fresh air and followed her out of the room.
She didn't return for about ten minutes but when she did Kitty
fancied she looked a little better, and some of her colour had
returned.

She was still standing at the window anxiously watching for her
father's return when the motor drew up outside, disturbing the
square's late Sunday afternoon somnolence. A little later Thomas,
a young footman who was new to the household, came in and
spoke to Aunt Ursula in a low voice. Ursula looked at Kitty
and said, 'It's Marcus, Marcus Villiers, my dear. Do you feel up
to seeing him?'

'Yes, of course. Why not?' Kitty had had a few minutes to prepare
herself, having seen the motor arrive and watched Marcus leap
from the driving seat, divest himself of driving goggles and toss
them on to the seat before running up the front steps. She hadn't
mentioned his arrival because she was too busy trying to work
out how they were to face each other. It was not going to be
easy. In the shock of it all, she didn't think any of them had so
far taken into account what a terrible experience the whole thing
must have been for him.

In the interval before he was shown in, Aunt Ursula summoned
up the social aplomb Kitty firmly believed she had been born
with. 'Marcus, my dear boy!' she said, rising as the door opened
and Marcus stood there, a dark presence on the threshold, changed

from the clothes Kitty had last seen him wearing. Maybe there had been blood on his riding habit. The thought made her skin creep. He was now dressed impeccably: a beautifully tailored, dark suit, stiff high collar and sober tie. He said abruptly, 'My apologies if I am intruding. I came to see Mr Challoner but they tell me the police have taken him away. Can this be true? What reason did they give?'

Aunt Ursula and Jon spoke together. 'They can't keep him,' said Jon, with all the authority of one who knows the rights and wrongs of those who have trouble with the police. His face was grim, though even in the exigency of the moment and his evident distress, he had been scribbling on a scrap of paper, possibly fired with the prospect of a challenge to bourgeois authority.

'Just formalities, they said.' Aunt Ursula stepped forward and held out both hands. Marcus bent his head over them in an oddly courtly gesture, but didn't move from his position in the doorway.

'I am so very sorry this has happened. I should have protected her,' he said stiffly.

'Marcus, what nonsense! How could you have possibly done that? Why are you standing there? Come in, come in.' The situation had eased the slight reserve she always showed towards him but the tightness of his face did not relax. Guilt. Kitty could understand that. It was what she had been feeling, too, for the last two or three hours. If she hadn't been too wrapped up in herself, or too eaten with curiosity about her mama's private affairs to go riding with her, as she ought to have done, maybe she would have been the one at the unlucky end of that shot. Or maybe she might have got some help to save Mama after the bullet had hit her . . . But no. They said she had died immediately.

At last Marcus stepped forward into the room.

The contrast between Jon in his flannel bags with the thick, untidy hair that he'd run his fingers through more than once, and Marcus, stiff and correct, was considerable. There seemed to be a slight constraint between them and Jon acknowledged him somewhat guardedly.

A cup of tea was pressed into his hands. He drank thirstily and the low murmurs of shocked disbelief were expressed until nothing new could be said. Presently he came to where Kitty was still standing a little apart in the window recess. 'Miss Kitty,' he said simply, taking her hand, and then for her ears alone, a low-voiced, 'Keep your chin up, all will be well, you'll see. Trust me. We'll speak later.'

Kitty could find no answer, though perhaps none was needed. The words, though meant to be comforting, did nothing to melt the ice that seemed to have congealed in her veins. All would be well, he had said, when patently it could not be, ever again. Trust him? That meant nothing to her, either.

The first few awkward moments having been negotiated, Ursula began hesitantly on the subject they all wanted to know more about. 'What we've been told of the accident is very sketchy, Marcus. Could you bring yourself to tell us more?'

'Accident?' He looked around him at the circle of faces. For a while he said nothing. 'No one is shot without a motive. I think one would have to be very naive to believe that was an accident.'

With a dull sense of dismay Kitty realised what he said was only too likely to be true. Looking back, she felt very sure now that the police had barely entertained the possibility of accident. Mama could only have been shot deliberately. And beneath the shock, her understanding took a small but perceptible shift. A lurch of the stomach. The police – and their enquiries about Papa's gun!

Into the appalled silence that followed Marcus's remark came the sound of a motor car. A moment or two later, the door opened and Papa came in. Aunt Ursula gave a little, strangled cry. He stood framed in the doorway for several moments, just as Marcus had done, looking around at the assembled throng. He took in first Jon, then Marcus. 'Well, well, quite a welcoming committee!'

Kitty ran forward to hug him. 'They've let you go!' Her father, who smoked only the occasional cigar, reeked so strongly of cigarette smoke she almost drew back. The policemen who had interviewed him must have been smoking continuously.

'Of course they've let me go, child.'

'What did they want of you, Louis?'

'Not now, Ursula, I can't go over it all again.' He looked un-utterably weary.

'But Louis—'

'Oh, what do you think?' he said impatiently then. 'They wanted to know if she had any enemies, quarrels with people – Lydia! Whether she had any Russian friends, for God's sake. What my relations with her were, if she had a lover, even. They wanted to know where my gun was, and if I had killed my own wife! And all *I* want now is a drink, an hour to myself, to get out of these clothes, have a hot bath and then some sleep. It has scarcely been a good day.'

'But that's ridiculous – those questions!'

'Ursula.'

She checked her shocked protest. 'Louis, I'm sorry. Have your bath and I'll have something sent to your room on a tray.'

'No, I don't want anything. Don't fuss, Ursula. I'm just tired. I've answered enough questions to last me a lifetime. I'll go to bed presently and we'll talk in the morning.'

'A little soup?' she coaxed. 'You must eat.' It was her way, to comfort with food, though they had all, including Louis himself, eaten roast beef and Yorkshire pudding not three hours before.

'Oh, very well. Soup, if you must, but later. Thank you for coming over, Jon, my boy. I'll see you tomorrow, Marcus.'

He disappeared into his study.

Once there, the first thing Louis did was to pour himself a glass of brandy. Next, he went to the safe, unlocked it and took out every single item it contained. He ranged them in front of him on his desk – private papers, deeds, Lydia's jewel cases, the lot. It went without saying that the pearls, diamonds and other jewellery were as intact as they had been when he'd opened the safe in the presence of the police; the papers he kept there were still in order. The gun had not miraculously reappeared. Nor had that other article. He shut the safe door, locked it and wiped the sweat from his brow. Leaning back in his chair he closed his eyes, the events of the day whirling round in his head like the pieces in a shaken kaleidoscope that stubbornly refused to make a pattern.

An hour passed without Ursula knocking solicitously on the door to see if he was all right. He must have frightened her off. He drained his third glass of brandy. Or was it his fourth? He'd always thought of himself as a reasonably abstemious man and dimly realised that, traumatic as the events of the day had been, he was letting them get the better of him. Perhaps they'd been doing that for some time. He did not normally drink so much. All the same, he went to pour another. It was only the glimpse he caught of himself in the looking glass over the mantel that made him stop with the decanter in his hand.

If Lydia were here now she would not see the handsome man she had married. She would be disgusted by the pouches beneath his eyes, his grey skin and the hair fast receding from his forehead. He was forty-nine years old, looked sixty and felt nearer seventy. After a long, considered moment, he put the stopper back into the decanter and returned to his chair. It was no use, he could at last admit, sitting here trying to make sense out of her death by drinking to the bottom of a bottle. For the sake of what Lydia had been to him he needed to take hold of himself.

Lydia and the mysterious person she had become in the last few weeks. He would previously have gone to the scaffold before admitting that in fact he had never really, deep down, known his wife, what and who she was. She had been a contradictory character, he had always known that, but it had been part of her charm: her warm, loving nature, her sense of fun as a counterbalance to the moods he had always put down to the Russian inheritance of which she'd been so intensely proud. The pride that had been so sedulously fostered by her father, Nikolai Kasparov – he who had been a passionate anti-Tsarist, a fighter all his life against the centuries-old tyrannies and injustices which the people of his homeland still endured. Lydia had grown up steeped in the dark history of their people, and with the conviction that one day wrongs must be righted, if necessary at the cost of spilled blood.

She had been extravagant, as much with money as with her emotions, but he had never minded that; he had shrugged and allowed her to spend as she wished. He delighted to see heads turn in admiration of her beautiful clothes and arresting presence when they appeared anywhere, Lydia outshining everyone, as she always did; he had shared her satisfaction when she came home with yet another costly trophy, some highly priced, ornate Russian work of art to adorn the house. It was only her bridge debts that he frowned upon, and even so only slightly, though his frowns had deepened of late, when their size had increased, the last one alarmingly so. She claimed they were debts owed to Fanny Estrabon – her dearest friend, although Louis had recently had moments of wondering if there had not been a cooling off there. He had been wrong of course; they'd remained thick as ever. He suspected the 'debts' were more likely to have been a loan Fanny was conveniently forgetting to repay. She was a bridge fiend, and notorious for running up liabilities, her excuse being that her husband was unbelievably stingy with money. Louis had smiled wryly at this – he knew very well it was likely to be true: her husband, Paul Estrabon, was not only his business partner but had been close to him ever since their schooldays together. The bond between them was as strong as that of many brothers, certainly stronger than that of Louis to either Henry in Shropshire or Barnabus in Australia.

He had never before had reason to suspect Lydia of lying to him, and that she might have had reason to do so pained him more than he could endure, but there had been no getting away from it. Had everything he had given her not been enough? What more could he have done? Why had she deceived him? And apart from Louis himself, only she knew what had been kept in the safe. Only she could have gained access to his keys. Louis knew the two detectives hadn't been slow to deduce this.

He opened the bottom drawer of the desk. From under a pile of papers he retrieved the letter, folded into four. Opening it, he held it for a while between finger and thumb, like something unclean, before carrying it to the empty grate. He struck a match and held it an inch from the paper. But before it had more than caught the corner, he pinched out the flame with his thumb and forefinger. Then he refolded the letter and put it back in the drawer.

Six

After leaving the Challoners, Marcus drove back to his sister's home, where he was presently staying. He crawled through a noisy chaos of buses and cars held up by slow horse-drawn traffic, frustrating the urge he had to move as fast as he could, away from what he'd left behind: the brief glimpse of Louis Challoner, very nearly on the edge of going to pieces, and Kitty – looking lost, but so grave and contained. Dry-eyed. Grief so controlled he feared it.

Kitty, he thought, with something approaching despair.

Eliza was, unsurprisingly, not at home when he arrived. He asked for whisky and soda to be brought, and went into what had been his late brother-in-law's study, shrugged off his jacket and threw himself into a deep, leather armchair. For once he was glad of the emptiness of this luxurious mansion flat, one in a gloomy block off Bryanston Square, which usually oppressed him with its cold atmosphere, so different from the warm one, even in its present despair, of the house he had just left. Tonight, he did not want to share with anyone the rage and self-disgust that consumed him, least of all with Eliza.

His sister lived here alone, apart from servants, and she had been happy enough to have Marcus stay with her as long as it did not interfere with the ceaseless round of social activities she had embarked upon since the premature death of her husband. In the event he might as well have been staying in a hotel for all the family intimacy they shared. She rarely came home before three in the morning and never rose until eleven, in order to prepare herself for the next engagement in her diary. The only times they saw each other seemed to be at the homes of mutual acquaintances or if they caught glimpses of each other at the theatre, or across a dance floor. As it was, Marcus might as well have been living with his father, had it not been for the fact that Loddhurst was inconveniently situated thirty miles out of London . . . inconvenient for present purposes, at any rate. And in any case, he and his father . . .

He took a long pull of his whisky, savage with himself for playing fast and loose with opportunities that would never be granted to him again. He was at a loss to know why he had got himself into this situation – or rather, he knew perfectly well, but damned himself all the same and just wished devoutly and with all his being that he had never agreed to it. It had been done for the wrong reasons though mainly, like some errant schoolboy, to appease his father for disappointing him so badly.

Until his retirement Sir Aiden Villiers had been a career diplomat, holding various posts in places as far apart as Warsaw, Constantinople, Vienna and St Petersburg, the latter a place where he had served for eight years. Marcus's mother had died when he was a child of seven and his sister Eliza eighteen. The large gap in their ages and the fact that Eliza had married young meant that brother and sister had never had the opportunity to get to know each other well. Sir Aiden had chosen to keep his son by his side while he lived abroad, delegating his education to a succession of tutors rather than sending him away to school. As father and son they had developed an easy relationship, though not too close; they were perhaps too alike, keeping a tight rein on their emotions. Marcus, who was always adept at his lessons, had delighted his tutors and Sir Aiden had expected great things of him when he went up to Oxford.

What had come over him there? A certain arrogance that led him to believe he was so brilliant he didn't need to work as he should have done? Perhaps. More to the point, life as the child of a diplomat in often turbulent countries had been a protected and sheltered one, since freedom was necessarily curtailed. The unaccustomed association with sometimes wild young undergraduates, many of whom regarded time spent at Oxford as nothing more than a lark, a rite of passage they were expected to go through as a nod to education before taking their place in the social milieu, had led him to drift into bad habits, although to do him justice he had never succumbed to excess. Rather it had been three years of wasted opportunity, fooling around, and ending up not with the brilliant degree, which had been predicted, but with a mediocre one, which had shocked and shamed him and devastated his father. In a mood of self-disgust Marcus had taken himself off to knock about the world in general until he'd worked off his own fury with himself.

He had returned to England to rejoin Sir Aiden, who was now living here in retirement and seeming hell-bent on turning back his home, Loddhurst, to its former glory as quickly as possible. It was a house they both loved; not too large but of some distinction, and his father was obsessed with repairing as quickly as possible the neglect that had occurred during his protracted absences abroad. He was still a comparatively young man, hale and hearty, and confidently expected to be master of Loddhurst for many years yet. Marcus did not enquire too closely into the reason for the hurry.

He himself had at last begun to turn his thoughts seriously to considering how he could make up for lost time, toward plans that would lead to an interesting and useful life, at least until it should be time for him to take over the running of Loddhurst – a prospect not likely to occur in the near future but one he thought he would at some time enjoy. In the meantime, it might still be possible to prepare himself, if not for attaining a post in the academic life as had once been his aim, then perhaps entering the Foreign Office himself. His father, reading him better than Marcus was aware of, had not rushed him into anything, although on that day several months ago when he had contrived to put him in a situation that required a firm decision, it had clearly been because he thought it was time Marcus moved forward.

He hadn't yet finished his drink but he couldn't sit still, and began pacing about restlessly. Dinner was not a regular occurrence here at this house, unless specially ordered, since both Eliza and he dined out most nights, but the events of the day had left him as tightly wound as a watch spring and he didn't feel up to encountering anyone he knew should he go out to find some supper. He made a sudden decision to ring for them to make him a sandwich. After which he would drive down to Loddhurst tonight, rather than wait to see his father the following day. When Marcus had telephoned him to tell him of the tragedy, Sir Aiden had immediately announced he would find time to interrupt his journey to Paris the following day so that they could meet.

Capital! thought Marcus grimly. There was a good deal his father himself would have to explain, even in the limited time there would be. It was not to be hoped or expected that he would put off his visit to Paris – it was one of the regular trips he made, to be with the woman who had been his mistress for many years, a Mme Estelle Bouvier, with which nothing was allowed to interfere.

Marcus had been aware of Mme Bouvier and her place in his father's life for as long as he could remember. Sir Aiden had never made any secret of his attachment to her, a charming and sophisticated Frenchwoman whom he had met when her husband had been an attaché in St Petersburg. Marcus knew nothing of Henri Bouvier, whether he was a complaisant husband, if there had been a separation, or even if he was now dead or still alive. The arrangement seemed to suit both sides, his father was obviously happy with it and he felt it was no business of his to comment on or question something so private.

The idea of doing something positive by going down to Loddhurst tonight having energised him, and having eaten his sandwich, there seemed no reason not to start immediately. As he passed through the hall on his way to his room to change into clothes more suitable for driving, his eye was caught by an envelope lying to one side of the mat. The afternoon post had already been placed on the usual salver; this had been hand delivered and must have escaped his notice when he came in – a plain, white envelope, with his own name written in block capitals. Just his name, no address. When he broke the seal he found inside a single scrap of paper with some sort of pencil sketch on it. The sketch had been roughly torn across: the piece he was holding appeared to be a partial drawing of a dog with a long, bushy tail, lean flanks and long legs. Puzzled, he felt inside the envelope for the rest of it but there was nothing. Glancing at the drawing again it now seemed to him the sketch resembled the hindquarters of a wolf rather than a dog.

In no mood for guessing games, he shrugged, crumpled the paper and envelope into a ball and tossed it into the fireplace, forgetting it was an unseasonably hot May day and there was no fire lit. It hit the fan of pleated, red paper in the grate and rolled out on to the hearthrug. He retrieved it but on second thoughts smoothed out the sketch. He stared at it but it meant no more now than it had a few minutes ago; it was nonsense. All the same, some instinct now made him fold it carefully and slip it inside his leather pocketbook.

Seven

It was an ordeal that had to be faced, going once more into her mother's room, and sooner rather than later. Otherwise it would be a hurdle she might never find the courage to surmount. So at the end of that terrible, unbelievable Sunday, Kitty nerved herself to do it.

The furious clatter of the typewriter sounded from behind the door of the little room Hester Drax used as an office as she went past. To work on the Sabbath was normally against her religious principles. She had, however, announced that the manuscript she'd been working on was finished for all save the last couple of chapters, but there were notes, full enough to make her confident of being able to knock it into shape in no time at all. 'If you should want to see it published, of course,' she'd added deferentially, leaving unspoken her own obvious wish that it certainly should be, and that Mama would undoubtedly have wanted it so.

'That would be up to my brother, but it's not something he must be troubled with at the moment,' Aunt Ursula had said firmly. But there could be no harm in having the manuscript typed and ready for when he was in a position to decide what to do about it, and she was sure Mr Challoner would have no objections to Miss Drax staying on until that was done. Hester had merely nodded briefly. Absolved now from attending to Lydia's personal wants, she was left free to concentrate wholly on the book, and she clearly had no intention of taking unfair advantage of the opportunity to extend her employment here by stretching out the time it was taking to finish the work. One could only admire her tenacity and determination. And her loyalty, of course.

Despite having screwed up her courage, Kitty found her footsteps dragging as she neared her mother's bedroom door, further along the corridor. This time the feeling that she was intruding was worse, so without giving herself time to think she pushed the door open.

There was no reason why the room should have changed, and of course it hadn't. Her mother's scent still hung in the air; the lovely icon winked sapphire and ruby lights from its corner; the silver-topped bottles on the dressing table gleamed; Marie Bartholemew's leather book still stood supported by its soapstone elephants on top of the bookcase. The firebird box had not been magicked from the back of the drawer where she had always kept it hidden away.

But her presence, like a ghost in the room, choked Kitty so that she could scarcely breathe. Like a thief, she lifted the box and slid the drawer shut. And then, hesitating for only a fraction of a moment, she picked up the exercise book which was her mother's next proposed work, the one numbered three, still on the desk where she had left it, and fled back along the passage to her own room as if pursued by Satan.

Once back there she flung herself on to her bed, where she curled up, her back against the headboard, the box clutched to her chest, getting her breath back. Her only thought had been to take the box to safety, as something precious that had been secret between herself and her mother and must not be meddled with by other people, especially the police, should they want to search Mama's rooms, as Jon had warned they surely would. Similarly with the exercise book, although she would make sure to replace that before Hester Drax should notice it was missing.

She ran her fingers over the rich, encrusted design on the box lid and as she felt the filigree gold work beneath her fingers, all at once the desire to open it left her. It was ridiculous to feel as if this familiar object gave out something dark and unwholesome. It was not Pandora's box which she should not open lest she should release all the evils of the world. She lifted the lid. No evil spirits flew out but as in Pandora's box, there was something lying there. Not Hope in this case. What lay there was nothing more than a blank, torn-off scrap of drawing paper – or blank until it was turned over. The reverse side showed a pencil drawing depicting the head and forequarters of an animal – the rest of its body was missing, presumably the half that had been torn away. The animal was recognisably a wolf, a *volk*, as Lydia had translated it.

Although she had never been known to pick up a needle Lydia

had tried at one time or another – and later rejected – most things considered to be feminine accomplishments, the sad little landscape painting that Papa out of kindness kept hanging in his study being the sole remnant of her enthusiasm for watercolours, for instance. She hadn't been too skilful with a pencil, either, but this was one of her better efforts. But . . . *a wolf?* And why on earth was it put secretly away, shut up in her firebird box? Even more curious . . . why was it only half a drawing? Where was the other half? The animal's long, pointed muzzle, the narrow eyes became more realistic, and more menacing, the longer Kitty looked at it. It was ridiculous to feel that small, cold chill running down her spine, and her flesh creeping.

That the box contained anything at all was surprising. All her life, Kitty had known and loved it. Why did Mama keep it empty, she used to ask when she was a little girl, and begged to have it to keep her own childish treasures in. But, normally so generous, she would not let Kitty have it. Perhaps it had been too cherished an object to give to a child, though she had loved the box too much to have maltreated it. Nor was it intrinsically valuable – the glowing red stones she had once thought of as rubies she knew now were only red glass.

'It will be yours one day, darling,' Mama had always said. She had never envisaged that day coming so soon, and in such a way. And that she would not want it when it did.

Later that evening, undressed and in her nightdress, Kitty sat huddled on the broad sill of the sash window that had been thrown up from the bottom, knees drawn to her chin. It was still hot and now humid. Thunder felt to be in the air. A feathering of clouds was massing together above the tops of the trees in the square garden; the branches were stirring, waving in the cold little breeze that was beginning to spring up. She shivered and when Papa's Viennese clock on the landing chimed eleven, though sleep seemed a long way off, she made herself climb into bed. There she lay, still as a statue, feeling too exhausted to sleep, but in the end sleep fell on her like a cloak.

During the night the weather broke. Thunder crashed over the city, waking up its sleeping inhabitants. Lightning flashed, changing London's river to a silver serpent, illuminating the streets and the buildings, the Tower, Big Ben and St Paul's . . . The rain crashed down and flattened the bedding plants set out in the parks and public gardens for the coronation; it ruined the bunting, but Kitty heard nothing of it; she was deep, deep in a dream . . .

A dark forest and a unicorn with silver hooves leading her through it. A golden feather that twists and trembles in her hand, and a huge grey wolf with yellow eyes and slavering jaws who tries to take it from her but then slinks away, his tail between his legs. A great golden bird in a tree who asks her what she wishes for, and when she cannot answer, there is Mama, saying, 'Be careful, little Katyusha. Wishes are liars . . .'

'Miss Kitty,' Emma says as she wakes in a panic, 'Miss Kitty, here's your tea.'

Eight

Joseph Inskip was resigned to having his Sundays disturbed in the line of duty, but as an unmarried man, free of the demands of wife and children, this didn't usually trouble him too much, unless it happened to be a day such as yesterday had been – a scorcher, and too hot to expect anyone to work. But there was nothing he could have done about that – the incident he'd been called out to attend, the shooting in Hyde Park, had had all the makings of Trouble with a capital T.

After the night's storm, the weather showed no signs of cooling off today. If anything it was hotter than ever. Arriving at New Scotland Yard, he took off his jacket, draped it carefully over the back of his chair. None of his colleagues had yet come in, and after considering for a moment, he took his waistcoat off as well. Only then did he pick up and read the note on his desk, from Gaines: a meeting, nine thirty, in his office.

Until recently the two men had been operating from different departments, then Inskip had been transferred from Leman Street in Whitehall to the Yard, and found himself partnered with Gaines, or rather, working as his subordinate. Pooling experiences and co-operating in the interests of solving a complicated case was a concept which should in theory work to the benefit of all concerned, and mostly did, but there was always the possible clash of personalities to take into consideration. That hadn't happened yet as far as he and Gaines were concerned, though Inskip thought it still might. They were still wary of each other. On the surface Gaines was easy enough, even if Inskip thought him too cautious. He was apparently well thought of by the top brass, whereas Inskip knew only too well that he himself was marked down as one of the awkward squad. Not that it troubled him in the least because he also knew that although they might get twitchy at his refusal to toe the line always, it had so far propelled him to where he now was.

The sergeants' office remained empty and he continued to sit

in his shirtsleeves and fancy braces, twisting the heavy, gold signet
ring on his little finger as he thought over the details of the
Challoner case, few as they were as yet.

Her family had chosen to believe it was an accident, which
was understandable. Lydia Challoner had been an ordinary, law-
abiding woman with nothing in her life to suggest that anyone
would have reason to shoot and kill her. But the police knew
just how unlikely her death was to have been accidental. For one
thing, she hadn't really been what one might call an 'ordinary'
woman. She was the wife of a well-to-do stockbroker, living in
a large, expensive London house with servants and a luxurious
lifestyle, and with an extensive social diary, a woman who gave
generously of time and money to various charitable organisations.
And unlike most other women, she had a profession: she was a
successful novelist. Definitely not ordinary.

She was also of Russian descent, Inskip reminded himself. But
that, he put on one side for now.

He picked up a pencil and rolled it between his palms. At the
moment, there were too many so-called ordinary women around
who were *not* law-abiding. Nice women who'd turned themselves
into screaming harridans. Suffragettes, causing damage to property
and untold trouble to the police – not to mention the public
– disrupting life in general with their uncouth behaviour and
outrageous demands. Plenty people out there who had been
at the receiving end and some of them wouldn't jib at retaliation
if they should happen to discover who the perpetrators were –
though not, as yet, to the extent of taking a gun and shooting
them.

There were a lot of women of Mrs Challoner's class lately,
women of leisure with time on their hands, who led lives secret
from husbands who'd have been willing to take a horse-whip to
them if they knew what they were up to. Inskip would've felt
the same way, if he'd had a wife at all, but he had not, a situation
he'd no intention of altering in the foreseeable future, either. Had
Lydia Challoner, despite what everyone believed, secretly been
one of those militant suffragettes? Had she committed some
terrible crime in the name of Votes for Women, against someone
who had decided to take his own revenge? They'd grown ruth-
less, these women, and cunning, adept at evading the police and

escaping detection. Her husband had given a definite no to the suggestion; he had sworn she'd never been active in the movement, or even remotely connected in any way with it.

They had had to let Challoner go, of course. Bringing him down here to the Yard hadn't been much more than a routine gesture, following the rule book; they could have continued to question him at his own home, but that had been the way Gaines wanted to play it. Inskip had a strong feeling the DCI might have had more instructions about this from on high than he was saying.

But Louis Challoner was by no means yet in the clear. If he had so wished, he'd had plenty of time last Sunday between leaving his club in St James's and arriving home in Egremont Gardens to have made a detour into Hyde Park. There was only his word for it that his hired taxi-cab had taken so long. His gun was unaccountably missing, and a search for it would be pointless; it could be anywhere, tossed into the Serpentine or even the Thames after using it. More importantly, such a gun as he owned wasn't capable of firing the distance from where the shooter had been spotted (by several other witnesses, as well as by Marcus Villiers). All the same, his reaction when he opened the safe had been unsatisfactory enough to give rise to some suspicion that all was not as it seemed.

Inskip glanced at the big round clock on the wall, donned his waistcoat and jacket and went to see Gaines.

The inspector's office was already building up steam and Gaines, himself in shirt-sleeves, glanced at Inskip but made no comment. He'd ceased to question why the sergeant insisted on dressing in full toff rig-out, even in sweltering temperatures like today's, or why it went harder for him than most of the others when he had to go undercover disguised as a docker or a navvy. He waved him to a seat and passed a paper across the desk. It was a report by the police surgeon saying that the bullet extracted from Lydia Challoner's body had come from a Mauser C96 pistol, known as the 'broomhandle' because of its long barrel, unhandy in some ways but popular because of its distance capabilities. Much more so than the pocket pistol (also incidentally a Mauser) allegedly missing from Challoner's safe.

It was after all no more than had been expected. From the first it had been evident that a long-range gun must have been used, capable of firing accurately from where it was assumed the marksman had been waiting. Because of this, Special Branch were taking an interest in the case – special in the sense that it had been created specifically to monitor the activities of foreign troublemakers. They had a wealth of experience in dealing with incidents involving firearms and special responsibilities for those calling themselves anarchists – and other like-minded troublemakers. The identification of the weapon and its implications were sinister: guns of any kind, in particular sophisticated Mausers, rather than the usual knives, were currently the weapons of choice for members of any one of the foreign revolutionary gangs who had been terrorising the community and causing the police so many big headaches over the last few months.

The East End of London was where it all happened. Violence roamed the streets of Whitechapel, Spitalfields, Stepney and surrounding districts untamed at present. Inskip had grown up around those parts. He had come over from Ireland as a child with his parents, who had sought a better life in England. It hadn't materialised for them. His mother had died, worn out by endless child-bearing, his father a few years later of consumption, a legacy from his famine-wrought childhood. Inskip and three of his brothers had survived, and they had all taken ship to America to join an uncle already settled there. Inskip had joined the Boston police, but he missed London and after a few years he'd returned and joined the Metropolitan Police as a constable. His knowledge of the East End where he'd grown up was one of the things which had helped in his transfer to the detective branch – he knew every hole and corner, every vice contained within it. Thieving and murder, men and women stabbed in drunken fights between wife or husband, some shopkeeper or other robbed and left for dead, a prostitute found strangled in an alley, homeless vagrants done to death for their broken boots and other rags – just some of the more mentionable occurrences the police had always had to deal with. The deprivation and hopelessness of the inhabitants had always seen to that. But now, over and above the violence which had never been far away, violence of another order had crept in.

The different ideologies, the confused and chaotic politics of the many ethnic groups who now made up most of the seething population had worsened the situation. Terrorists from Eastern Europe: rabid Bolsheviks and the more moderate Mensheviks, communists, anarchists, communist-anarchists, nihilists; Poles, Russian Bessarabians and Odessans mingled with the earlier huge influx of Jews who had fled from political and religious persecution and settled here. Some of them were idealists, working for when they could return to their own country; some had found asylum here, a better life, and wanted to stay; others were thugs, hardened by brutality and privation. Fighting between the various gangs was so common it wasn't worth remarking on, and infighting within the gangs wasn't unknown. Fists, knives and broken bottles, pitched battles were the order of the day – and now guns had entered the scene. Many of the newer arrivals were Letts – Latvians who had fled Russia after their bloody but unsuccessful revolution in 1905, which had made them enemies of the state, wanted by the hated and feared Ochrana, the Secret Police. These terrorists existed in lawless bands dedicated to obtaining funds by any means, criminal or otherwise, to smuggle back to their comrades in Russia in order they might carry on the fight. They were hard, dangerous men, and if they were apprehended, they didn't hesitate to shoot and kill, as the police recently had good reason to know.

But what had any of them to do with a woman of no importance to them or their schemes?

Gaines must have been reading his mind. 'Let's not lose sight of the fact there may be more to Mrs Challoner than appears. Why should she take that gun, for instance? Assuming she did. For someone who had such an avowed distaste for them, it doesn't make sense.'

'Unless she'd decided her husband was right, after all, and she did need protection.'

Gaines gave a grunt. 'All the same, it wouldn't be a good idea to ignore any possible connections, unlikely as they might seem at the moment, with our friends from the East.' He paused. 'Such as her being of Russian descent.'

'She's lived here all her life. And wasn't much more than a baby when she came here with her father.'

'And possibly growing up steeped in his views. Don't forget, he was an exile after he fell foul of the authorities in Russia, and he carried on his support work from here until he died.

And – he was a friend and disciple of Kropotkin. Possibly helped with the smuggling of arms to Russia, and certainly with subversive literature.'

Inskip shouldn't have been surprised at how much information the DCI had managed to gather in such a short time. George Gaines seemed to have a well of subterranean information he could draw on at will. An educated man, one of the new breed of policemen, he had already built up an impressive success record in CID though he was not yet forty. His mildness was deceptive. His bite was worse than his bark on occasions.

Inskip shrugged. 'Kropotkin – isn't he a spent force nowadays?'

'Men like Kropotkin are never a spent force.'

The Russian-born Peter Kropotkin styled himself an anarchist-communist, another exile who had escaped to England, where he'd now lived for many years. Philosopher, writer and revolutionary, he was loved and revered by his countrymen, and by now regarded as the Grand Old Man of the Russian extreme nationalist movement. But since this didn't extend to his advocating the overthrow of the British throne, he was allowed to spend his exile in England, tolerated and even much admired by many of the British intelligentsia.

'That's true, but do you really believe someone like Lydia Challoner could have been mixed up in all these plots, with those ruffians? That she did something to upset them and they killed her for it?' Inskip argued. 'It's surely more likely she was killed for some private grudge that had nothing to do with them. The Letts aren't the only ones who can get hold of Mausers.' He wanted it to be so: a man shooting her because she had played him false; a jealous woman, even, shooting her rival. Although it had to be said, chasing East End troublemakers was more to his liking. He didn't have much patience or understanding of people like the Challoners and the spheres they moved in.

'Open minds, Inskip, open minds. We don't know about any Russian connection, of course, but there's enough for us to keep at it. Find out more about who she associated with. It's a queer set up whichever way you look at it. Somebody had it in for her, even if it wasn't one of the Letts. Maybe someone who wants us to believe it was them. By the way, there's a nephew, too. Runs a paper called *Britannia Voice*.'

Inskip knew of the *Voice,* a newish paper with its offices in
Whitechapel, but not much of its editor. There were as many of
these little papers around here as there were political factions, all
with their own axes to grind. 'I've heard of him, that's all. Bit
of a Bolshie, like the rest, isn't he?'

'Socialist, he calls himself. Sent down from Cambridge. He
writes inflammatory articles, speaks at meetings, advocates protest
– though non-violent, as far as I'm aware.' Inskip raised his
eyebrows. Protest without violence in those parts was like bread
without butter.

The telephone rang. Gaines rose and unhooked the instrument,
held it to his ear and spoke into the mouthpiece. Inskip stood
up to leave but he was motioned to stay. The conversation seemed
to be all at the other end, and he sat back, thinking about what
had just been said.

Not one policeman in London had forgotten those Russian-led
murders in Houndsditch just before Christmas – nor were they
likely to, considering the three men killed and the two who had
been critically injured were their colleagues, unarmed against a
gang of Latvians intent on tunnelling into a jeweller's shop to
steal the contents of his safe. It had been a disorganised attempt;
the noise they had made alerted someone to send for the police.
Accustomed to the brutal methods of capture and torture by the
police in their own country, the robbers, armed to the teeth, had
had no hesitation in shooting before escaping.

The shock had run through the Force like an electrical charge.
The public's sense of fair play was outraged. Unarmed British
police, officers of the law going about their business, killed by
foreign immigrants? The affair was disgraceful.

But although it had taken some time, eventually the escaped
Houndsditch murderers had been traced to Stepney, to a house
in Sidney Street, and on a snowy day in early January the house
was besieged by the marshalled forces of the police, this time
armed. A detachment of the Scots Guards had been called in to
assist. The houses along the street had been evacuated and the
area cordoned off but the operations were not helped by the
general public crowding the surrounding streets, climbing on to
the roofs of nearby houses and hanging out of windows in the hope
of glimpsing something exciting. On the second day the Home

Secretary himself, Mr Churchill, was cheered when he appeared
and joined the police. The situation had been in danger of turning
into a farce, Inskip recalled. Though bullets were whizzing around
no one seemed to realise it was not a spectator sport, that the
gunmen inside the house were desperadoes, prepared to shoot to
the death.

The shoot-out had only ended when a fire broke out in the
house, either by a shot having ruptured a gas pipe or the gang
staging an unsuccessful smokescreen. The fire raged until eventually the house collapsed. Two charred bodies were subsequently
recovered but the man thought to have been the leader, the
so-called mastermind, was nowhere to be found. Peter Piatkov.
Peter the Painter, they called him. Artist or house painter, take
your choice. A weedy-looking individual but responsible for the
biggest police operation and search ever launched, but with now
no hope whatsoever of him turning up. Not after the lack of
response to the offer of an unimaginable five-hundred-pound
reward for information on his whereabouts.

Trying to link the killing of a lady such as Lydia Challoner
with this sort of intrigue would be flogging a dead horse.

Gaines finished his call. He hooked the receiver to its stand
and sat back, stroking his moustache. It was unfashionable and
made him look older. Perhaps that was why he wore it. Inskip
himself was clean-shaven – or until late afternoon, when he began
to look blue around the jawline. 'Marcus Villiers,' Gaines said.
'Looks like a visit to that young fellow's on the cards. Better still,
have him brought in here.'

Nine

Working here in Whitechapel, Jon had been prepared to find himself among like-minded people, which of course he did. This part of the East End now included any kind of political activist you could name. It was fruitful ground for seeds of discontent to grow and flourish, nourished by the sort of propaganda the *Voice* was intended to put out. Fiercest in the midst of this melting pot of different ideologies were the escapees from the bloody but unsuccessful Russian revolution of 1905, who had nothing to lose and to whom human life meant less than nothing.

'That is true,' agreed Lukin. He was the owner of the *Voice*, a big, blond Russian with wide cheekbones and light blue eyes. 'It is sometimes necessary, even to take the life of a Tsar,' he had shrugged, totally uncomprehending of the British enthusiasm for the forthcoming crowning of a king. The Tsar he was referring to was the Emperor and Autocrat of all the Russias who had been assassinated by a bomb – twenty years ago, but not in any way forgotten, Jon reflected. Nor for that matter had it succeeded in halting the hated and repressive Tsarist rule it had been meant to bring to an end.

He had no idea who Aleksandr Lukin was, apart from being a man educated enough to speak the fluent French that was used by the nobility of his homeland as being more elegant and sophisticated than the barbarous native Russian spoken by the backward, illiterate peasants. His English, too, was excellent. Jon supposed, without any basis for the supposition, that he had been born into the ruling classes, but about what had led him into exile he could only speculate. Lukin gave away nothing on that subject.

Nor had the precise nature of any beliefs held by the owner of the *Voice* been made apparent when he and Jon had first been introduced. He thought now that the Russian had been careful *not* to make them too evident. Seemingly wealthy, he had only made it known that he wanted a British editor for his new venture, someone capable of putting radical ideas forward to the British public without using the violent rhetoric of his own compatriots. He had discovered that far from influencing those who were in a position to support their cause, that sort of inflammatory language served only to give reactionary English politicians and those otherwise in power a reason to dismiss such. Jon, delighted to have been approached, eager to throw himself into something he considered worthwhile, had not, with hindsight, given enough serious thought to what might be expected of him. Although by no means averse to stirring up and urging strike and protest for the basic human rights of better wages, shorter hours and decent living conditions for working people, he was no anarchist. Unlike them he had no wish to see the state abolished, and it was becoming apparent that these lukewarm beliefs did not go far enough for Lukin. He had recently hinted at the possibility of closing the paper down if circulation didn't improve – if Jon's future editorials didn't have more fire. He was in any case considering the possibility of returning to Russia.

This Monday morning, however, after the traumatic events of the weekend, as Jon stood looking out of the second floor window on to the busy street below, his thoughts were not concerned with the growing problem of his association with Lukin. He was eaten up by guilt.

The office, and his own sparse living accommodation, was situated on the second floor above a pie-maker's shop. On the first floor lived the pie-maker himself, his wife and three children, while the attics above were the occasional venue for meetings of what Jon had discovered to be a group of hard-drinking Latvians. From his vantage point, he could see along the length of the street, its tall, narrow buildings housing shops and stalls at street level, a decent enough street for these parts, but which hid the maze of filthy, squalid tenements, noisome, narrow alleys and dark court-yards that crowded behind it, where no one was safe and policemen walked in twos. Already the street was thronged – though not yet as congested as it would later become – with people going about their concerns, and the business of the day already well under way. Electric trams clanged and swayed along their rails, cleaving their way through the busy traffic of horse-drawn carts and motorised delivery vehicles. Bicycles – an unimaginable luxury for most people in this part of London – were notably absent, and the only private motor cars were those passing through. Today Jon couldn't summon up his usual lively interest in what was going on; he barely noticed as two ragged-trousered street urchins, each clutching an apple and chased by a shouting stallholder, dodged between the traffic and knocked into a thin-chested errand boy pushing a handcart piled high with fresh bread. The lad staggered, the cart tipped and spun across the cobbles. In the consequent brouhaha the grinning urchins escaped, giving cheeky gestures and followed by a string of invective from all sides. The bread cart was righted and the loaves picked up – doubtless to be wiped off and sold – and the usual cheerful, noisy life of the street resumed.

Jon remained where he was in front of the window. He had taken off his jacket and his hands were thrust deep into the pockets of his flannel trousers, his shirtsleeves were rolled to the elbow, pencils bristled in his waistcoat pocket, ready for work. Yet the weight of sadness he felt was making him reluctant to move. Light footsteps sounded on the stairs and Nolly entered, in the grey coat and hat she wore to the office in the mistaken belief that it made her inconspicuous. On removal the coat revealed a businesslike striped blouse with a short tie, the blouse tucked into a dark skirt, tightly belted in stiff petersham. She was glowing, and had brought in with her a small bunch of sweet violets. She buried her nose in them. 'Aren't they heavenly? Too delicious for words! Old Anna was selling them and I simply couldn't resist. I'd have liked her whole basketful but I thought I'd better not. I don't suppose it's likely you have anything I could put them in?' she added doubtfully, belatedly realising the impulse might have been less than practical.

'You might find a jam jar or something next door,' Jon replied vaguely, gesturing towards his living quarters. As she disappeared, he moved over to his desk, where he thrust his hands through his untidy brown hair and then began to shuffle papers about a bit. When she came back, his head was bent over them.

'Do smell, isn't the scent divine?' She wafted the violets under his nose before setting them down on her desk.

She had put them into a large cut-glass inkwell taken from a stand given to him along with a few embroidered cushions, pretty knick-knacks and other things he didn't need, by his mother. The result only served to emphasise the shabbiness of everything else. Lady Devenish had not, of course, any idea what his rooms were like. Jon had been careful not to invite her here.

'Mm, yes, lovely,' he replied absently. 'What's happened to the ink?'

'Oh, I poured it away. These sweet little things won't last long, I'm afraid, so you'll soon have the inkwell back. It was only the red ink, anyway.' She beamed at him and uncovered her typewriter.

When she had first arrived, Olivia Brent-Paxton had instructed him that she was to be known as Nolly, the pet name her three older brothers had bestowed on her, one of whom had been a fellow undergraduate with Jon. It was he who had persuaded Jon to give her the job. 'For God's sake give her something to do! She's driving us all mad since she came home from being finished in Switzerland. Too much energy and nothing to expend it on.'

Jon was in need of an assistant, but he said quickly, 'Oh, I don't think so, Pax, round here ain't the sort of place for nicely brought up young women—'

Will had waved away the objections. 'You'll be here to see she's all right. Anyway, you don't know Nolly. She can take care of herself. And she's a dab hand at organising,' he added pointedly.

Jon was not efficient at keeping his papers – or anything else for that matter – in order, and in the short time he'd been here the one not very large room that comprised the office of the *Voice* had become crammed to overflowing, the walls papered with anything that needed keeping and for which there was no room on his desk or the floor. The residue sometimes overflowed into the room next door, where he lived.

'Give her a try, old chap,' his friend pleaded. 'Her heart's in the right place – she'd love what you stand for. You won't regret it.'

He owed Pax a favour – many favours – for getting him out of scrapes, waking him up in time for lectures after a rough night – and the rest. All the same . . .

'Look here, I'll bring her round, and you can see for yourself.'

'I can't promise,' Jon said weakly at last.

He quickly saw what Pax had meant when he met her. The diminutive Miss Brent-Paxton was not at all shy, and within minutes was giving it as her opinion that she could cope with all this mess, and making several suggestions as to how it could be accomplished. Avoiding Pax's grin, Jon was left with a dazed feeling that it was he who had been interviewed and that he'd had no option but to agree to employing her.

His reservations for her safety were soon put at rest. At first, she had arrived at the door in a taxi-cab and Jon had escorted her safely towards home at the end of each day. But the cab was fairly soon taken only as far as Aldgate, from where she made her way on foot to the office, making frequent stops to chat to the owners of shops and stalls on the way, buying bagels or warm latkes, honey cakes and pickled herrings, Polish bread, sausages and smoked cheese from the foreign food-sellers, which she insisted they shared at midday, correctly guessing that Jon existed mainly on pies from the shop downstairs. She had become a familiar figure in the street. Now that they knew who she was and where she worked, men touched their caps to her, women smiled, stallholders slipped her extra treats. Mrs Ostrowski, the old Polish woman who did what she could to clean amongst the chaos of the office and Jon's quarters, was her slave within half an hour. And though he still escorted her to where she could take a taxi-cab home in the evenings, his first worries abated.

She had a whirlwind energy and a private life that Jon could only speculate on. He'd found it expedient never to answer the telephone himself when she was there, since it was just as likely to be one of her admirers, with whom she had giggling conversations. But she rapidly had the workings of the paper at her fingertips, chivvying Jon along to make sure it came out on time, deciphering the articles he tended to scrawl on odd bits of paper then rattling them out briskly, if sometimes inaccurately, on the noisy, second-hand Remington typewriter they'd acquired.

All the same, she was really a complication he could do without. He thought about her more than was good for him – like now, when his eyes constantly strayed towards her desk. As usual, her hair was scraped back anyhow for severity, but the effect she tried for was spoilt because the silky, dark curls refused to be confined by pins and constantly tumbled around her piquant little face. Enchanting. Distracting. Especially when she gave him her wicked, beautiful smile or said with a perfectly straight face something that made him laugh.

'Shall I type this ready to take to the printers?' she asked now, holding out a paper he'd left on her desk.

'Mm, yes, I suppose so.' She gave him a quick glance but said no more and resumed her typing, while he continued to watch her, the scent of the violets she'd brought in wafting across the room. She was quite without inhibitions, determined to be emancipated, and had declared herself in favour of free love. As the weeks went by it had fleetingly crossed his mind more than once to wonder how accommodating she might be if he were to suggest she move in with him, but his courage failed him there. She was, after all, the daughter of a rural dean, and despite her frank, uninhibited way of talking he was pretty certain where she would draw the line when it came down to it. Perhaps he ought to offer to marry her – though in the manner of St Augustine, not yet, he amended hastily. At any rate, in view of Lukin's implied threat to close the paper he supposed he ought to get rid of her before it should happen, in fairness to both of them.

He became aware that the clatter of the typewriter keys had stopped and that she was looking at him with concern. 'What's wrong, Jon? Is it Lukin again?' She did not care for Lukin and thought he harassed Jon.

'No, it's not Lukin, not this time.' He fell silent. 'You haven't heard, then?' he asked at last, unnecessarily, since it was quite evident she had not.

'Heard what?'

He could scarcely bring himself to voice what had happened, the impossible thing that unfortunately was only too true. 'You don't know about my Aunt Lydia?'

'No, what?' He didn't answer immediately. 'Is it something too awful?' she asked, her eyes wide.

'It couldn't be more awful. She's – she's dead, Nolly.'

'*Dead*?'

'She was shot yesterday by some madman while she was riding in the Park.'

The silence that followed his disclosure took him aback. He had anticipated sympathetic tears but not that she would also lose colour so rapidly. 'Not . . . not Hyde Park?'

'Which other park would she be riding in?'

She went on staring at him. 'It . . . it wasn't meant to be like that,' she said faintly. And then she burst into tears.

* * *

The day before, Paul Estrabon's Sunday afternoon had been disturbed by a distracted call from Lady Devenish, giving him the devastating news about Lydia, and the almost equally incredible information that the police had taken his partner Louis Challoner away for questioning. She hadn't made much sense, but later that evening, when Paul telephoned back to enquire further about Louis, she seemed to be in more control, saying he was back home but firmly refusing to call him to the telephone. 'He needs to rest, Paul. He's been through quite an ordeal and he's thoroughly shaken. Don't expect him into the office tomorrow, either.'

Paul didn't argue. 'I'll come round first thing in the morning. I won't trouble him, but there are things we shall need to sort out.'

The next morning, his wife, Fanny, had broken the habit of fifteen years and had risen at the same time as he. It was unusual for her to be out of bed before eleven and unheard of for them to meet at the breakfast table. But the circumstances were hardly usual. It was not every day that one's dearest friend was shot dead. Not every day that Fanny needed to catch her husband before he left for the office.

'I scarcely slept a wink last night,' she remarked, nibbling on a piece of toast.

'Understandable, my dear Fanny,' he replied absently, polishing off the last of his ham and eggs and reaching for the marmalade.

It was evident to Fanny that he did not appreciate the effort she had made to rise in time to breakfast with him, a meal he had heretofore eaten alone, his only company *The Times*. She observed him critically, this man she had married fifteen years ago and still didn't know completely, perhaps not at all, she sometimes admitted to herself. This powerful, darkly handsome man, with brown eyes and very white teeth, all due to his Latin-American inheritance, far back as that was. A man who, when he was young, had given every impression of being possessed of a smouldering, passionate nature, when she knew (perhaps the only one who did) that he was really a cold fish, interested only in his business and making money which he was disinclined to share.

'Don't you simply hate being without money, Lydia?' she had asked her friend not too long ago.

'I can't hate it because I've never been in that condition – not since I married Louis, at any rate.'

'You can have no idea how fortunate you are not being married to a man who doesn't spend a penny if he can help it – on his wife, at least.'

Lydia had heard this before. 'But you have a lovely home, clothes – look at those diamond earrings Paul bought you for Christmas. He has never struck me—'

'You simply don't *know*, my dear.'

'Well, I suppose he wouldn't have chosen to be a stockbroker if he weren't aware of money. Louis is, very much.' She laughed. 'They're all as dry as dust in that direction.'

But Louis had never been remotely mean to Lydia, though she had been too spoilt to appreciate him. And she hadn't taken the broad hint that Fanny so desperately needed a loan. Trying to get money from her had been almost as bad as trying to squeeze it from Paul.

She toyed with her toast, plotting how she could get round Paul and persuade him to part with the money she must have. Not only for her gambling losses, of which he disapproved most strongly – which was shockingly unfair considering the far greater monetary risks he took every day, though that of course was with other people's money – but to pay for the other expensive necessities for which she had run up bills here, there and everywhere, many of which could no longer be disregarded. An idea slid into her mind. Should she approach Louis and ask for the money Lydia had owed her? She was not a sensitive woman, but even though it hadn't been much, in the circumstances she thought it would not be advisable. Louis Challoner, however generous to his wife, was not a soft touch. Unless . . . Her heart began to beat rather fast.

Nothing else came to her and as she watched Paul getting on so calmly with his breakfast she began to wonder, as she did rather too often nowadays, why he had married her. She knew why she'd married him – he had been very rich, and was still incredibly good-looking. Although he was the same age as Louis Challoner, in appearance he was ten years younger, mainly because he kept himself fit with regular exercise such as tennis and riding. At the time of their marriage, he had declared himself very much in love with her. But his attention had wandered after a few years. He had sworn his affairs were the sort of distractions men were expected to have and did not affect his feelings for his wife, and they had eventually managed to come to an agreement, but unsatisfactory to Fanny, at least. She had a jealous temperament and the rumours that reached her constantly stirred up emotions which could only be appeased by gambling at cards and spending exorbitant amounts on new clothes and other luxuries. Or by taking her revenge in malicious gossip of her own instigation.

She poured herself fresh tea. 'Don't you feel anything?' she asked, eyeing him narrowly through the steam as she raised the cup to her lips. 'Lydia was your friend, as well as mine. The wife of your best friend,' she added carefully. 'And what about Kitty? You've always said she feels like a daughter to you.' They had never had children, something he had minded more than she had. 'They were – almost family.'

He looked at her then, for much longer than was necessary, it seemed to her. 'And of course, you would know all about family, my dear, wouldn't you?' he said silkily. The blood rushed to her face.

He folded his newspaper neatly, in the way he did everything, and stood up. 'She was indeed a friend . . . to both of us. But Lydia is dead, my dear, and nothing can bring her back.' He stood up and looked at the unusual apparition of his wife at the breakfast table, in her morning dishabille, her little cat-face devoid of paint or powder. 'How much do you want this time, Fanny?'

It was only after he had gone and she was regarding the meagre offer he had made with more than usual dismay that the idea which had come to her hardened into determination.

Ten

Kitty couldn't believe it was nine o'clock on Monday morning as she struggled out of the dream and back into consciousness. 'Goodness, can that be the time?'

'Yes, it's nine o'clock, Miss Kitty. I thought not to disturb you before, you were so deep asleep.'

As Kitty turned her head and felt her pillow wet with tears, yesterday returned. She wanted nothing more than to close her eyes, sleep again and forget everything, but a cup of tea steamed on the bedside table and Emma, determinedly cheerful, was crossing the room to draw the curtain a little against the sun streaming into the room. 'Goodness, what a storm we had last night! Looks as though you had a fine old storm in there, too.' She waved towards the bed sheets, tangled into a knot.

'I had a dream,' Kitty said groggily.

'More like a nightmare by the look of it.'

'No, just a dream. Strange, but not precisely frightening.' Yet she shivered. Mythical creatures that didn't exist. A wolf, a unicorn. A golden bird. What was there to be afraid of? She almost reached for the diary she kept at the side of her bed to write down what she could still recall, but this wasn't something she was likely to forget.

She washed and dressed in a hurry. Yesterday, she'd felt incapable of thinking; her mind had blanked out, her body felt as though she was dragging leaden weights around. But the tears that had wet her pillow last night seemed to have dissolved the hard knot of disbelief. However sad this new situation was it was real, and she must face the fact and act responsibly, be a help to her father. She was no longer the little girl who had sat on Mamoshka's knee listening to tales of magic; she had grown out of all that. She must stop the silly, needless worries that had been lingering in the corners of her mind . . . what did they amount to after all but a misplaced Russian cross and a scrap of paper in a normally empty box? Although they must have preyed on her mind and been part of what had induced that strange, lingering dream, they were nothing more than small inconsistencies. And they couldn't matter a jot now.

After breakfast, at which Louis didn't appear, she steeled herself to go along to his study and talk to him. He wouldn't be going into the office, he would for the present be taking time off, Aunt Ursula had said. Anything important, he would deal with from here for the time being. Mr Estrabon had already been to see him this morning, when presumably the necessary arrangements for his temporary absence had been made. Kitty felt an enormous wash of relief to hear this. A strong shoulder to lean on, a cool, sensible and practical man, Paul Estrabon could be relied upon to help her father. As a child, she had called him uncle, until she felt herself too old to do so, with the result that she hadn't yet found another way of addressing him. Mr Estrabon was too formal and to call him Paul was unthinkable.

She was very disappointed that he hadn't stayed to speak to her and must have shown it. 'He was in a hurry, Kitty – there will be a great deal for him to take care of now,' Aunt Ursula said gently.

'Of course.'

In point of fact she discovered he hadn't yet left, although he was about to do so when she crossed the hall to go to her father's study.

'Kitty, my dear!' Not normally a demonstrative man, he held her hand warmly, then suddenly gave her a great hug, sat down with her and asked her how she did. She was surprised at how much affected by the news he was; there was an unmistakable tear in his eye when he spoke of her mother. He was such a distinguished-looking man, elegantly dressed as usual, tall and slim, his once-black hair just beginning to turn grey, with the patrician, rather haughty look of a Spanish grandee. Haughty until he smiled his brilliant smile. He and Papa had been at the same school and then gone into business together. He was very rich and something of an art expert, especially on Japanese porcelain. All his passion was centred on his collection of rare Celadon ware which Kitty had once been privileged to be allowed to handle. Mama had gone into raptures over it but it was all pale grey-green or grey-blue with little or no decoration and failed to appeal to Kitty. Perhaps she'd been too young to appreciate its subtlety.

'I've already offered your father whatever help I can give, your aunt too, and it goes without saying that is extended to you, Kitty, my dear,' he said now. 'I'd very much like to think you can approach me or my wife, if you should need to talk to anyone. Promise me you will?'

From a childless couple, Kitty realised this was a magnanimous offer, and she promised she wouldn't forget. He was so kind, she could readily see herself asking him for help, should she need it . . . but his wife? Fanny Estrabon was a small, pretty woman with a tip-tilted nose, a penchant for gossip and an apparently insatiable passion for cards. Sharp and brittle, she was not the sort of woman Kitty could envisage seeking kindness from.

He put his hand on her shoulder and surprised her further by depositing a light kiss on her forehead before he left.

When Kitty went into his study she saw her father looked a little better this morning than the hag-ridden old man he had appeared after his return from the police station, but it was still painful to see how much he had aged. He was a broken man and looked weary to his soul.

'Good morning, Papa.' She kissed him gently and he patted her hand absently. There was an awkward pause.

'Well, Kitty.'

She still hesitated. She had never been shy of asking anything of her mother; no subject had been taboo between them (at least, until those horrid doubts had arisen lately) but with Papa it was different. Although she'd never had any reason to question his affection for her – he had always been a kindly, indeed an indulgent father, though not outwardly expressive of his emotions – Kitty had always been conscious of a distance between them; there had never been the same closeness that had existed between herself and Mama. Perhaps that had simply been the bond between mother and daughter; perhaps if she'd been a boy it might have been different. Or maybe if she had never existed, Lydia herself would always have been enough for him. It was not by any means the first time this had occurred to Kitty; it made her sad sometimes but she knew it was true, and it seemed to her it had never been more evident than now. All the same, she was her father's daughter, as much a part of his world as Lydia had been and now that they had lost her she must not admit she would never be able to take her place.

Her nails were biting into her palms in the effort not to let this thought go further, to do what she'd come here to do. She couldn't bear to look at his tortured face but something urged her on. She had to start somehow, somewhere. She swallowed hard and plunged. 'Papa, who do you think could have opened the safe?'

Although he had papers on his desk to give an illusion of busyness he had been doing nothing when she went in except staring aimlessly into space. Now he picked up a pen and began fidgeting with it, rolling it between his fingers. Suddenly he threw it on to the desk, scraped his chair back and walked to one of the two tall windows that faced the square, where he stood rigidly with his hands clasped behind his back.

'Papa?'

He still didn't reply. Kitty had never known him struck dumb like this. He was normally a good conversationalist, amusing and charming, an excellent raconteur. Ladies liked to sit next to him at dinner and be entertained by his sometimes mischievous wit. Maybe the silence meant he was trying to control his anger at a question she should not have asked. It was one to which they both knew the answer – and one it wouldn't have taken the police long to figure out. There was only one key to the safe; it was kept on Papa's watch chain, which on his own admission never left his person – except, of course, when he was in bed and sleeping. Who else could have taken it but Mama? How easy it would have been to wait until he was deeply asleep, then to take it quietly, slip downstairs and open the safe. If one could imagine why she would want to.

She took a deep breath. 'It was Mama, wasn't it?' He still didn't answer. His hand was gripping the tassel of the curtain tie-back until his knuckles showed white. At last he turned and came back to his desk. He sat down heavily and after a moment or two he shrugged and spread his hands, palms uppermost.

'But whatever did she want with your gun? She refused to have one of her own to carry around.'

At last he found his voice. 'Perhaps she changed her mind.'

'You don't believe that!'

He sighed, and then seemed to come to a decision. 'No, not really. No, it wasn't the gun.'

'You mean there was something else she wanted from the safe? But you told the police all her jewellery was still there.' And in any case, there would have been no need for her to steal downstairs like a thief to take out what she had merely to ask for. 'What was it?'

He shook his head and was silent again. Then with an effort he roused himself. He wiped his hands across his face and said, 'No. It's best that you shouldn't know, Kitten. Believe me, it's best that way.'

This use of the pet name for her which he hadn't used for years was not to be borne, a crushing dismissal of her ability to understand. She drew herself up. 'I think you have forgotten that I am not a child now. If there is something about Mama you are keeping from me, don't you think that's being unfair?'

He gave her a sharp look of surprise, perhaps at the coldness he heard in her voice, then picked up the pen and began toying with it again. 'She . . . your mother . . . she had . . . expensive tastes.'

Well, that was no secret to anyone. But apart from her bridge debts it had never been apparent that Papa disapproved of her extravagances, he was wealthy enough not to mind what she spent his money on – the inordinate number of white kid evening gloves she seemed to need, the silk stockings she bought by the dozen pairs, the array of perfumes on her dressing table; the furs, the trinkets – and not least the costly works of art to adorn the house.

'She owed a large debt to Mrs Estrabon.'

'*What?*'

Fanny Estrabon? Kitty had seen Lydia shaking her head the morning after playing cards with Fanny, deploring the eye-watering debts her friend had incurred the previous evening. It seemed odd, to say the least, that she should have allowed herself to run up debts in the same way, and even odder that it should be Fanny to whom she owed money. But . . . 'I suppose that means she took something from the safe to sell? Some of her jewellery?'

'No, no, the jewellery is all there. It was . . . oh, it was just something else.' He waved a hand as though whatever it was had been of little importance.

'Such as what, Papa?'

He avoided looking at her. She sensed a struggle in him – whether to tell her or not. 'It was the icon,' he said at last.

'The icon? But it's still upstairs in Mama's room, I saw it last night.'

He shook his head. 'Not that one.'

His head was bent. He had a bald spot she had never noticed before. Bewildered, she waited for an explanation As far as she was aware there had only ever been one icon: the most precious thing in the house, and precious not only for its monetary value, which was supposed to be fairly considerable. It was said to be unique and her mother had loved it passionately. Now it seemed there had been *another* icon in the safe, unknown to her, and presumably just as valuable, if it was worth stealing. But all this was posing more questions than answers. Why should Mama have taken it – and presumably the gun with it? If it was an attempt to make it look like a robbery, it didn't sound like her. She had been too astute to believe that would hold water for long.

'Did you tell the police about it?'

'No, I did not,' he said quickly, raising his head and looking directly at her, suddenly alert and startling her with the harshness of his look. 'And neither will you, do you hear me, Kitty? It has nothing to do with what happened to her. Besides which – the icon upstairs, you know, hanging on the wall in her room, that one is only a copy.'

'*What?*' This was getting way beyond her. 'I – I don't understand.'

He studied her for a while then he stood up and came round to the chair where she was sitting. His face softened and he drew her back towards the small two-seater sofa which stood between the two windows. 'I'm sorry,' he said when they were seated. 'Oh God, all this has knocked me off balance. I haven't been thinking straight.' With a sudden awkward gesture he drew her nearer. He smelled not of acrid cigarette smoke as he had yesterday but cleanly of the bay rum he used after shaving. 'You're right,' he admitted, 'it will be hard for you to understand but it might be better if you did know.'

She leaned back a little to look at him and the movement caused her to brush against the looped-back velvet window curtain. The hairs on her arm stood on end, though she was not sure whether the frisson that went through her was due only to the friction of the curtain or the growing feeling of apprehension at what Louis was about to tell her. 'How much do you know about icons, Kitty?' he asked at last.

Icons? Not very much, she had to admit. Mama had taught her their religious significance, of course. She understood that an icon, a depiction of either the Virgin Mary, Christ, or a saint, was to be venerated as a holy object, a devotional tool for prayer. And indeed, the icon of the Madonna which had its place in her bedroom was the very one Lydia's once childless mother, Mariya Ivanovna, had prayed to, asking for a child. Lydia had miraculously been born, though Mariya had not lived long after her birth. The precious icon had been kept safe by Nikolai when the two of them had escaped from Russia, along with Mariya's amber jewellery, to be cherished until he died, when it had passed to Lydia herself. Though Mama had professed herself not religious, she had nevertheless cherished it too and set it up in the traditional holy corner, where she saw it daily.

'Yes, well, I don't know too much about them myself,' Papa admitted, 'but I'll try to explain.'

He had always been willing to explain patiently to Kitty anything she didn't understand. She settled herself to listen and as he spoke, it became clear that simple as an icon might seem, the wider subject of iconography was more complicated. 'It's an ancient tradition, you know, Kitty, to tell the story of the Gospels in pictures for simple people who were unable to read. Here as well as in Russia. Think of St Andrews at Southfields.'

In the village church which Aunt Ursula attended the Bible story was told in its beautiful ancient stained-glass windows. But also there were remnants of a medieval Doom painting of the Last Judgement surviving on the west wall, bodies writhing in the torments of Hell behind the congregation as they knelt, prayed and sang hymns. Kitty shivered a little, as though a goose had walked over her grave. 'But Russian icons are not in the least like that.'

'No. In Russia religious teaching took the form of icons

painted on wooden panels, or on cloth glued to wood. They look Byzantine because that's what they were, basically. When Christianity spread from Constantinople their art spread with it. And the older they are the more precious they become. You have to understand that iconographers, the artists who made them, were skilled artisans but they never became famous since their work was never signed. It was deemed an honour to paint such a subject . . . done for the glory of God, not for glorification of the painter himself.' He waved a hand. 'Nowadays it's possible to make icons by machine, to produce them in quantity, so they're relatively worthless, whereas your mama's icon was very old and . . . almost, one might say, priceless.' He searched for the right words to continue. 'That was why we had a copy made, years ago. An excellent copy – so good it's probably worth a considerable sum in its own right, but a copy all the same.'

It just wasn't possible that the glowing icon in the corner of Mama's room was only a *copy*, was it? But if she was to believe Papa, it seemed that it was, that the real one had been kept locked away. Had been, until he had opened the safe in the presence of the police and found it missing.

If you had looked at something for years, a perfect copy of the original work of art in every tiny detail, studied it and believed it to be beautiful, and loved and worshipped it for its sheer perfection, where was the difference in the two – apart from the fact that you knew one had been made by the hand of the master who had conceived it? Kitty's mind was in too much of a turmoil to try and sort out the complications of that. Other things intruded: such as how was it possible Mama's debts had been so enormous that she had resorted to selling the original? And to whom did she owe them? Not to Fanny Estrabon, that was surely not possible. 'And you really believe she took' – she could not bring herself to say stole – 'the original to *sell* and pay her gambling debts?'

'What other reason could there be?'

She kept silent. I don't believe you are telling me the truth, Papa – or not all of it, she thought. There's something you're keeping back. If his intention was to save her more pain, it was having the adverse effect. He was still excluding her. And that hurt, very much.

'You must not be so mistrustful, not with me, Kitty,' he said softly, but with a note of coercion in his voice that jolted her. 'Say you are not.'

'Of course I'm not.' She couldn't say it with any great certainty, though. She felt this wasn't her father she was seeing, but a stranger. The last two days had made him different, in a way she couldn't put her finger on. And she didn't feel it was only due to the shock of Mama's death, and the way she'd been killed.

'Then trust me and we'll consider the subject closed.'

'Trust me.' The same words Marcus Villiers had used yesterday. Immediately, she began to wonder what *he* knew about this? She felt even more certain now that there had been something inherently mysterious about his relationship with Mama. She had not been mistaken. The word 'collusion' sprang immediately to mind. As her daughter, Kitty did not want to believe that possible, but as a woman she knew it was. But . . . collusion about what, for goodness sake? It seemed obvious he had known Mama in ways they – or at least she, Kitty – had never suspected. In which case, how much more did he know about why Lydia might have been killed than he had been willing to admit?

Her father brushed his hand across his eyes, as if to erase what was too painful for him to think. 'Don't look so stricken, child. Be brave, for your Mama's sake, as well as mine. Give me time, and all this will be cleared up. Meanwhile, be careful what you say to the police when they come back, as they will. They will question you and try to put words into your mouth.'

He was right about the police coming back, at least. When Kitty left the study, Bridget approached her. 'Oh, there you are! I've been looking for you. One of those policemen is back – he's been talking to everyone and now he wants to see you.'

'Me? What does he want to see me about?'

'Only the same silly questions they've asked Uncle Louis and all of us about your mama, I suppose. Such as had she quarrelled with anyone, had anything been worrying her, had she seemed different . . .?' She sounded impatient but she looked shaken – thinking of her own differences with Lydia, probably. 'It's the chief inspector, not that sergeant. He won't bite your head off, he's quite reasonable.' She added, 'For a policeman. All the same, I'd watch my step if I were you.'

What did she think she, Kitty, had to keep from the police? For a moment, she actually wondered if Bridget knew about the icon, but she could hardly think that possible. Had she guessed those secret things about Mama that Kitty had been worrying about? Was that what they had quarrelled about? She had been in a very edgy, unaccountable mood since yesterday. But suddenly, in a very un-Bridgetlike way, she quite gently kissed Kitty's cheek. 'Don't worry, my love.'

Kitty didn't know who was the more surprised of the two.

Eleven

She was indeed relieved it wasn't Sergeant Inskip waiting for her, but the other detective, Gaines. Unlike Inskip, he didn't set her teeth on edge. He seemed to be a calm and matter-of-fact sort of man, though something warned her not to underestimate him. When she went in, he was finishing a cup of tea someone had brought him and immediately put it down and stood up. He held out his hand. 'I won't keep you long, just a few words, if you don't mind.'

'No, I don't mind.' But she felt bound to add, 'Though I can't see there's anything I – or any one of us, for that matter – can tell you that's going to be of any use.'

He studied her for a moment and his voice was noticeably cooler when he said, 'I'm here to help find who is responsible for your mother's death, Miss Challoner. She may have left clues that will help us find that person, whoever it was.'

'What kind of clues?' she asked sharply, and instantly regretted such a crass question, as if she was expecting him to creep around on all fours with a magnifying glass, like Sherlock Holmes.

But Gaines didn't give any sign that he found it anything but a reasonable query. 'Clues that may give some indications of what sort of life she led, what people she may have associated with, what may have led to this shooting.' This sounded very much like a hint that he thought she might not have been altogether blameless for what had happened, which gave Kitty a distinctly hollow feeling. After a pause he said quietly, 'Your mother, Miss Challoner, was a victim, not a suspect.'

'Then how can her friends matter?'

'If any of them were Russian, it may have a great deal to do with it.'

'One or two acquaintances were, but none of them were close.' This was the same question they had asked Papa. To the police, Russians would signify trouble, she supposed, after those shootings earlier this year which had so appalled everyone, but they must be clutching at straws, surely, if they were trying to link her mother's death to that sort of person, simply because she too had been shot, and because her father, Kitty's grandfather, had been Russian. He had, however, been Nikolai Kasparov, and it was clear his activities in support of his countrymen, blameless or otherwise, could not have been unknown to the police.

'I see.' Gaines stood up. Her answer seemed to have satisfied him for the moment. Perhaps, then, he could begin by seeing her mother's bedroom, and where she had worked? He added unexpectedly, 'I'm aware this may be a trifle upsetting but I'll try not to be intrusive.'

Her bedroom? 'Yes, of course,' Kitty said nervously. 'I'll get someone . . . my father, my aunt?'

'Perhaps you'd be kind enough to do the honours yourself? We can have our little talk at the same time.'

Kitty shrank at the thought of going into that room yet again, never mind having a 'little talk' and she wondered for a moment what he would do if she refused, but of course she knew she had no choice. He was politely waiting for her to lead the way.

His keen interest in everything was evident as they went up the wide staircase that curved gracefully between polished mahogany banister rails to the rooms off the first landing where the bedrooms were situated, and then upwards again to the next floor. It was such a familiar background to Kitty, having lived in this same house ever since she was born, that it was something she rarely noticed. Certainly, it had never occurred to her before how it might appear to strangers, but now, seeing it through his eyes, she was suddenly aware of how the rich reds, blues and greens of the Turkey-patterned carpet echoed the stained-glass window on the first landing, how in turn the window threw lozenges of light on to the pale walls. Of the huge, dark blue vase, reputedly from the Imperial Porcelain Factory in St Petersburg, hand-painted and lavishly ornamented with gilt, standing four feet tall in the angle of the staircase, and of how the rich oil paintings on the walls contributed to an overall impression of taste and discrimination. Seeing in this light the collection of beautiful objects chosen and arranged by her mother made her catch her breath and once again, she was rather glad it was Gaines, and not Inskip, who was here. Inskip was certainly the sort of man who would despise such expensive comfort.

'Here we are,' she said abruptly, pushing open the bedroom door and standing back to let him in.

'Thank you.' He waited for her to step inside before following. His gaze went immediately to the icon in the corner and she had to remind herself that he knew nothing about it; he could have no idea that it was only a facsimile of something far more valuable that had been kept locked in the safe in her father's study and was now missing. It was hard for Kitty to believe, yet, what she had just learnt about it, that something so beautiful and arresting could be a mere copy, or that her mother, for whatever reason, should even have contemplated selling the original. Gaines seemed to be looking at it a long time – but it would have been strange if anyone seeing it for the first time had *not* stared at it. Its glowing beauty immediately drew attention away from anything else in the room, prettily furnished in cream and a deep rose colour, but otherwise unremarkable. 'Striking,' he said.

'It was her most treasured possession. It had belonged to her family for generations.'

Eventually he took his gaze away. 'I need to look in the cupboards and so on, Miss Challoner, you understand?'

She stood back to watch, but all he did was to open a few doors and drawers and take what seemed to be a fairly cursory glance at the contents, almost as if he was just going through the motions. An elusive drift of perfume escaped from the rows of silks, velvets and chiffons as the two wardrobes were opened. A shoe was dislodged from its rack – champagne kid with a buttoned strap across the instep, Louis heels. She had worn that pair last week with – Kitty turned away, unable to bear it, but he quickly replaced the shoe and shut the doors again. She could only suppose that detailed searches, if they were deemed necessary, were normally delegated to someone of lesser rank, and that those clues Gaines had spoken about and hoped to find were perhaps less tangible. He did what he had to do with efficiency and with little fuss, hardly disturbing anything at all, throwing out the odd question here and there as it occurred to him. Questions about her mother's state of mind recently, whether Kitty had been aware of anything worrying her, had anything unusual or untoward occurred? Kitty shook her head. Which church had she attended? The Russian Orthodox Church, she told him, adding that she very rarely went at all lately. What sort of recreations did she enjoy? Theatre, music, reading – and riding. He asked what Kitty knew about Marcus Villiers. She was in such a quandary over Marcus just then that it was as well she had little more to tell Gaines other than that he was a friend who went riding with her mother and sometimes escorted her to the theatre or a concert which her father did not wish to attend after a tiring business day.

He made no reply to this, and it was only when he came to the polished inlaid trinket box, lifted the lid and saw the ambers inside that he spoke again, his interest apparently aroused, asking if any of it was of great value, or if anything was missing.

Kitty could say with certainty that everything was intact, or at least as intact as it had been when she had seen it on Sunday morning, and that the box contained nothing particularly valuable, but at his request she checked it again and reminded him that there was other, more expensive jewellery in the safe downstairs. 'It's all here,' she repeated. The pendant-cross was something of such little significance it could add nothing to his enquiries, certainly nothing that could have anything to do with Mama being killed, but in the end she added, 'Apart from a silver cross which is usually kept with the other things. It's nothing important. I expect it'll turn up somewhere else.'

'What sort of cross?'

'A crucifix – what they call a three-barred cross.' She described it to him: the upright with its two horizontal bars at the top, one shorter than the other, and a third diagonally angled bar near the feet. 'It wasn't of any particular value and my mother never wore it. It was too heavy, for one thing. She may have got rid of it.'

Not for one minute did she believe that, and if Gaines didn't either he didn't say. He had moved over to the pretty little walnut writing table and the nearby bookcase with the Russian novels on the shelves, and was looking at the book bearing the name of Marie Bartholemew between the soapstone elephants. 'So this was where your mother worked?' he asked. So, he had been told about her writing. The thing she had been so insistent on keeping a secret was in the open now. Soon, everyone would know.

'Yes, except when she was working in the office with Miss Drax, who types her manuscripts.'

'My wife enjoyed reading this.' He tossed out the information as he opened the desk's single, shallow drawer, finding nothing in it but pens and pencils, India rubbers, blotting paper and the like. 'No new work in progress?'

'No,' Kitty answered, reflecting this was at least the second time she had lied to him within a few minutes, salvaging her conscience by trying to believe none of it was a direct lie. In any case, the few pages in the exercise book labelled number three that she'd picked up and which was still in her own room, though she hadn't yet attempted to decipher Lydia's scribble, could hardly be described as work in progress. 'Miss Drax is working on getting her second novel ready for the publishers. When you're ready I'll take you along to see her if you wish.' And there she could leave him. She desperately wanted to be alone. She was beginning to feel there wasn't enough air in the room to breathe. Her chest felt tight.

'Are you all right, Miss Challoner?'

'Yes, it's nothing.' But she'd caught a glimpse of herself in the dressing table looking glass a few moments ago and knew Gaines had every justification for concern. She looked pale and drained and unattractive. The black dress didn't help. She'd never worn black before and it leached all the colour from her face. Aunt Ursula had sent for ready-made mourning clothes from Swan and Edgar for Kitty, Bridget and herself, tutting over the cut and quality when they arrived, but thankful that they need only be worn until they had all been measured and fitted for better ones, though they would of course still be black. 'It's just a little warm in here, that's all.'

He crossed to the window and opened it wider. She breathed deeply, aware that he was studying her and then, seemingly satis-fied she wasn't going to faint at his feet, he turned his attention to the Russian tracts and pamphlets that occupied the bottom shelf of the bookcase, while Kitty stood near the window, through which came a dancing breeze, the scents of summer, the hum of traffic and the sounds of a distant hurdy-gurdy. An ordinary day for other people. Below, a nursemaid in a round felt hat wheeled her charge round the garden in a wicker perambulator, with a terrier on a lead. A small boy jumped alongside, astride his hobby horse. A cat arched its back at the dog, but when the dog began to show interest in a fight thought better of it and melted into the bushes.

Back in the room Gaines was picking up one booklet after another. He paused in flicking the pages over, and she sensed some sharpening of interest in him. 'I'd like to take these away, if you don't mind,' he said at last, gathering them together. Politely, as though it would have made any difference if she had objected. 'They'll be returned to you, of course.'

'They were my grandfather's. I mean, he wrote them, years ago.'

'Not all of them.' He indicated names on the front covers of one or two. The pamphlets written by Nikolai Kasparov were by this time a little ragged, timeworn and well-thumbed, but the ones Gaines seemed more interested in looked newer. She saw the reason for the small leather attaché case he had with him when he packed them into it.

'People used to send my mother this sort of thing, you know,' Kitty told him. 'It annoyed her considerably. Some of those who wrote those pamphlets are very violent in their opinions, I believe, and she hated violence of any kind.' But a small voice inside was whispering that she had kept them, hadn't she, and not thrown them away, and though he didn't say so, she felt certain he must be thinking the same thing.

He said suddenly, 'Why don't we sit down for a moment, Miss Challoner?'

'Oh. Oh, very well.' There were several chairs in the room, and she chose to perch on the edge of the rose-coloured velvet armchair in front of the window, leaving him to take one of the straight chairs. If he had brought her here on purpose to this room, which he must realise held such emotive echoes for her, to trap her into saying something unwary, she didn't want to be facing the light. But he sat stroking his moustache for a while without saying anything, then took the wind out of her sails by saying abruptly, 'You have a cousin who edits a radical newspaper called *Britannia Voice,* I believe?'

'Jon?'

'Jonathon Devenish, yes. He has quite advanced socialist

opinions, I gather. Like those of the Russian revolutionaries who wrote these booklets.' He tapped the attaché case which he had deposited on the seat of the chair next to him.

A sense of teetering on the brink of disaster made her heart give an uncomfortable thump in her chest. 'Perhaps you should look at the name of the paper again, Inspector Gaines. *Britannia*, it's called,' she said as steadily as she could manage. '*Britannia Voice*.' She put a heavy inflection on the '*Britannia*'.

'Owned by a Russian called Aleksandr Lukin.'

Kitty tried not to show that this disagreeable titbit was news to her. 'Well, not every Russian is a troublemaker. And Jon does have a strong social conscience, yes, but he isn't interested in turbulent Russian politics. Or in violence at all, for that matter. Quite the opposite. He's a pacifist.'

He sounded rather tired when he answered. 'Everyone with a social conscience today is interested in the terrible news coming out of Russia, and in its politics. It's a country in turmoil and what's happening there is arousing sympathy throughout the world, as I'm sure you know. You may be surprised how many people in Britain are showing their support for a revolutionary movement.'

'Including my mother?' She knew what he was hinting but it was outrageous to suspect Lydia of being in league with those thugs when she had been so adamantly against them. 'I can tell you she felt very strongly that those who were robbing, stealing and killing while calling themselves patriots were doing actual harm to their cause rather than good.'

'From what I have gathered, however, Mrs Challoner was a generous and compassionate woman. Is it feasible she wouldn't have wanted to help her countrymen?'

'Well, of course she did. In a sensible way. She – and my father – gave to many refugee charities.'

'Yes,' he said softly, 'and your father has told us she was a member of SFRF.'

A silence fell between them. The Society of Friends of Russian Freedom. 'Well, yes, I believe she was. But not an active member,' she said eventually, hating the defensive way she heard herself speak. And she couldn't help asking herself with a sick, shocked feeling: how do I know? Lydia had been British in all that mattered, but how could anyone deny her obsession with her Russian roots?

Gaines stood up. 'All right, Miss Challoner, don't upset yourself. We'll leave it at that for the moment. I shall probably have to talk to you and the other members of your family again, but for the moment I'd like to see your mother's secretary – Miss Drax, you say her name is? Perhaps you can tell me where I may find her?'

'I'll show you where she works.' Kitty hoped he had been trying to be kind to her, yet she had sensed the steel under the velvet glove. She was more than willing to leave him to the tender mercies of Hester Drax, though she felt bound to give him some warning. 'She can be a little intimidating, but she really is awfully efficient. My mother was not especially good at spelling and grammar and that sort of thing, but she used to say Miss Drax wrought marvels, tidying it all up.'

The SFRF was a society dedicated to stirring public opinion outside Russia against the iniquitous system of government prevailing in that country, where basic human freedoms were denied, and where suffering, deprivations and even the torture of its oppressed people were the norm. As well as Russian émigrés resident in Britain, the members who made up the society included many British and American sympathisers, among them not only hot-headed students, but also intellectuals, political thinkers of left wing tendencies, and writers such as the famous playwright Mr Bernard Shaw.

The aims of the society were to make the stark facts of what was happening in Russia known to other peoples in the world by means of lectures, the distribution of literature and the publication of its newspaper, *Free Russia*. Anyone who read it – as in fact Kitty herself had, from time to time – would know that it was not in any way sympathetic to the criminal methods used by those confessed anarchists now causing such trouble in Britain – like those who had attempted to rob the Houndsditch jeweller (expropriation of funds, they called it, money to send home to their revolutionary-minded contemporaries, though to everyone else it was just plain theft) and which had ended with such tragic consequences. She was furious that merely being a member of the society and reading its newspaper should be held against her mother.

Some people, of course, might have been mistaken and believed that it should be. Had Mama been shot by someone like that, some wildly illogical, mad person who in some twisted way thought that because of her Russian birth she must be on the side of the terrorists and therefore deserved to be killed?

And Jon. What had Gaines meant when he had made the point about the newspaper he edited being owned by a Russian? Kitty didn't really know why that surprised her, yet although she had to acknowledge it must be true, it didn't follow that Jon could possibly have anything to do with the death of an innocent woman – his *aunt*, for heaven's sake! To whom, she reminded herself, he had always been so close.

The unanswered questions hovered, gathered, like an impending storm, an incipient headache. She was utterly confused and her overwhelming feeling was that she desperately needed to talk things over with someone. They came to mind one by one, but one by one she rejected the idea of approaching any of them: Papa, too wrapped up in his own misery at the moment; Aunt Ursula, practical and bracing but a little biased in the matter of her mother, to be honest; even Bridget, especially Bridget: clever, clear-headed and usually all too willing to give advice but not now, for some reason.

There was, of course, Marcus. Marcus Villiers, who had been with Mama when she died. He was a large part of what Kitty didn't understand. Yet she knew suddenly, with certainty, regardless of her ambivalence about him, that Marcus was someone with whom she felt she should talk. This despite the fact that there was so much that was unexplained, mysterious even, about him. And in any case, where was he? He had not put in an appearance yet, though he had promised they would speak soon, and whispered that she should trust him. He had looked stricken as he had said, 'I should have protected her.' Why was he blaming himself for something he surely couldn't have prevented?

Gaines, left in Miss Drax's workroom with her, began by asking her the same questions he'd asked everyone else: how had Mrs Challoner seemed recently? Had she been worried about anything? Acted unusually? He received the negative answers he'd expected, the sort most people gave when a loved one had been murdered – no one was going to admit that she'd been anything less than perfect. He then said he would like to examine any papers and so on Mrs Challoner had left behind, to which she tightened her lips further and remarked tartly she hadn't supposed he was there for any other reason.

She seemed to be living up to her reputation as a bit of a Gorgon, though apart from the primly folded mouth and a frown of disapproval, she was in fact a handsome, if rather cold-looking, woman, somewhere in her early thirties, he estimated. The thick bottle-bottomed spectacles she was presumably forced to wear did her no favours of course, drawing attention from a good skin and classic features, thick and glossy dark brown hair, which it was a pity she chose to wear severely drawn back like that. She was thin, flat as a washboard, but wore her unobtrusive clothes with a certain elegance. A glance told him she worked meticulously on an uncluttered desk. He noted a top copy and two carbons rolled into her typewriter; on the right of her desk were three separate piles of finished pages, precisely squared up, and to her left was an open exercise book. A tray of sharpened pencils stood handy. She sat with her hands poised above her machine, as if she wished to dissociate herself from the proceedings and was only waiting to recommence typing immediately after this unasked-for interruption to her work.

Hers was not the only desk in the room, though it was the largest, a sturdy, workmanlike construction. It stood at right angles to one of the two windows in the room, which was a smallish, corner one; there was a less imposing desk, which Miss Drax said was the one her employer had used only when they needed to work together. As he looked around for somewhere to sit she indicated its chair.

'A kind of collaboration between you and Mrs Challoner, was it?' he asked, turning the chair to face her.

'It was not.' She sounded affronted. 'I merely typed out each day what she had written and prepared the manuscript for publication.'

Which might, he thought, have been no easy task, if the incomprehensible squiggles he could see as he squinted at the exercise book from the wrong side of the desk were anything to go by. 'That seems like a hard day's work.'

'Not at all. I was able to offer a few suggestions as to spelling and so on, but that was all that was needed, indeed all I could contribute. I have no imagination,' she said flatly.

'Very well, then, Miss Drax, if this was Mrs Challoner's desk, I'd better have a look inside it.'

She seemed to take great pleasure in telling him that he wouldn't find anything which was going to help and when he began to open the drawers he saw this was likely to be true. Like those in the little writing table in her bedroom, they were almost empty of anything interesting. Apart from a small book he picked up, there was little more than a good supply of new, marbled-covered exercise books and one or two other odds and ends. He was beginning to adjust to a different view of authorship. Not the author starving in a garret, this one, tearing her hair, constantly crossing out, altering and rewriting; nor yet a modern-day Ouida, reclining on a sofa with a cigarette in a holder, dictating ad lib. Or perhaps that *was* what Marie Bartholemew had done. 'Did she dictate her work?'

Miss Drax looked rather as though this was a suggestion beneath contempt. 'Never.'

'Did she write anything other than novels?'

'No,' she said dismissively, adjusting her spectacles and bending over the exercise book once more.

'Miss Drax.' She looked up again, her eyes immediately drawn to the little book he was still holding, elegantly covered in grey watered silk and fastened with a pretty little gilt clasp. 'I think I need to take this with me.'

'I'm afraid you can't. That's her personal diary. It's private.' She held out her hand for it.

'Is there something in it you think I shouldn't see?'

'How should I know? I was not party to her private thoughts.'

'I'm sorry, but I must insist.'

'It's locked.'

It was. Tiny as the decorative clasp appeared, it was actually a lock – pretty useless as a security device, but enough to deter casual curiosity. 'Then I shall need the key. Otherwise, I must force it open.'

He had succeeded in disturbing Miss Drax's icy calm. She had flushed in a dull, unbecoming way and opened her mouth as if to argue the point, but he forestalled her by putting the diary into his attaché case along with the Russian tracts he had picked up in Lydia's bedroom. Eventually she opened one of the drawers in her own desk and took out a tiny key which she offered reluctantly. 'Thank you. I'll give you a receipt for it, of course.'

He put it into his attaché case and as he raised his head he caught a glimpse of her unguarded face. She looked anguished. After a moment he said, 'Are you sure there isn't anything you want to tell me?'

'Why should there be?'

A few minutes later, after writing his receipt and handing it to her, he was at the foot of the stairs, in the hall.

For a while he contemplated talking once again to Louis Challoner, the only one he hadn't seen this morning, but he was pretty certain they'd got out of him yesterday all he was prepared to give, for the time being at any rate. He was already sweating. It wouldn't do any harm to let him sweat a bit more.

His visit had been disappointing, he decided as the front door closed behind him and he ran down the steps. He'd expected to gather more from the interviews he'd had with the people who had lived with Lydia Challoner and known her best. But this was often the case in the first days after a family tragedy, especially when it had been as traumatic as this. They might have had second thoughts and found reasons to be more forthcoming with what they were presently holding back the next time he interviewed them.

Twelve

Inskip, after having failed to make contact with Marcus Villiers, made his way towards the *Britannia Voice* offices in Whitechapel, where he instantly felt more at home amongst the familiar clamour of everyday life, regardless of the stench issuing from the glue and soap-boiling factories and the odours of foreign food permeating everywhere from the main streets to the noisome back alleys. It was all malarkey in his opinion, thinking the Bolshies had anything to do with this murder. But he was happy enough to do as he was told and to leave the other side of the enquiry to Gaines, though he wasn't the only one working on the same lines: as well as liaising with Special Branch, as many men as Gaines could justifiably spare had been detailed to check on those foreigners under constant surveillance, most of them speaking barely a word of English, or acting sullen and uncommunicative. Gaines was right to insist every line of enquiry should be pursued, of course, but Inskip privately believed it ludicrous to contemplate a lady of Mrs Challoner's class having anything to do with these foreign gangs, simply because of some tenuous Russian connection. Their lives were as far apart as the North and South poles; they were from different worlds . . . she from very near the top and the others from somewhere near the dregs of society. For all her supposed gift with words, he doubted if even her imagination could have extended to encompass the way these desperadoes she was supposed to have associated with existed – little more than cut-throats, thieves and robbers, when you came down to it.

The assistant behind the counter in the pie-maker's shop over which the premises of the newspaper were situated directed him to a side door which opened on to a narrow, shabby, lino-covered staircase, but he found his means of ascent presently barred by the heavily built person who was coming down the stairs. He stepped aside, raising his hat politely. 'Mr Devenish?' The big fellow, who Inskip now saw was probably too old for the young chap he'd come to see, gave him a look, jerked his thumb upwards but said nothing and continued on his way down.

Inskip shrugged and carried on to a half-landing. Another leg of the staircase went up to the next floor but here was a door with peeling green paint and a slightly tattered piece of cardboard pinned to it, a temporary-looking expedient which hadn't stood the test of time. BRITANNIA VOICE, it announced in large, black, printed capitals, underneath a crudely drawn logo. The untidy young chap at the desk facing him when he opened the door looked up and smiled pleasantly. The smile still held but became ever so slightly strained when Inskip introduced himself and produced his warrant card, but he stood up and came round the desk, offering his hand.

'I'd like a few words with you, Mr Devenish. Is there somewhere we can be private?'

'Miss Brent-Paxton is entirely discreet.'

The pretty, dark-haired young woman who had been following what was being said with bright-eyed interest, lowered her gaze, picked up a sheaf of papers and began reading intently.

Inskip mentally shrugged. If Devenish didn't mind discussing his private affairs in front of his staff, that was up to him.

'I know why you're here, Sergeant, I've been expecting someone.' The young chap had an engaging air of frankness, waving him to a chair and perching himself on one corner of his desk, projecting nonchalance with a swinging foot. Inskip noticed at once that he had on odd socks. 'It's this sorry business about my aunt, I presume?'

'Mrs Lydia Challoner, yes. What can you tell me about her?'

'What is there to tell? Except that I was extremely fond of her – as most people who knew her were.'

'Someone wasn't. Someone made a point of shooting and killing her.'

The assumed nonchalance slipped and a curious expression crossed his face. He was evidently upset about his aunt's death but Inskip could recognize anger too when he saw it. Devenish folded his arms across his chest and drawled, 'So what steps, may one ask, are our police taking to find him?'

Inskip did not respond to the jibe. 'Every step we can, sir.

Which includes talking to anyone who knew her well. Especially her family. Where were you, for instance, at midday on Sunday?'

If he'd been expecting a visit from the police, he must have known this would be asked but it evidently nettled him. 'I? What does it matter where I was? My God. You are unbelievable.' It was to be hoped he meant the police in general and not Inskip in particular. 'I was here, working.'

'On Sunday?'

'Yes,' he replied shortly. 'I live through there.' He indicated a door at the far end of the office. 'I was here until my mother rang me with the news. After which I went straight away to Egremont Gardens to see if there was anything I could do. And if you want to know if anyone can corroborate my being here, you should speak to the paper's owner. He was in the office with me until about half past twelve.'

'And the owner is?'

'His name is Lukin, Aleksandr Lukin. You've just missed him. He was here until a few minutes ago.'

'Ah.' The blond giant he'd passed on the stairs – he should have known. 'The name sounds Russian.' Jon nodded. So the information given them about the proprietor of the *Voice* had not been mere speculation, then. 'Your aunt was Russian, too, wasn't she?'

'Not really. Not in any meaningful way. She happened to have been born in Russia, that's all. To all intents and purposes, she was as English as you or I.'

Inskip let that pass. 'Your paper's a newish venture, I understand, Mr Devenish. Doing well?' He had already made it in his way to read through several back numbers. The paper was small, both in size and content, and seemed to have been written mostly by its editor, the other contributors being regular but extremely few in number. It could hardly be paying Devenish much, if anything, and could even be running at a loss, Inskip suspected. These small newspapers came and went, but he knew Devenish was Sir Jonathan, a title he disdained to use, and presumably he had a private income which he very likely did not. One of the new breed of young idealists who'd been stricken with a social conscience and felt able, with the weight of privilege behind them, to challenge the prevailing class system without undue hardship to themselves.

'What sort of woman was your aunt?'

'She was beautiful. Not in the accepted sense but . . .' He spread his hands helplessly. 'Exceptional.'

'And talented.'

'That, too.'

'Did she have any connections with this paper?'

'The *Voice*? What on earth gave you that idea?'

'She was a writer, wasn't she? And never mind her Britishness, she was of Russian descent. You tell me the owner of your paper is Russian. Did your aunt never write anything for you?'

Jon didn't hide his amusement. 'Have you read that book she wrote? No? You should. Not great literature, admittedly, but not a penny novelette.'

Why should that preclude any other type of writing? Words were words, as far as Inskip could see – nor would it have prevented her from using a pen name, as in fact she had done when she'd written that novel as Marie Bartholemew, but he didn't think it necessary to say this. Devenish had taken the point.

'Look here, I'll tell you frankly, Sergeant, you're wasting your time pursuing that line. Added to which I've no more idea than you how my aunt came to have been killed. But I can tell you it had nothing to do with any sympathies or otherwise she might have had with Russian politics.'

'She was shot with the sort of gun these anarchists favour – a Mauser pistol, to be precise.'

'Then I don't follow your logic. If she was, as you seem to think, on their side, why should they have shot her?'

Hard to explain the reasoning.

Devenish, who had resumed the chair behind his desk, leaned back to a dangerous extent and regarded Inskip over his steepled fingers. He smiled, as if he had divined what the other was thinking. 'You *are* wasting your time, you know,' he repeated. 'Even if it should turn out to be one of those gang members, you're unlikely to find which one – wouldn't you say?'

The tone nettled Inskip, but it was only echoing what he thought himself. It was only too true that they didn't have a cat in hell's chances of finding the perpetrator – much less nailing him for it, even if by some miracle they did. All the same . . . His glance fell on the large round clock on the wall and he did a double take. 'Is that the time?'

The young woman put aside the papers she was allegedly reading. 'Oh, take no notice of that, it's useless – gains like mad if I don't remember to wind it up, which I don't always. Jon never notices. He doesn't know if it's today or tomorrow.' She smiled. 'Would you like some coffee, Sergeant? I'm sure you'd like some, Jon, wouldn't you?'

'Thank you, Nolly.'

Inskip said he would be glad of a cup before he left. He'd been wondering where he'd seen her before and suddenly he remembered where, as she disappeared into what Devenish had said were his own living quarters, from whence could be heard water running into a kettle, the rattle of china. Presently there came the smell of coffee. Silence fell while they waited. Devenish seemed absorbed in his thoughts. He leaned sideways from his chair, idly reaching for a paper which was on the floor beside his desk and then ineffectively shuffling other papers together on his desk, while Inskip took stock of his surroundings. Fanatically neat himself, he wondered how anyone could work in all this mess, how anyone could have managed to accumulate such a mass of paperwork in the less than four months of the paper's existence. But then he saw that although the walls were practically invisible under posters, notices, and other unidentifiable papers, with one wall devoted to crammed bookshelves, he began to see there must be some kind of organised chaos about the way they were assembled together in piles on the shelves. There was even a battered row of mottled grey box files, clearly labelled. It was probably due to the young woman, who now placed a cup of steaming coffee in front of him and held up a sugar bowl. 'One lump or two, Sergeant?'

'Three. Please,' said Inskip.

'Well,' said Nolly when the sound of the sergeant's boots on the lino-covered stairs had died away and the door to the street slammed behind him, 'that was a close shave.'

'You mean your timely intervention to get me off the hook?'

In fact Nolly had suggested the coffee because she noticed Jon had looked as desperate as her brother did when he was in need of a cigarette. Jon didn't smoke but she had rightly guessed he might be in need of a diversion. 'Well, it did, didn't it?' He raised his eyebrows and she gave a short laugh. He was pleased to hear it. He'd missed that laugh. She'd been unusually subdued since hearing about Lydia, after that burst of tears when he'd told her what had happened, and the remark which she had refused to explain. 'Oh, come on,' she added, 'don't pretend not to understand.'

'I don't. Understand, I mean. I don't know what you're talking about.'

'Oh yes you do, Jon dear, you do.' She began to gather the used coffee cups together. 'But that sergeant's pretty sharp. He already suspects you were fibbing, and it won't take him long to put two and two together.'

His gaze travelled to the paper he'd picked up from the floor, now covering the latest article submitted by 'Cicero'. Maybe he'd been too late, attempting to hide it. If Nolly had noticed, maybe Inskip had, too – though he couldn't have made the connection – could he?

'Lord, Nolly, nothing gets past you, does it?' She looked as pleased as though he'd paid her a compliment. Which indeed, he had. He liked to think he could lie as well as the next man when the situation demanded it and thought he'd deftly steered the police sergeant away from tiresome questions. 'You and my sister – you should meet, she's another one for mind reading.'

'Oh but we've already met.'

He stared. 'You know *Bridget*?' Not for the first time she was flummoxing him. 'How in the world did that come about?'

'We were introduced at a meeting at the Caxton Hall.'

He said slowly, 'You're talking about a women's suffrage meeting? Nolly, Nolly, please tell me you're not mixed up in that!'

'Well, if agreeing with them means being mixed up, then yes, I am. And I do a bit of work for them. In a menial capacity of course. My talent for stuffing envelopes knows no bounds.' She was smiling but he could see that behind it she was deadly serious. She said, 'Oh, you! You're telling me that you with your quick perceptions . . . you never even guessed?'

'No. I didn't.' He'd been blind, because this explained a good deal that had puzzled, even worried him. The times she'd been late (no doubt after one of those meetings which he knew from his own experience of meetings of that sort tended to go on and

on, or perhaps working for those suffragettes until late the previous
night), those telephone conversations, probably not always from
her admirers, he now realised. The visits – which he had not
encouraged – from women who had not perhaps just come to
goggle at the strange sight of Nolly actually working.

'I wouldn't have known who Bridget was, of course, but Devenish
isn't all that common a name. She was astonished that I worked
with you but after that we got on famously. She's top-hole, isn't
she?'

'Who? Brid? Well, I suppose she does have her moments . . .'
He was taken aback, but only momentarily. 'Strangely enough,
I'm not altogether surprised. She's always been wayward – but
I'm astonished that she's prepared to let something like that get
in the way of her future prospects.' He was astonished, too, to
find himself angry about it, because he was one of the minority
of men who believed strongly that women had as much right to
be enfranchised as men. He had a profound belief that universal
suffrage was a basic human right for everyone, man or woman,
at present denied to the female half of this country. Hugely
admiring of the courage of those women who were fighting for
it, he had occasionally gone to their meetings, joined in the
heckling of politicians, though he had been too busy, too involved
with the problems of the *Voice* to respond to invitations to speak
on platforms on their behalf. He had, however, once written –
cautiously – on the subject in his paper, though it had not been
well received and would not be repeated. He wasn't sure where
Lukin stood on the subject and daren't risk more of his disapproval.
But Jon didn't subscribe to militancy and the whole thing was a
different matter when it came to his sister – and even more, he
realised, to Nolly. It wasn't some game those women were playing,
they were deadly serious in their aims, their cause was to them
a matter of life and death. Disregarding the element of martyrdom
which undoubtedly fired some of them, they were prepared not
only to suffer imprisonment and the horrors of force feeding but
also to go to the stake if necessary, he was convinced.

'How deep into this is she – my sister?'

'I don't know.' She hesitated. 'I'm not sure I should be telling
you this, but there's a woman she admires called Rina Collingwood
who's very persuasive and . . . Bridget admires her a lot.'

'Bridget is not a woman who's easily persuaded.'

'We're all sisters under the skin – when it comes to fighting for a cause.'

Nolly, and Bridget. He felt winded, as though he'd been given an actual blow to the solar plexus, and for once in his life was speechless. And dismayed, too, to detect traces of hero-worship when Nolly spoke of his sister. He could find nothing to say except, 'Well, you women!' As if they were after all a species hitherto unknown to the human race.

Thirteen

Kitty's diary was usually a mundane thing, just a record of what had happened during her normally not-very-exciting day, with random thoughts and observations that occurred to her from time to time, rarely amounting to more than a page, or maybe two. But tonight, writing it up as she always did before going to sleep, she had covered page after page, as if recording every detail of yet another endless day would lessen the horror of it, perhaps even help her make sense of life turned upside down.

It was another stifling hot night and after she'd finished writing and turned out the light she threw off the bedclothes. She was bone tired, emotionally exhausted, and though she kept her eyes closed she lay wide awake, unable to get to sleep, however much she told herself she needed to. The truth was, she was afraid of dreaming again, that tonight her dreams would not be so pleasant as the last one. This time, the grey wolf was snarling, his yellow teeth ready to snap.

Eventually, tossing and turning, she must have fallen into a semi-doze. She didn't know how long it was before she was suddenly jerked awake, her heart thumping, by the soft click as the knob on her bedroom door was turned and the door creaked open. She shot bolt upright. Hardly had she drawn breath to scream before the intruder whispered, 'It's only me, Kitty. I couldn't sleep.' She sat up and leaned over to switch on the electric lamp; her heart resumed its normal beat and her panic receded. Only one person would come into her room like that.

'No. Don't put the light on,' Bridget said.

'What on earth are you doing here?'

'I couldn't sleep,' she said again. She stood by the bed, clear in the moonlight. Kitty could see she was shivering. She reached out for her and Bridget slid in beside her, as Kitty used to do with her when they were children, when she'd had a bad dream and Bridget had been there to comfort her. Only now it was she who was trembling. Bridget – so self-reliant, in need of comfort!

'Why couldn't you sleep?' Kitty asked, taking hold of her hand, uncurling her clenched fingers.

'It's been so awful,' she said after a moment. 'And I don't know whether I'm being a fool or not. To even think of jeopardising my chances. And then what happened yesterday – to Aunt Lydia . . . Kitty, I never remember two worse hours than those after the police came to tell us.'

This was Bridget she was hearing. Rational, sensible Bridget, who never lost her cool hold on every facet of her own life. Making no sense whatever. Or rather, a vague idea as to what all this might be about had begun to stir, except that Kitty couldn't see in the least what it might have to do with Mama.

'What have you done?'

She seemed to have grown a little calmer. 'I haven't done anything, nor has Emma. Nor has anyone else, for that matter. Or not much, as it happens.'

'You're not making sense.'

After a silent moment or two she said, 'You're right, I'm not. Let me see if I can do better.'

'You can start by telling me about this Emma, then. Emma who?'

'Emma Pavell.' Her whisper was exasperated. 'Oh, Kitty – Emma – your maid!'

Kitty had never before heard Emma's surname. The servants here were never called simply by their last names, as in some households. Although Lydia had never actually said so, Kitty knew she would have thought that demeaning – to both parties. 'What has Emma to do with you?'

'Well, we – she and I – she's become quite a friend.'

'*Emma?*'

'Sh! Why not? Kitty, you should get to know her better. If you knew what she's like, you'd see her quite differently.'

It was true that Kitty had never seen Emma as a person, never looked beyond the cheerful, brisk young woman who brought her a cup of tea in the morning, who had lately been doing up the complicated hook-and-eye back fastenings of her new dresses, and sometimes helped her to put her hair up. Until now, she hadn't needed a maid of her own but she soon would have done if things had gone as expected, and it had been understood that

Emma would be offered the position. She was quite handy with a needle, Mama had said, and would be quick to learn all the other things she must know. But perhaps Emma – this unknown Emma that Bridget seemed to know better than Kitty did – wouldn't be interested.

'What you mean to say, Bridget, is that she's one of those suffragette women as well.'

Bridget went quiet but after a while she repeated, 'As well? You know then, Kitty.'

'You shouldn't buy white dresses with purple and green sashes if you don't want anyone to know where your sympathies lie.'

In fact Kitty had had her suspicions long before seeing that dress. For all her avowals about not wanting anything to do with them, she knew Bridget had been itching to join those protesting women, which had frightened her. Being Bridget, Kitty doubted she would be content to play a passive role in anything, and what could happen to those who chose not to be passive, those who saw themselves as activists, soldiers for freedom, was simply too awful to contemplate.

After a while Bridget said, 'I should have had the sense not to underestimate you. But I'm not "one of them", as you put it.' She did not say 'yet' but Kitty couldn't help feeling it was there. She went on to say how she had found out about Emma's sympathies, and how much she admired her for the work she put in after her long, hard day's work here. 'But she's willing to do it because she's really dedicated. A woman in her position, the sort of life her mother has led – and all the other women she knows – has more reason than most of us to want things to change. It's so hard being a woman, Kitty, but for women like them, it's a hundred times harder.'

She wouldn't have liked to hear it said, but it struck Kitty that Aunt Ursula was right – there wasn't that much difference between Bridget and her brother Jon, when it came down to it.

'She comes from the East End, you know. You can't imagine what life is like for them. I've begun to feel so – so sheltered and pampered. It's so unfair.' Her voice shook with emotion.

At first Kitty could find no answer. She had no experience of those sort of things Bridget was talking about, any more than Bridget herself had. She longed to stretch her wings but she'd hardly been allowed to venture further than the streets around Chelsea or Mayfair, or to look out of the bars of her cage on to anything but her own tiny, proscribed world. Now, she was suddenly conscious that there was all London out there and she who'd lived here all her life knew hardly any of it. Especially not the East End, where all those terrible shootings had happened – where the murderous men who called themselves anarchists lived. The men the police suspected her mother of being involved with.

They were speaking in low voices, though no one was likely to hear them, unless they too were wandering around the house in the middle of the night. The whispers made what Bridget went on to say seem all the more alarming as Kitty learnt how she'd gone with Emma to that first meeting – purely out of interest, of course – and then to several more.

'Let's hope it hasn't got to the college authorities in Cambridge, then,' Kitty said. They wouldn't be pleased to hear that someone who'd gained one of their coveted places was preparing to throw it away.

'Why should it?' Bridget answered quickly, then sighed. 'The truth is, I'm in such a muddle, Kitty. I almost wish now I'd never made that first move. You can't go and listen to what they have to say without sympathising with what they're trying to do. You get drawn in—'

'You haven't—!'

'Of course not.' She said it as though what Kitty was implying was unthinkable, but Kitty wasn't so sure she was telling the truth. Visions of Bridget hurling bricks through shop windows and facing arrest by the police, prosecution and even prison didn't seem too far-fetched, yet she could see she was being pulled both ways, one half of her on the side of those who advocated a rational and more cautious approach to the problem of women's suffrage, the other, more aggressive half leaning the other way. She felt horribly afraid because if it came down to it, she didn't see Bridget as being reasonable where something she truly believed in was concerned.

'No,' she repeated, but this time so forcibly Kitty heaved a sigh of relief. 'You know me. I'm almost sorry to have to admit it but I do have my priorities, and I can't – I won't – throw away everything I've worked for, so you needn't worry. Besides, your mama might have had a point, saying all this violence only achieves the very opposite of what we want. Only hardens the politicians' attitudes against us, reinforces their opinions of us as viragos.'

Kitty began to have an inkling as to what the quarrel with her mother had been about, but she didn't want to get into a circular argument, the sort she knew from experience her cousin could keep up indefinitely, the sort Kitty never won. 'What did happen on Sunday?' she asked.

After a moment, Bridget told her. It was half a dozen of the more militant suffragettes out of a group she attended, despite the truce that had been agreed, who had planned that demonstration in Hyde Park during which Lydia had been shot.

'Bridget, you don't mean—' Kitty was so choked by suddenly seeing the obvious explanation for Bridget's terror when they had heard the news about Lydia that she couldn't continue. *No!* Such a thing was impossible.

Bridget understood immediately what she was thinking. 'No, of course I don't mean that! There are plenty of hotheads in the movement, Heaven knows, but they wouldn't go as far as shooting anyone, or even carrying a gun. Only think what that would mean if they were apprehended by the police.'

'Then why were you so worried after we heard what had happened to Mama? You were, I know – until Emma came back and presumably told you that her being shot had nothing to do with your friends. What made you think they might have had anything to do with it?'

'Kitty, I was only relieved that the demonstration hadn't come off. I always did think it was a mistake.' Kitty knew she was prevaricating, but before she could say anything else, Papa's clock on the landing struck the hour and Bridget slid out of the bed. 'Thank you for listening, I needed to get it off my chest. I'm going back to my room now to get some sleep. You try and do the same.'

Kitty grabbed her hand, held it tight and refused to let go. 'Not before you've told me what you really came to tell me.'

She was called Sabrina, Bridget's new friend, but she only answered to Rina.

'You want to watch her, Bridget,' said Emma, who had at last agreed to drop the 'Miss', at least when they were away from the Challoner house. She had lost her reserve with Bridget, who for her part was becoming accustomed to the forthright opinions Emma voiced. It meant they were friends, and usually what she said was common sense. But this time . . .

'If you mean watch her and catch some of her enthusiasm,' Bridget returned rather sharply, 'then I couldn't do better. She's awfully keen, you know.'

'Keen to get you involved.' Actively, Emma meant.

Rina Collingwood was a woman who was in the top echelons of the movement, a member of the more militant W.S.P.U., the Women's Social and Political Union. She never smiled and rarely spoke, unless it was to give one of her pep talks, expounding on such subjects as the enthusiasm of the working women and factory girls in the north whom she had been meeting with recently, holding them up as peerless examples. She was a striking-looking woman. Tall and slim, with pale, flawless skin, she wore her shiny black hair wound in a coil around her small, neat head, giving the impression she was wearing a coronet. She had extraordinary grey eyes, so light they might almost have been silver, with a mesmerising quality when she fixed them on anyone. She was uncommunicative about her private life and held herself rather aloof. Everyone except Emma seemed to be intimidated by her, but Emma's opinion didn't really count. She was welcomed into the Sisterhood of course, but it was clear she was also expected to help serve the sandwiches and cakes, and with the washing up.

'Oh, nonsense,' Bridget said sharply in answer to Emma's warning about Rina. 'It's just that she's so committed herself she feels everyone else should be, too.'

'She hasn't got a place at Cambridge waiting for her.'

'I don't see why the two should be mutually exclusive.'

Emma raised an eyebrow. 'Well, keep your eye on her, that's all I say. Before you know it, she'll have you chaining yourself to the railings at Number Ten.'

It was Rina who had tried to persuade Bridget to approach Lydia with the intentions of enlisting her interest and support, but Bridget couldn't do this, recalling her previous rebuff. So

Rina had taken it upon herself to write to Lydia. It had been a woeful mistake.

'You must have warned Rina that Mama wouldn't agree,' Kitty said.

'And she didn't. A polite refusal would have been enough, but perhaps Rina's letter wasn't quite tactful. Aunt Lydia seemed to feel she'd almost been threatened. Emotionally blackmailed, I suppose, is the phrase. At any rate, her reply was very sharp . . . she said she could never support those who didn't understand there were more appropriate ways in which women could gain power. By being so aggressive, the W.S.P.U. was simply demonstrating why they should *not* be allowed the vote and thereby gain power and a right to help run the country.'

Rina had been coldly furious at the response. 'You didn't tell me your aunt was a member of the Women's Anti-Suffrage League.'

'Aunt Lydia? There's nothing more unlikely.'

'Really? Then it's remarkable how similar their views are.'

Kitty said, into the silence after Bridget finished speaking, 'And on Sunday, you thought she'd actually—'

'What I thought doesn't matter, Kitty. It was ridiculous even to have contemplated such a thing in the first place. Even Rina wouldn't – well, it didn't happen anyway.' She jumped up and left, and this time Kitty didn't try to stop her.

But why had Bridget even mentioned that woman? Kitty was beginning to dislike this Miss Collingwood intensely. But she was heartened by the feeling that Bridget's initial enthusiasm for her was wearing off.

Fourteen

Marcus had stayed with the decision he'd made on Sunday evening: rather than spend an impatient night waiting until he could see his father the next day here in London, he'd driven down to Loddhurst, only to find on arrival they'd missed each other. While he had been driving down, his father had been on a train travelling in the opposite direction, to London. His manservant informed Marcus that in order to give himself more time the following day before he needed to leave London for Paris, Sir Aiden had decided to put up for the night at his club; he himself had telephoned Mrs Stanhope's residence to leave a message for Marcus that his father would call on him shortly after breakfast, but he had been too late.

Marcus cursed himself for not telephoning his own intentions to drive down to Loddhurst, but at the same time he didn't feel inclined to drive straight back to London. He would stay the night at Loddhurst, set off very early the next morning and catch his father breakfasting at his club. But even in that he was frustrated. A puncture on the way back (a commonplace hazard of motoring on unmetalled country roads) held him up and he arrived to find Sir Aiden was already on his way to Paris.

He also found a note had been left for him to say that Sergeant Inskip had called. He would be obliged if Marcus would present himself at the police station at the earliest possible moment. Inskip. What did he want? Marcus had spoken to him and to Chief Inspector Gaines after the shooting had happened and he didn't want to talk to either of them any more until he'd had the chance to speak with his father. In the circumstances, with Sir Aiden in Paris, this might not occur for some time. He felt himself in a dark mood. Hiding in a corner of his mind, still waiting to spring out, was that demon asking whether he had unwittingly done anything – anything at all – that might have contributed towards the death of a woman he had come to consider a friend. Albeit one whom he felt he had never really known, a woman outwardly so extrovert, but who he'd discovered had secrets even from her family. It wasn't, however, in his quick, impatient nature to mope, and certainly not over something that might only exist in his imagination. And over and above that was the need to see Kitty.

Nothing had passed between himself and Lydia on the subject of Kitty but he was fairly certain she had known how he felt, and had not been entirely averse to the idea of a match between him and her daughter. Why else had she tried to get Kitty to join them on those morning rides, left him alone with her for long periods while she herself was dressing, if not to encourage their acquaintance? At the same time she'd made it clear that Kitty was to be allowed her first Season. Girls so looked forward to the excitement of it, she had constantly stressed, and with good reason. It was a time in Kitty's life that would never be repeated, a glorious time when the world and all its possibilities would be opening before her, when she would learn the ways of the world, make friends and acquaintances who would stand her in good stead all her life. Kitty should be given opportunities she herself had never had.

The word 'opportunity' hadn't fallen on deaf ears and Marcus had with difficulty conceded that he must hold back. He'd known it might be a risky strategy not to make his intentions clear to Kitty, or even to hint at how he felt without actually declaring himself. There was more than a chance that during her year out she might meet some sprig of the aristocracy who would sweep her off her feet, or be a better proposition than he would ever be, and she would become spoken for before he had the chance to ask her. The devil of it was the uncertainty about Kitty herself. He was by no means sure if she even liked him. You never knew with women, and Kitty was always so cool. She seemed to draw into herself whenever he tried to reach out to her and he couldn't make out if this was natural reserve or whether he actually aroused some antipathy in her. Which didn't bear thinking about. Caution had never before been a word in his vocabulary, but he was learning his lesson; this was too fragile a situation to risk by making the wrong moves, in the wrong direction, too soon. For the first time in his life Marcus appreciated what the term 'falling in love' actually meant. He felt he had literally tumbled into a vertiginous spiral, totally astonished that he should have fallen for this grave young woman with the clear hazel eyes.

He went straight to Egremont Gardens after dutifully presenting himself to the police as requested in the note. He considered that what transpired there had been a waste of time for everyone concerned: with the best will in the world he hadn't been able to summon up any more detail about what he'd witnessed in those few fatal minutes in the Row. It was not that he had no remembrance of it – every single moment was still there in his head, and would be forever – it was simply that everything had happened at once and was all over within such a short space of time. There was little that could be told which hadn't in any case been corroborated by the many other witnesses to the shooting.

Although the request had been left by Inskip, DCI Gaines had also been there when he arrived, and after a while it had become clear that he'd been summoned not only because he'd been a witness to the shooting, but also to give them opportunity to probe further into his relationship with Lydia. Alerted, he had parried questions about how he'd come to know her, why he'd been so friendly with her and in the end they had let him go. He had left them, he hoped, with the impression that he was just one of those young nincompoops dazzled by a mature, fascinating older woman.

Since Louis Challoner had declared himself not yet equal to replying to the letters of condolence which were arriving by every post, Ursula had taken on the task, assisted by Hester Drax, who was at that moment sitting bolt upright at the table, addressing envelopes in her neat, careful script. She'd suggested that typing them on the machine she had in her office upstairs would be quicker and more efficient but Ursula had been shocked. 'My dear, that would never do! People would think us quite ill-bred.'

Ursula was not the woman to break with convention, and it was frightfully bad form to answer personal letters other than by hand, especially those following a bereavement. Lydia had been popular and many, many such letters expressing genuine sorrow and sympathy had already been received, though perhaps fewer than might have been expected. Obviously a number of people were waiting to see how the wind blew, whether they should in future receive a family mixed up in the mysterious circumstances

of a death which was involving police investigation. Gossip was
rife. There was no smoke without fire. However inconceivable
it was to her family that Lydia could have been mixed up in any
kind of questionable activity, it was now plain by the amount of
police interest that the fiction of her death being due to an accident could no longer be sustained, and it would not have taken
long for rumours to circulate. It was a harsh fact to accept, but
there were those who would want nothing to do with the family
of a woman who had been sufficiently connected with the sort
of scandal which had ended in her being murdered.

This was an attitude which Ursula fully understood, and in fact
had a great deal of sympathy with. Had her own family not been
concerned, had she been on the other side, she would have behaved
in the same way. As it was, she had been careful not to allow, even
to herself, that it was somehow a breach of bad taste for Lydia to
have got herself into such a scandalous situation, and she had dealt
competently with the myriad tasks necessary in a house suddenly
deprived of its mistress, the burden of which must sooner or later,
of necessity, fall on Kitty's unprepared shoulders, poor child.

Meanwhile, she had been grateful to Miss Drax for her help
in fielding telephone calls and attempting to fend off the atten-
tions of the press, who hadn't been slow to latch on to the story,
while Ursula herself attended to the dreary business of cancelling
the arrangements for Kitty's coming out, now unthinkable.
Originally, those preparations had been a self-imposed task she
had willingly taken on when Lydia had thrown up her hands and
declared she wouldn't know where to start. Now it was her job
to see to the orders being countermanded:

> The ball to celebrate the coming out of Miss Kitty
> Challoner has regrettably been cancelled, owing to a
> recent, sad bereavement in her family, therefore arrange-
> ments made with you for catering at the home of Lady
> Dunstable, Curzon Street, will not now be necessary . . .
>
> Flowers will not be needed for the event scheduled
> for the 29th June . . .
>
> Please cancel the order for champagne . . . for the
> appearance of the Quintus String Ensemble and the Roxy
> Ray Dance Band . . . for the carriage attendants . . .

As for the funeral . . . There would first have to be a post mortem, according to DCI Gaines – a routine procedure in cases of violent death, he'd been quick to reassure them. After which there would be an inquest, which would be adjourned until the police had completed their enquiries. Mrs Challoner's body would be released for burial, since it was clear how she had met her death, though enquiries as to why she had been killed, or by whom, would continue.

The funeral would be a small, private affair with only the family and a very few especially close friends, and Ursula had suggested to Kitty that afterwards, they might go down to Southfields – just herself, Kitty and Bridget. She was gratified to see how the suggestion had been received: it was as though a blind had been lifted for Kitty and the sun had come out. 'Southfields? Oh, Aunt Ursula!'

Southfields, Ursula's pretty, comfortable house with its own distinctive smell of woodsmoke, old timbers and beeswax, spices at Christmas, roses in summer, its unchanging country house traditions. Tennis, and tea on the lawn. A hammock under the trees. No constant, painful reminders, as here in Egremont Gardens, of how things had been this time last week, last month. When Ursula, who was desperately missing her home herself, had made the suggestion, Kitty had smiled, for the first time in days. Not a polite, social smile, but a real smile, although it had vanished almost as quickly as it had appeared. 'But I can't. I can't leave Papa alone, here.'

'I've already spoken to your father. He's willing to stay at his club.' Ursula only just stopped herself from saying that he might as well be miserable there as at home.

'I can't let him do that!'

'He will do very well, Kitty. I've told him it's more than time he went back to business – it won't attend to itself for ever and it's hardly fair to Mr Estrabon to leave him with all your papa's responsibilities as well as his own. He has promised – he will go back full time to his office tomorrow. It will do him no harm, he needs to be occupied,' finished Ursula, whose remedy this was for all ills.

To tell the truth, her patience with her brother was wearing a little thin, despite the sympathy she felt for him. The tragedy seemed as though it might have left its permanent mark on him. He made sporadic visits to his office but for the most part he shut himself away in his study and hardly came out, except for meals, where he made no effort to pretend, as everyone else was valiantly trying to do, that things were as near normal as possible. They were not, of course, and never could be again, but one had to make an effort.

Although she was a little out of temper with Louis at the moment, she was actually very worried about him, too. Apart from the shock of what had happened to Lydia, something else was weighing on his mind. Of course, knowing her brother so well, she was aware that he was simply acting as he often had when he was a boy: easygoing if things were comfortable, but thinking only of himself, withdrawn and sulky if they were not. He appeared to have forgotten Kitty and even when he was prompted to comfort her, so caught up in his own grief the attempt was counter-productive. An exodus to Southfields would do them all a great deal of good. She had other reasons, too, for wanting to be there, and not only because her own dear home was beckoning. Bridget was not as clever at hiding things from her as she thought. Far more aware of her children's concerns and what motivated them than anyone gave her credit for, Ursula knew that being here in London was not good for Bridget; she was absorbing too many of these outrageous feminist views. She didn't intend, if she could help it, to allow her headstrong daughter to involve herself in indiscretions she would certainly regret later. Cambridge, however much Ursula deplored it, was turning out to be the lesser evil.

The door to the small room she'd appropriated for their task opened. 'Kitty, there you are! Just the person to help me with these envelopes.' Smiling, she turned to the other woman. 'Miss Drax, I'm most awfully grateful for the time you've spared to help me, but now Kitty's here I needn't keep you any longer from your work.'

'It's nothing, Lady Devenish, I'm glad to do what I can. But – if Miss Kitty has the time . . .'

'I've all the time in the world,' Kitty said. How could anyone think she had not? her words implied.

'I can get another hour or two on the book then . . . I'm hoping it will be ready for the publisher in a very short time.'

'Well done, Miss Drax. You've done us a great service.'

'No more than anyone else would have done, I'm sure.'

Ursula sighed after the stiff, departing figure. 'Really, I don't know! But she is so good at this sort of thing.' Kitty saw Lydia's open address book, the pile of black-bordered envelopes and the box of matching, black-edged writing paper which had been ordered by Hester and delivered at express speed. 'And I'm afraid she is not often given credit for it. What a pity one cannot like her.'

Kitty was turning over the stack of business letters. 'You've been awfully busy.'

'They're all finished now, everything cancelled.' Ursula hesitated. 'Dear Kitty, I'm so sorry you should have missed all this.' She waved a hand over her now unnecessary lists of arrangements. 'Perhaps, when everything is over . . . next year . . .' She faltered, seeing Kitty's expression, and then went on hurriedly, 'Well, well, we'd better get on. It's only a matter of addressing envelopes.'

Kitty took Hester's place, after which they worked in silence, and were still busy when the flowers came, an enormous basket of them, brought in by young Thomas. 'For me?' No one had ever sent Kitty flowers before, and she looked overwhelmed at this huge extravagance of pink and red roses, white carnations and freesias set in damp moss, filling the room with their perfume as she extracted and read the card and then passed it to her aunt. '*May I call on you? If not today, at any time, whenever you wish. Marcus.*' She blushed as red as any of the roses and looked bemused, bereft of speech.

'How delightful! How very kind,' Ursula said.

Thomas coughed. 'Mr Villiers is in the hall, Miss Kitty. He said he would wait for a reply.'

'You must go and thank him, Kitty.' With the cool edge towards Marcus back in her voice she added, 'He probably still feels guilty. Go and forgive him.'

Kitty woke up at last. 'Thank you, Thomas. I'll come right away and see him.' Still holding the flower basket, she fled the room.

Fifteen

He was waiting for her in the hall. He stepped forward, resisting the urge to take her in his arms, which would have shocked a girl as well brought up as she had been – or even to kiss her gently on the cheek, which would not have been *comme il faut* either – and instead took her hand quite correctly. He did, however, keep hold until she herself withdrew it.

She was still flushed. 'Thank you so much for the flowers. They are beautiful.'

'It's my pleasure,' he said, his face unsmiling. 'Will you sit down and talk to me? And forgive me for not coming round before?'

'Of course.'

She was in deep mourning, which only enhanced the translucency of her skin, and the soft blondeness of her hair. The gleam of amusement, and sometimes mischief, was sadly absent now from her eyes. Dark, well-defined brows lent emphasis and character to her face, adding up to something far more than mere prettiness, and all the more appealing because she wasn't aware of it. He suspected she might always have felt herself eclipsed by Lydia's vibrant looks, although she and her mother had been sufficiently different for there to have been no danger of that ever happening. No doubt her Aunt Ursula was exaggerating when she had lightly remarked one day that Kitty was all set to take London society by storm when she came out – but whether it was an exaggeration or not, she would not have been short of admirers, that was for sure. She had been deprived of all that by what had happened, pitched into a sort of limbo – but he knew instinctively that she had left being a girl behind that moment on Sunday when the police had entered this house. Still grave and contained today, she looked around now for somewhere to put the flowers she was holding. Having found a space on the window sill, she gently tucked a sprig of fern in the basket into place. He noticed her glance briefly out of the window as she raised her head, then stiffen and abruptly turn her back, fingering the only piece of jewellery she wore, the jet mourning brooch at the neck of her dress. Where did women get these things? Did they have them all ready for any such eventuality? Probably. Death, sudden or otherwise, was not after all such a rare occurrence, even in these enlightened times. But dear God, no one could have envisaged one such as this!

'I noticed someone I took to be a member of the press hanging around as I came in. Is he still lurking? And do you want me to go out and deal with him?' he asked, looking and feeling quite capable of it.

'It would be a waste of time. They just come back. We're news just now but they'll get tired of us presently.'

An awkward silence fell. This was not going to be the kind of conversation they had ever had when he was waiting for Lydia to put in an appearance, nor could it be, ever again. Conventional murmurs of sympathy, the anodyne phrases used at such times need not be repeated; they had been said on Sunday, and in any case that wasn't what he was here for today. There were other things that needed to be said. 'Have the police been here again?' he asked.

'Yes. They spoke to all of us.'

'And what did they tell you?'

'Nothing! They told us nothing. All they wanted to do was to ask us questions about Mama and any connections she had with those Russian refugees who are causing so much trouble. The inspector – I think he suspects she sympathised with them. Which is absolute nonsense. Isn't it?' She searched his face with troubled eyes. 'You do believe that, don't you?'

Eventually he said, as carefully as if treading on eggshells, 'I do believe, Kitty, that she might have got herself mixed up in something she didn't fully understand.'

'I'm sorry, I don't see what you mean.'

'Sit down. Please sit down.' He waved her to a chair, sat down opposite and leaned forward, elbows on his knees. 'I came to know your mother quite well over these last few months. I don't for one moment believe there was anything – underhand – in what she was doing—'

'In what she was doing? Underhand?' she repeated. 'What's all this?'

Instead of answering, he sprang up and took a stance before the fireplace, its empty grate hidden behind a huge, colourful and lavishly embroidered fire screen, where he stood with his hands clasped – almost clenched – behind him. The silence extended, broken by the longcase clock in the corner striking the hour in an effortful sort of way, running down because Louis had neglected to give his clocks their usual weekly attention. He glanced at it impatiently then came back, sat down again. 'I have things to tell you,' he began. 'Most of which you are not going to like, I'm afraid. But – they have to be said.' Without waiting for her assent, he added, 'It's a long story.'

'There's no hurry, that I can see.' She was not smiling.

He took a deep breath, afraid he might gabble once started, but although he felt a distinct chill in the air, she listened mainly in silence as he nerved himself to explain as best he could, without excusing himself in any way, knowing that when she'd heard everything, she would never look at him with the same eyes again.

Still he hesitated, then plunged. It seemed a crude way of beginning, but perhaps as good a way as any. 'Three months ago, I didn't even know your mother existed . . .'

After returning from a long and strenuous ride that February morning, he had found his father entertaining a visitor – none other than the Home Secretary, Mr Winston Churchill. Although he was now retired, Sir Aiden still had friends, colleagues and connections within the Foreign Office and as an experienced diplomat his advice and opinions were often sought. Marcus suspected that his father was still more of a power behind the scenes than he would ever admit. Urbane and affable, accustomed to social interaction, he often entertained people from his former life, but Churchill was not someone Marcus had met before.

The three of them had taken lunch together and afterwards, in his father's study, in an atmosphere heavy with rich cigar smoke, it was made known that a proposition was to be put to Marcus. He assumed that Sir Aiden's years of diplomacy would ensure a reasonable discussion of whatever was to come, but in fact his father had discreetly left Marcus alone with Mr Churchill, pleading a pressing need to consult the builders who were presently working on a section of the roof. The Home Secretary was a man full of charm and wit, not to say charisma, plus a bulldog determination to succeed, and a boyish enthusiasm for becoming personally involved in anything that was engaging him. He was at present locked in combat with the suffragettes over their demands for the right to vote, though that problem didn't seem to be on his mind just then; in his official capacity his avowed intention was to get to the bottom of, and eradicate, the present trouble caused by the murderous gangs of foreign anarchists who were terrorising the East End of London. Despite his urbanity he was evidently rattled by the situation, though he avoided any mention of the strong criticism he was under for putting in a personal appearance at the now infamous siege in Sidney Street. That subject had been made very public and by now no one could have been unaware of the storm it had raised. Pertinent questions had been asked in the House as to why the Home Secretary had felt it necessary to join the soldiers and police already there at the scene, why he had endeavoured to take part in directing operations, and had even commandeered ordnance to be sent from the Tower of London.

However, Marcus now learnt from him, it was believed in certain quarters that that particular anarchist gang had not been working alone, that there were people of influence behind them, possibly British citizens who sympathised with their aims. The intelligence amassed over the business had thrown up several names and all were being followed up. Was it the disapproval of Churchill's behaviour at the siege, considered inappropriate and interfering, Marcus asked himself later, that was causing him to justify himself by having even the most unlikely leads pursued?

The man himself had not seen his arrival at Sidney Street that snowy January day as anything untoward. In his younger days he had been a man of action, a brave soldier who had taken arms against Afghan tribes on the North West Frontier, fought Dervishes in the Sudan. He had been a newspaper correspondent in the war with the Boers, where he'd been captured as a prisoner of war while defending an armed train, had escaped and returned home a war hero, thereafter entering Parliament. He had written several books on his experiences. At the end of last year he'd been attacked, personally, by a militant suffragette wielding a whip. He was still only thirty-seven.

At first Marcus didn't believe the man was in earnest about what he was asking him to do: the proposition made to him seemed not only simplistic but slightly bizarre, so preposterous it might have come out of the *Boy's Own Paper*. Except that it wasn't in the honourable tradition and moral principles of the *Boy's Own Paper* stories. To put it bluntly, it was not playing a straight game. In fact, Marcus was damned if he would act as lapdog to a bored society woman (Lydia Challoner, a name unknown to him then) while at the same time keeping an eye on her and reporting on what she did and whom she met, simply on the off-chance that she might be up to something suspect – and only on the flimsy pretext of her origins, it seemed. If she had been acting suspiciously, Marcus thought cynically, it was more than likely there was a lover somewhere in the wings. Moreover, he was apparently expected to accept what had been put to him without question, which obscurely irritated him. After a while, it occurred to him to wonder if it was some sort of test: if he came through this well, he would be offered more in the same vein. 'If I am not mistaken, you are asking me to spy on this woman, sir,' he said outright.

Churchill had looked as pained as if Marcus had committed a social gaffe.

But you did not lightly refuse the Home Secretary, especially if he happened to be Mr Winston Churchill. Marcus began to feel himself no match for the combination of his eloquent, persuasive and forceful arguments and the intimation that it was his father's desire he should comply with the suggestion. That was how it had been couched: a suggestion that he was at liberty to refuse if he wished; he was not under any obligation to agree. But of course, it was in the national interest that everyone should do what they could to root out all these troublemakers; it was one's patriotic duty to do all one could to assist the authorities.

In the end, it was that which had clinched it. His conscience, his patriotism, his humanity, were stirred despite himself. That, and the impulsive streak in his nature that said what the hell? Persuaded that in any case, until he had made up his mind about his future, anything was better than kicking his heels at Loddhurst or wasting his time on pursuits in town that increasingly had no point.

'It goes without saying that you will keep this under your hat.' The faint smile masked a steely glint in the Home Secretary's eyes.

He was told little more about the object of his potential attention, except that she had been deeply attached to her Russian father, a man named Nikolai Sergeivich Kasparov, who had lived for many years in this country, a disciple of the notorious Peter Kropotkin and one in the vanguard of the seemingly endless struggle for his own country's freedom. Well, Marcus had shrugged, what had he to lose by making himself agreeable to an attractive woman, escorting her around, noting what she did and with whom she associated?

The weight of the argument had prevailed but although his heart was not altogether in it, he set himself out to do what was expected of him and acquaint himself with Lydia Challoner.

It was easy enough to contrive an introduction. Southfields, the house where Mrs Challoner's sister-in-law, Lady Devenish, lived was not above twenty miles from Loddhurst, making them pretty near neighbours. Sir Aiden had been well acquainted with Ursula in their youth, and he threw a party to celebrate the recent improvements he'd made at Loddhurst, to which he invited all the local gentry. At the party Marcus had made himself agreeable to Lady Devenish, reminding her that as a young boy he had been invited to her children's parties at Southfields on the rare occasions when Sir Aiden and he had made visits home to Loddhurst. She was charming to him (she had an unmarried daughter, Bridget, of course) and invited him to call on her when she went to stay with her brother and sister-in-law in London for the coming out of her niece.

When he eventually met Lydia, they got along famously, mainly due to their shared interest in all things Russian and his ability to converse with her in her father's native language. Nikolai had always spoken to his daughter in Russian, with the result that she had grown up bilingual, and Marcus's sojourn in St Petersburg had made him not only fairly fluent in the elegant French the aristocracy used but also, following his father's example, in the native Russian they so despised. Their mutual interest in literature and the great Russian novelists also helped to form an immediate bond between them, and after that it was plain sailing.

Yet he had constantly wondered what he was doing, wasting his time escorting her to aimless social pursuits. And increasingly, he began to feel a downright hypocrite, though by then he would have found it difficult to extricate himself. He had been warmly accepted by the family as well as by Lydia – Louis no doubt because Marcus was willing to ride with his wife and occasionally escort her to occasions which he himself found tedious, and Ursula who had her own motives in fostering his interest in Bridget (though she must soon have seen that she need not trouble herself on that score).

The main reason Marcus didn't extricate himself was because he did not want to. A complication he had never anticipated had arisen: he had met Kitty, Lydia's daughter. And after that, there was no question of abandoning the Challoners.

Now, when he thought of how he might possibly, though entirely inadvertently, have contributed to her mother's death, his heart misgave him. In the light of something he had recently witnessed, and then, incredibly, her murder, he unwillingly had to allow that he might just possibly have been mistaken in Lydia, that she really might have had connections with those fanatical Russian émigrés . . . In which case, had her association with Marcus himself caused them to assume she was betraying them, and they had therefore shot her? Worse than that was the thought that the shooting might have been done by one of those who were ranged against the anarchists and all those who were in league with them, that some sort of double deal had been set up . . . nothing was impossible, as he had been brought up to know, in the dark world of spying and intrigue that surrounded the seeking out of such people.

Realistically, he knew he could not have prevented the tragedy, yet still felt obscurely to blame. He couldn't dismiss from his mind the feeling that he ought somehow to have protected Lydia. He could only take comfort in the fact that he'd given nothing away because he had found absolutely nothing whatever about her to give away.

Or nothing until recently, and nothing he would have revealed to anyone else.

★   ★   ★

There was a silence from Kitty when he had finished his story. Understandably. He knew it had been an abject confession which apologies could do nothing to lessen.

'Who are they, these people who wanted you to spy on her . . .?' she asked at last. 'You are saying that they suspected her of . . . of . . .' She could not find words to continue.

'Of nothing, or not in any specific way. The Home Office don't seem to need suspicions. They're willing to grasp at straws in their war against the anarchists. I think they're watching anyone at all likely to have the remotest connections with them. In the same way, I don't think for a moment I was specially chosen. I just happened to be at a loose end when the Home Secretary came to see my father, and that was all. Spying – or reporting – on her. Where's the difference? You've every right to despise me, Kitty.'

She looked at him steadily, silently, neither agreeing nor denying it. 'You were following your conscience,' she said at last.

'If I was, look where it led! Oh, I haven't acquitted myself well over this, but I did it of my own free will – so enough of excuses. Is it too much to ask you to try and understand, if not forgive me?'

Her smile was strained. 'Let's say no more of it, Marcus.'

'Except – let me say one thing – there *was* no reporting, you know. In the first place because there was nothing to tell – and . . . well, I found I couldn't. She had become a friend. And besides – she was your mother, Kitty.' His voice took on a deeper note and suddenly he reached out and took hold of both her hands, raised them to his lips – to the devil with propriety, it was too late for that!

She didn't shrink from him.

'You have a forgiving nature, but I . . .' He pulled himself together. 'No doubt I shall recover.'

Kitty walked over to the window and nudged the curtain to one side. 'He seems to have gone, that reporter,' she said absently. After a while she came back to where he still stood beside the fireplace and sat down on the sofa that was set at an angle to it. 'I have something to say, too.' She hesitated. 'You said there was nothing to tell – about Mama – but that's not quite true, is it? No, please don't pretend, Marcus, I know there was. I saw it myself.' Her hands twisted tightly together, she went on, 'I know she was meeting – someone. She forgot that my bedroom window overlooks the square garden, and when the trees are bare . . . My window isn't the only one on that side of the house, either. Anyone else might have seen.' They had *kissed*. 'It was not – very discreet of her, was it?'

Lydia had never been that. Not at all. Even as she spoke, it flashed once more through his mind, that day, a miserably wet and blustery morning, more reminiscent of autumn than spring, just before the present heatwave had set in.

He had arranged to meet her at Burlington House, at the Royal Academy, for a new, much-talked-of exhibition of Byzantine art. He was early and wandered through the various rooms, killing time, prepared for the usual wait before she arrived. Reaching the gallery where the exhibition was held he saw that Lydia, never before on time, was already there, sitting next to a man on one of the central seats provided. Hands clasped, they were talking, her eyes never leaving his face. After a while, something passed between them – a book, some sort of parcel, Marcus was too far away to see either shape or size – which she had taken from the large leather bag hanging over her wrist on a long strap. They sat for about ten minutes in earnest conversation while Marcus hovered out of sight near the entrance and then Lydia touched the man's cheek gently with her fingertips, and he was gone. Marcus would not easily forget the glow, the unmistakable expression on her face of a woman in love. He turned and also left the exhibition room, to return by a roundabout route ten minutes later at the appointed time for their meeting, ready with a joke about her being there first for once.

It had been a rash thing to do, meeting that man, whoever he was, in a place where at any moment one of her friends might appear, but Lydia was hardly the cautious type, nor one to dissolve into the background, unnoticed, for that matter. That day wearing a sable-trimmed coat, the colour of autumn leaves, a velvet hat of the same shade, modishly wide, perched on the heavy coils and puffs of her hair. Charming, stylish. Ridiculous on this wild day. The wind – or perhaps that meeting he'd witnessed – had whipped colour into her cheeks. She was attracting attention as she always did, but perhaps she'd been confident none of her acquaintances would venture out in such weather, fearful for their hats, or their hair.

He saw Kitty was waiting now, hoping perhaps for him to tell her that what she herself had seen – at a distance, through a window, screened to a certain extent by trees – must have some innocent explanation, but the coincidence of the two rendezvous made the lie stick in his throat. That encounter at the Academy had not been the meeting of mere acquaintances. Nor, despite the furtive exchange of whatever had been taken from Lydia's handbag, was it in any way consistent with two people having nefarious purposes in mind. But how could he tell Kitty that? He sprang up and began to pace about again.

After a moment she said, 'Do stop and sit down. This – person I saw with Mama. Tell me the truth. Could he have been one of those people the police are convinced she was mixed up with?'

He stopped pacing. 'Perhaps.' But he'd hesitated too long, and then not put enough certainty into his reply. If she hadn't already done so, she would soon reach the same conclusion as he. I've lost her, he thought. I've shown everything in the wrong light and put thoughts and suspicions into her mind that ought not to be there. He sat down and told her, playing it down as much as he was able, about the man her mother had been with at the Academy.

She did not become as upset as he expected. Looking steadfastly at the flowers he had brought, she merely nodded as if it had confirmed what she had already thought. 'Did you – did you know about Marie Bartholemew?' she asked suddenly at last, bringing her gaze back to him.

'Marie Bartholemew?' The unexpectedness of the question completely threw him. 'Oh – er – yes, she did tell me about the book, though I was sworn to secrecy. Your mother was a remarkable lady. Who would have thought that of her?'

'It seems there may have been rather a lot of things one would not have thought of her, Marcus.' She turned to leave the room. 'Wait a moment, if you please, there's something I'd like you to see.'

Somewhere in the past was her other life. She was living a new one now, in unknown territory, and she was a different person in it. She had sloughed off Kitty Challoner's schoolgirl preoccupations like an outgrown skin; her new skin was thicker and less easily bruised. She would never be so easily hurt again, so gullible or trusting. As she had listened to Marcus telling her of his part in all this, she had gone through a series of conflicting emotions: first wondering at the astonishing naivety in someone like him; then thinking that perhaps it was not naivety, but cleverness, doing what he had done, that all along he had been acting for his own good, the hope that it would lead to some future prospects for himself with these people who had persuaded him to work for them . . . And then, the moment he told her that Lydia had confessed to being Marie Bartholemew, her doubts about him dissolved. Not even Fanny Estrabon had known that her dearest friend had a secret life, another persona. If Mama had trusted him with that, the only one outside the family as far as Kitty knew, could her own trust in him be misplaced?

For the space of a moment she was back in that dream she'd had, that search for something that was evading her, the golden feather trembling first one way and then another in her hand. The silver-hoofed white unicorn, with one foot raised, stood waiting for her in the shadows, ready to lead her on. But the legend told how you needed more than one helper to find the firebird.

She hurried back to where Marcus was waiting in the hall, which was filled with the scent of freesias from that extravagant basket of flowers he had brought. He needn't have gone to such expense – they were lovely but she would have been just as touched had they been a handful of buttercups and daisies. With the firebird box in her hands she sat down beside him. She decided to say nothing in explanation but simply opened it and took the drawing out. She had been prepared for surprise but not for the utter astonishment that crossed his face when he saw it. 'I keep telling myself it's silly to think this could mean anything, but all the same . . . Marcus?'

'It looks very much like a wolf.'

'It is a wolf, or part of one.'

For answer he took out his wallet and from it another sketch, this time one of a wolf's hindquarters. He spread both halves on the small table in front of them. The torn edges precisely matched.

They looked blankly at each other. 'Do you have a magnifying glass? I think there's something here.' He pointed to a very slight smudge in the corner of Kitty's half of the drawing.

'Somewhere, I suppose, I'm not sure. I'll see.' Without asking what he thought the mark might be, she went to look for the glass Louis used for his stamp collection, kept in a cabinet in the book room where Bridget usually worked, though she wasn't there today.

When she brought it back, Marcus had switched on a lamp above the table where the two pieces of paper lay. It was possible now to see that the smudge was the residue of what had once been a pencil mark, and with the help of the glass, to identify the indentation the pencil had made. It didn't make any more sense than the torn drawing itself, revealing itself as nothing but a curly squiggle.

Marcus explained how he'd come by his half of the drawing. As they puzzled over why it had been sent to him and what the two torn halves could possibly mean, Kitty found herself telling him about the missing pendant-cross, and even about the copy icon that hung in Mama's bedroom, which of course he had never seen. She didn't even pause to wonder what Papa's reaction to including Marcus in the secret would be. The relief at having someone to share it with was like a weight being lifted from her shoulders.

'The police should know,' he said at last.

'What? What is there to tell? A silver cross I can't find, and this silly business of the wolf?'

'Is it silly? I'm far from sure. But I wasn't thinking so much of either of those. A valuable icon and a gun have gone missing – and yes, I do see the dilemma, Kitty. Your father is choosing to believe Lydia took them and so feels there's no necessity to tell the police, and I don't see how we can go against him. But they should be told, really, you know – we should do something.'

'Papa surely has compelling reasons that we don't know about for keeping the truth about the icon from them.'

'Hiding the truth is rarely a good idea,' he said with feeling, frowning darkly at the two matched halves of the sketch lying on the table. 'I don't understand this any more than you. And I can see you feel the business of the cross is puzzling, though there's probably a simple explanation for that not being where it's always been. But the icon, you know – that's a different matter. The police really should know about that.'

He must have seen the consternation she felt reflected in her face. 'We can't tell them, Marcus.'

'Of course we can't.' His brows came together in the familiar way. 'So your father must somehow be persuaded to tell them himself.'

'He won't listen to me! He can be stubborn when he wants to be.' And more than a little bit frightening, she thought, remembering how insistent he had been when he'd told her the truth about the copy icon. 'But it's more than just being stubborn, there's something behind all this that he's not telling me.'

'Perhaps I should add my weight to the argument.'

'Then he'll know I've told you. After I promised him I wouldn't.'

Sixteen

Fresh from a meeting with Detective Superintendent Renshaw, the DCI and his sergeant regarded each other glumly. Emergency meeting, that was what Renshaw had called it. It turned out that the only urgency was his need to know that the enquiry was in no danger of losing momentum, which he suspected it was. Over a week had passed, and there should have been developments. He had given them to understand, in no uncertain terms, that he – and those even higher up – wanted no pussyfooting around with this case. Trouble fermented in this sweltering heat. Everyone was touchy at the moment – a shooting in Hyde Park was just another complication they could have done without. He even had a map of the coronation processional route pinned to the wall, strategic points on it marked with red crayon, buildings where would-be assassins might hide themselves. The assassination of a monarch would be nothing to any of those Russian revolutionaries who'd sought refuge over here – they hadn't hesitated at killing their own Tsar. To a marksman competent enough to shoot a woman horse-rider from two or three hundred yards the new King's coach would offer little challenge.

A directive from Renshaw, a blunt, expatriate northerner nearing retirement, was not something you took lightly. He dealt fairly if you did your job as you were supposed to do, but he hadn't got where he was by pulling punches or being nice. He was experienced enough to know the problems they were facing; at the same time he expected to see more in the way of progress. Sharpish, understand? As they left his office, Inskip had noticed a line of sweat on Gaines' brow, whereas he himself had stayed cool and collected . . . hadn't he? Though now he did desperately need a smoke.

The trouble was, Renshaw was right. He wasn't a man to jib at underlining the obvious and as he pointed out, the news of the shooting would have the whole anarchist community on the qui vive. Sidney Street was still very much alive and the chances of finding the marksman among their number were minimal.

'Has it struck you that the shooting of this woman might possibly have been some sort of rehearsal?' Renshaw had demanded, the coronation concerns still obviously uppermost.

'Yes, but I don't think it's likely,' Gaines replied, not giving his reasons. Renshaw was being overly touchy. The coronation was being used as an excuse for anything at all untoward that happened, which was having the opposite effect from what was intended, making people shrug and grow careless – or even take risks. Besides, the Russian sharpshooters didn't need any rehearsals. The super-intendent sighed and didn't pursue it. He was aware of the need for informants but dubious about trusting them. A rumour (though not without a certain amount of truth to it) had gained credence after someone had come forward with information on the Sidney Street murderers. After the shooting of Lydia Challoner several low-life specimens had emerged from the woodwork with something to sell, but so far all of them had been discounted. On the other hand, if the information was good, if it should turn out to be the Russians, the Letts, those who were responsible for the Sidney Street debacle and the loss of those police officers, he wanted them nailed. To the floor.

Gaines rubbed his forehead, evidently more worried than he'd so far appeared to be. 'Renshaw has to have something to complain about, I suppose,' he grumbled. But he was thinking hard, steepling his hands together in a way that reminded Inskip of Jon Devenish. He said, 'Loath as I am to say it, I believe I might be coming round to your idea – that the answer to this might lie closer to home than we first thought.' Inskip's jaw dropped. That was a first, Gaines admitting he could be wrong! 'It won't do any harm to dig deeper into Mrs Challoner's personal life.'

The sergeant jumped up and moved restlessly about the room. He thought better on his feet; he wasn't patient, like Gaines, now silently following the train his thoughts had set up, though it wasn't helping now.

Lydia, Gaines was thinking, a lady apparently following the usual frivolous pursuits of one in her position, except for the career she'd had as a writer – and which for some reason she'd deemed necessary to keep secret. It had never occurred to him to question why. Writers used pen names for different reasons and rightly or wrongly he'd assumed it might be thought infra dig in the circles she moved in to write for money. Nevertheless, writing books didn't seem to have prevented her from leading a very full and interesting social life. Her husband hadn't given them much help with insights into anything else she might have been involved in, but Louis Challoner was an enigma himself. Take the pistol allegedly missing from his safe. That was still a puzzle.

'Supposing Challoner did shoot his wife?' he said suddenly. He was, after all, still the chief – the only – suspect. Everything pointed that way and it was true that the obvious solution was usually the right one – in this case, murder by someone known to the victim. 'What motive could he have? Jealousy? A quarrel? But if so, why choose such a method? I'm sure a man like him could think of other ways of getting rid of an unwanted or troublesome wife.'

'Not if you want to kill two birds with one stone. Shooting someone from a distance isn't close up and personal, as might be expected of a husband, and doing it with a Mauser C96 was bound to throw suspicion on the Letts, as we've just said.'

'But that gun of his – it struck me at the time it should have been obvious it wasn't there as soon as he opened the safe door – it's only a small safe – yet he fiddled around a hell of a long time looking for it. And he looked pretty damn sick when he turned round – as if he wasn't really all that surprised. Maybe the gun was never there – though if it had been, Mrs C was the only one who had access to the safe. Which he well knew.'

'Why would she take anything at all, especially the gun? They all claim she hated guns.'

'If she was up to something shady, maybe she'd begun to fear a time might come when she was likely to need it, at least in self-defence.'

'Do you think he suspected she was? Doing something she shouldn't? And did something about it?'

On the surface, Challoner as a murderer seemed unlikely. He didn't seem as though he'd have the guts. But so far, it was at least as likely as any other theory they'd played around with. Certainly more so than the random killing they'd mooted, for instance, done for some obscure reason: to bring attention to some grievance, real or imaginary, that was held by some disaffected member of the public? Those who habitually rode in Rotten Row were more often than not perceived to be plutocrats, toffs with means and leisure to ride and own horses, and if some member of a less privileged class had taken it into their heads to make an example . . . Well, it wasn't impossible. All was not milk and honey in this glorious year of celebration, especially in view of the amount of money that was being spent on what a lot of people saw as an unnecessary public display of pomp and pageantry. Hostility against the moneyed classes was sweeping through the labour force of the country. The dockers and others were threatening strike because of lowered wages and longer hours, backed by the Trade Unions and the memory of starving miners being forced back to work after that unsuccessful strike the previous year, poor devils.

And you couldn't ignore the Irish terrorists either, a constant thorn in the flesh of Parliament – the extremists fighting for Home Rule for Ireland. That was a debate which had dominated British politics for decades. Dynamite was more in their line, though, preferably in a public place. Still, a threat posed by them or anyone like them was a particular headache in this coronation year: there had been a bomb plot against Queen Victoria in her Jubilee year. That suffragette protest? An unlikely possibility that it had gone as far as that, already discounted. In any case, if it had been them, they would have claimed responsibility. That was what their actions were all about – publicity. They'd come a long way along the path of violence, but not so far as murder yet, thank God. All of which indicated that this murder hadn't been a random, symbolic act. It had been personal. Lydia Challoner had for some reason been deliberately targeted.

'Bringing us back to where we started with Challoner – and to what motive, if any, he could have had. Jealousy? Insurance, even?' Gaines stroked his moustache.

'Jealousy, maybe. Insurance – that would depend on how much for. He hardly seems to be in need of money.'

'Hardly without, that's true. All that Russian stuff they have in the house, the vases and what not, I'm willing to bet it's worth a fortune, and it couldn't have been inherited. Not from Lydia's father, anyway. Nikolai Kasparov left Russia without a penny in his pocket and he couldn't have earned much after that, not in the way of life he chose to follow. She bought the stuff, I suppose, with Challoner's money. Wealthy family, aren't they?'

Owning a house in Egremont Gardens clearly indicated no shortage of funds. But appearances could be deceptive; people put up a front, for themselves as much as for other folks. Behind the prosperous façade there might be real desperation. There could be business worries. Jealousy and money were prime motivators. Gaines flicked through his file. 'Challoner and Estrabon, Stockbrokers. Challoner is the third generation in the firm. Paul Estrabon? Personal friend as well as business partner. Fancy a visit?'

Seventeen

The exercise book still lay on her dressing table, reproaching her like a neglected chore, its faux-marble covers reflected in the looking glass behind it. It was time she made herself read it – if only to stop herself thinking about what Marcus had told her of his association with her mother . . . and whether they should go to the police about the icon. He was convinced they should but he'd given in when he saw how horrified Kitty had been. He'd seen that for her it was a question of loyalties: the promise to Papa that she would say nothing, and even more the feeling that she had no right – more so, now that she was dead – to reveal something to outsiders her mother had been at pains to keep secret. Including that secret affair. But Kitty was so afraid of what that might mean that whenever it came into her mind, she resolutely shut it out.

She wasn't sure why the exercise book should be bothering her, what difference it would make, if any, even supposing she could decipher it. Would it be worth the effort? Maybe not, but the wretched thing had been lying there too long, nagging her at least to give it a try.

Half an hour after opening the covers she was still no further than the second page. How was it that Hester Drax had not gone quietly mad with frustration, if this was what she'd had to cope with during the writing of the previous books? Kitty knew how loyal she had been to Lydia but even so! Dedication such as that – Miss Drax rose in Kitty's estimation. Quite apart from Lydia's large, untidy scrawl, the sentences were long and rambling, the punctuation negligible, the spelling . . . well, picturesque, if you were being kind. Was this how Marie Bartholemew's other novels had begun, with six or seven pages of almost illegible notes? If so, it was a mystery how that first one had turned out so readable. All sorts of ideas and theories that Kitty realised now had been swimming around in her mind for some time began to bob their heads above the surface, though she couldn't really see any of them as being very likely. There was something elusive here that she felt she should know, yet she was failing to grasp it. She had shown the book to Marcus but he had only looked at it casually, not seeming as puzzled or intrigued by the chaotic nature of its contents as Kitty now was, having forced herself to try and read it. 'I suppose all writers work in different ways,' he had said. 'Why don't you ask Miss Drax?'

She had no particular desire to face the unresponsive Hester with the question of how she had coped – she invariably became uptight and prickly when anything connected with Lydia's writing came up. But at the same time, it was something of a mystery, if not as worrying as the greater mystery surrounding her mother, which Kitty could no longer pretend didn't exist, no matter how much she wanted to believe that. It hung over her, with imperative questions demanding to be resolved, but the answers that were coming to her were so far-fetched and outrageous she refused to entertain them. She pushed the exercise book away but she couldn't forget what Marcus had advised. He was very likely right. And since she'd now made herself read those few pages, she knew she wouldn't rest until she'd done something about it. In the end she took the book along to Miss Drax's office.

She was sitting in her usual position at her desk in front of her typewriter, looking as if she'd scarcely moved an inch since the last time Kitty had seen her there, rigid as if a ruler had been placed down her back. She looked up from her work as the door opened and her glance immediately went to what Kitty was holding. She held out her hand. 'If that's what I think it is, I've been looking for it. It's Number Three, isn't it? Where did you find it?'

'It was on Mama's writing table on Sunday, and since then it's been in my bedroom. Why were you looking for it? It won't be any use now, will it?' There was no answer. 'As far as I can make out, it's only the bare outlines of the plot that are scribbled down. Nobody can do much with that.' There was a longer pause and then Kitty didn't know who was the more startled when she heard herself asking bluntly, 'Who wrote those books, Miss Drax – my mother or you?'

She could have sworn she hadn't known she was going to voice the suspicions that had slowly been building up in her mind, only half acknowledged but gathering force. If she had known, and could have anticipated its effect on the other woman, she doubted very much whether she would have spoken.

For the first time in her life she saw Hester Drax bereft of either an acid comment or a meek reply. And then, dreadfully, her face began to crumple. To blur, almost disintegrate. It was quite shocking to see her – Miss Drax of all people! – in that state. Her eyes behind her thick spectacles began to fill with tears. She pulled them off angrily and groped blindly in her pockets for a handkerchief. Failing to locate one immediately, she sniffled and tried to rub away the tears with her fingers. Kitty saw the edge of the handkerchief protruding from her cuff where she'd tucked it and she pulled it out gently and handed it back to her. 'I'm so sorry,' she said, though she didn't know whether that was pity, or an apology for her own clumsiness. Hester blew her nose, hard, but the tears still came. The only comfortable place to sit in this room, apart from the two desk chairs, was a cushioned seat under one of the windows, and she allowed Kitty to lead her to it. It was impossible for her to speak through her sobs.

After a while, Kitty pressed the bell. 'I'm going to ask them to bring us some tea. If you don't want it, I do.' She thought brandy might be a better proposition but to ask for that would be to make everyone curious as to what was going on. She knew Papa was out and she could have slipped downstairs for some from his study but she was afraid if she left Hester the opportunity would slip away. They sat in silence, the weeping Hester hiding her face, until Emma had answered the bell and brought them a tray. By then the sobs had begun to subside and when she'd taken a few sips of the scalding liquid her colour came back. Finally, she put her glasses back on and said drearily, 'Well, now you know. How did you guess?'

'I'm not sure.' It hadn't come to Kitty as a blinding revelation or anything at all like that. She had somehow, thinking and puzzling so much over it, come to realise it was just possible that was how it might have been. How utterly improbable it was that her mother, Lydia Challoner, with no education to speak of, no necessity to earn money – and possibly no real talent, to be honest – should have produced two books, if you counted the one Hester was still working on. The longer she brooded on it, the more likely the only explanation that came to her seemed almost equally incredible in itself. The only thing she hadn't been able to work out was why. Lydia obviously hadn't been seeking fame. She had never pretended to anyone else outside the family that she had written those books. Any credit for them had gone to the mythical Marie Bartholemew, not even to poor Hester, who had slaved so long and hard over them.

'What was it all about, Miss Drax? It seems . . .' Pointless, rather silly, was what she would have liked to say. A fabrication they'd constructed between them, another secret, yet something quite apart from the other, hidden life of Lydia's that was emerging. But for what reason?

'She paid me for them, you know,' Hester said quite suddenly, her voice hoarse from the storm of tears which had left her face blotchy and swollen. But Kitty was relieved to see that after that temporary loss of control, she was in command of herself again. 'I – I have a brother, he's in a private institution near here, and the fees . . . Your father never knew. He thought she spent it all on herself. Every penny she earned, she insisted on my keeping it.'

'But they were your books. You wrote them and did all the work, didn't you? What she wrote in these exercise books was rubbish.' Kitty didn't feel it necessary to point out that the money must have been irrelevant to Lydia, anyway.

She shook her head. 'No, it wasn't like that. It wasn't rubbish. You don't understand.'

'You're quite right, I don't. I don't see why you needed her at all. Why you didn't just write the books yourself . . . make your own name. Why didn't you?'

'I couldn't,' she said simply. 'I wouldn't know where to start. She was the one with the ideas – she was *full* of ideas, and she just dashed them off! I could never have thought of such people and stories. But,' she admitted sadly, twisting the damp ball of her handkerchief, 'to tell the truth, she really had no notion of how to develop them, whereas, once I get started, provided with ideas . . . well, I seemed to be able to build it up to make it come right. I always had silly notions of wanting to be a writer, you see, but somehow, it seemed beyond me,' she finished sadly. Before Kitty could think of anything to say to this, she added, 'You know what she – your mother – was like. She had this knack of getting people to tell her about themselves and they did because she was always so willing to listen, and help. She found me tearing up the first story I'd tried to write, one day, and when she heard what my difficulty was – that was when it all started. She said why didn't we put our heads together, she would help me. So we did, and after the first book was successful – well, we just carried on.'

'I still don't see why she had to pretend she had written them. She didn't contribute much, after all.'

'Oh, no, you're quite wrong. I couldn't have done it without her.'

'You could now though, Miss Drax. You have experience – and such a lot of talent.'

A blush ran up from her neck, right to her hairline. 'That was what she said, but she was only being kind. Anyway, it doesn't matter now. It's all in the past.' Something of her old acerbity came back as she compressed her lips. 'I'm sorry you had to find out, but you must never mention it to anyone, Kitty. It wouldn't be what she wanted. It must not go beyond these four walls. Never, do you hear?'

Such intensity, in so controlled a person as Hester Drax, was alarming. 'Why must it not? It's not such a terrible secret, after all.'

'I should never have spoken. I've broken my promise to her.'

Another part of Lydia's life that must be kept secret? She had made poor Miss Drax promise not to tell this sad little secret. So unfair, thought Kitty, and not at all like her mother, who, whatever else, had always had a great sense of fair play. She felt bound to point out that Lydia could not have known she was going to die so suddenly but at the same time she longed to know why Hester hadn't yet told her what had been behind all this unnecessary secrecy.

'Miss Drax, nothing you've told me, surely, can prevent you from carrying on writing as Marie Bartholemew?'

'Oh, no!' Hester exclaimed, sounding and looking more shocked than Aunt Ursula when Hester had suggested typing the envelopes to the sympathy replies. 'I couldn't do that! Not even her publishers knew who she was. They communicate with her through a box number.'

'Can't you do the same, if you must?'

'No.' She shook her head. 'It's no good, it can't be done.' But something in her tone made Kitty feel that perhaps the suggestion hadn't entirely come as a surprise to her, that somewhere deep down in her subconscious the possibility, the hope perhaps, had already occurred to her. She thought that surely if Hester did indeed want to write so badly, she would teach herself how to cope with what she saw as her deficiencies. If she'd been able to develop Lydia's original bright but wild ideas – the sort of thing Kitty had just read – she could most certainly do that.

Meanwhile, they seemed to have reached an impasse, without getting much further on the subject of why all this had been necessary. And Hester Drax was once again – Hester Drax. She stood up and went across to her desk and sat down again, her face set, her hands ready to poise above the keyboard. 'Thank you for the tea,' she said primly. 'It was kind, Miss Kitty.'

So what had just passed between them was to be ignored, as though it had never happened. Which was not in the least satisfactory, but Kitty couldn't see what alternative she had, other than to leave her to it.

Eighteen

Another London square, other houses slightly smaller but no less prosperous-looking than the ones in Egremont Gardens, and not far away – this particular one belonging to Paul Estrabon. A telephone enquiry had ascertained he was not expected in his office until later that day; no reason was given for this and Gaines didn't enquire further, merely asking if he would be found at home. The snooty-sounding young man who had announced himself as Estrabon's secretary couldn't or wouldn't say, and Gaines had decided to take a chance. He thought it better to see the man in his own home, in any case, in his own surroundings, hopefully with his wife, rather than in the more impersonal surrounds of his office.

At about ten a.m. Inskip knocked on the door and after an examination of Gaines' warrant card and a head-to-toe inspection, the manservant reluctantly let them in while he enquired if the master would see them. 'He'd better,' muttered Gaines.

They were left to wait, standing awkwardly in a room that could scarcely have been more different from any room in the Challoner home. The furnishings were spare and elegant, the colours cool. It was uncluttered; here and there were pieces of iridescent glass or smooth, plain silver displayed in isolation on stands or in small alcoves. The eye was drawn to the only focus of colour in the room – two large cabinets built into either side of the fireplace, lined with Chinese red silk against which were displayed porcelain bowls, plates and vases in muted greens and blues, as well as plain white. Gaines stared at one of the three pictures in the room, the sort he thought of as 'modern', as incomprehensible to him as they were to Inskip, judging from the sergeant's expression as he too surveyed them.

In fact it was not Paul Estrabon but his wife who entered after a considerable wait, enveloped in a cloud of scent. She was perhaps wearing mourning, of a sort. Her elaborately fashioned dress was of very dark grey silk, but it was trimmed in shades of turquoise, peacock and pale blue. Jewels winked at her ears and elsewhere on her person, a vulgar affectation at this time in the morning, Gaines had always been led to believe. A small, sharp-featured woman, set amongst these aesthetic surroundings she looked like an exotic bird that had lost its way and found itself in the wrong nest. Summing them up with a critical glance, she told them her husband was busy at the moment and was due to leave the house in half an hour.

'We won't take up much of his time,' Gaines said imperturbably, making their business known.

'Very well, then, I'll see what I can do. Please take a seat.' She rang the bell, perched herself on the edge of a graceful ebony chair upholstered in ivory damask and waved them to similar ones. They waited. Fanny Estrabon had once, no doubt, been attractive but by now she had a look of being slightly worn at the edges, likely to become haggard in the not too distant future. Her mouth drooped discontentedly and her thin fingers played restlessly with her rings. The manservant presently appeared and she spoke to him in a rapid undertone; he inclined his head and went out. 'I've told him to tell my husband you are here, and to ask him if he'll spare you a few moments, since it's about this terrible thing that's happened to Mrs Challoner. Though I should not pin your hopes on what he can tell you.'

'While we are waiting, perhaps we can have a few words with you. I believe you might have known Mrs Challoner well, as the wife of your husband's business partner?'

'Of course I did. Lydia and I – I am utterly devastated.' Producing a scrap of lace, she dabbed at what seemed to be a dry eye.

'A bad business, I'm sorry.'

'She was my best friend, almost like a sister to me, but I'm afraid I don't have anything that will help you, either. I was not with her when – when it happened. Who could have done such a thing?'

'That's a mystery we're hoping to find the answer to. Hopefully by talking to people like you, who knew her.'

'Well . . .'

'How did she strike you, recently? What I mean is, were you aware of anything that might have been troubling her? Or indeed anything different you might have noticed about her?'

'Oh, goodness gracious, no. On the contrary. She was quite her usual self. In fact, she was extremely happy at the thought of all that was to happen in the coming weeks. Her daughter's coming out, Inspector,' she added, seeing his blank expression. 'Parties, balls, everything needed to launch the child into society. Poor Kitty. It won't happen now, of course, it wouldn't be right.'

'No, of course not.' He waited while she dabbed at her eyes again. 'Well now, Mrs Estrabon, presumably you and Mrs Challoner met often? As you were such friends.'

'Of course, several times a week. Shopping, tea, at social evenings and so on. And, of course, bridge. We were both extremely fond of the game.'

'Would you know if that caused her to have any debts? You ladies can get quite carried away at bridge, I've heard.'

'Not Lydia, heavens, no! She was never in debt – or nothing you could call *debt* – but in any case, what has that to do with what's happened to her?'

'It's a matter of covering all aspects, Mrs Estrabon,' said Gaines, who had read the notes Mrs Challoner had kept in the back of that little grey silk diary he had found in her drawer, and to which Miss Drax had reluctantly produced the key. 'There might, for instance, be people who had grievances against her.'

'Grievances?' She waved away the suggestion impatiently. 'If you had ever met Lydia, you'd know she was the kindest soul imaginable.'

'Which makes the tragedy even worse, ma'am. Do you think you might oblige Sergeant Inskip here—' Inskip had already taken out his pocketbook '—with a list of her other friends, those she played bridge with, and otherwise?'

'All of them? She had a great many.'

'As many as you can bring to mind, then.'

'I really don't understand all this interest in her bridge playing.' Annoyance had brought a spot of colour to her cheeks. 'And to suggest that any of her friends might conceivably have had any involvement in – in shooting poor dear Lydia, is really in extremely bad taste.'

She was working up to be obstructive, but any awkwardness was averted by Estrabon himself entering the room at that moment. His appearance was a surprise although, considering his name, perhaps it should not have been. His once-black hair was threaded now with silver, he had an olive skin and liquid brown eyes. He was tall, about fifty years old, and carried more weight now than he probably had when he was younger, but he still moved with the ease of a man who took regular exercise. He smiled a Latin-American smile and held out a manicured hand to each of the police officers in turn, asking pleasantly what he could do for them.

'I'm sorry for the intrusion, and we realise you're going out so we shan't keep you long. You understand it's necessary in this sort of case to speak to those who knew the victim and we've been told you and your wife were as close to Mrs Challoner as anyone.'

'Indeed, to both the Challoners. Louis and I are in business together and we've managed to stay friends as well for many years – no mean feat, that. Since we were at school and Cambridge together, in fact.' He slid open a drawer, took out a photograph and held it towards them. Boats in the background, two laughing young men in rowing apparel, squinting against the sun, leaning together, each with his arm around the other's shoulder. Two indecipherable signatures across the corner, the date 1884. 'University Boat Race, the year we won and broke Oxford's run.' He put the photograph back and when he turned round again his smile had disappeared. 'Catch him, Inspector. Catch whoever did this thing and your police benevolent fund or whatever you call it will not be the loser.'

Inskip's head jerked up. He opened his mouth to speak but Gaines forestalled him. 'That won't be necessary, Mr Estrabon,' he said coolly. The other man raised his eyebrows, but said nothing more. 'As I understand it, you socialised a good deal with Mr Challoner – outside of business, that is.'

'Indeed yes, we dined together, perhaps two or three times a month. My wife and Lydia also saw each other frequently, played bridge together.' He shook his head. 'This is an unspeakable business . . . shooting, for God's sake!'

'Yes. Were you aware that Mr Challoner's gun is missing from his safe?'

'So he tells me. Pocket pistol, little more than a toy. Not one of those he used regularly.'

'He has other guns?' Challoner had said nothing about that.

Estrabon smiled slightly. 'He has several, mainly for when he goes down to Shropshire to his brother's place to shoot. He keeps them locked up at the shooting club where we're both members, in the armoury there. They are very obliging in that way, in the interests of greater security.'

'So you enjoy shooting, too?'

'I keep up my membership but – enjoy? Let's say I was persuaded to join the club. It was formed after the South African war for training to shoot in case of another, so they say. Useful, no doubt, but as for actually enjoying it? No. Nor can I claim to be anything like the marksman Louis is. In fact I was there on Sunday attempting to improve my skills.'

And incidentally giving yourself an alibi, thought Inskip, the idea that Estrabon might be one of those who needed an alibi not having occurred to him before. 'How long were you there for, sir?'

'From eleven to around two. I lunched there. With several other gentlemen,' he added.

Inskip wrote, and a short silence ensued. 'As you and Mr Challoner have been in business for many years, I assume it's a profitable concern for both of you,' Gaines remarked.

'As far as the present government will allow. All these new social reforms they're introducing interfere with market forces and that's not good for anyone.'

'But your firm's otherwise in good health?' He saw no profit in getting into political discussion.

'No one is complaining.' Estrabon took out his pocket watch. 'And if that's all, I must ask you to excuse me, gentlemen. I am due to attend a sale that starts at eleven. There's an important piece of porcelain I should be mortified to miss.'

'Another collector, are you? Not of Russian art, I presume?'

'My preference lies in acquiring Japanese porcelain.' He waved towards the cabinets. 'Celadon ware. A few pictures here and there, as well, but porcelain mostly. An all-consuming passion, you might say, in fact. Just as my wife's passion is bridge.'

'As Mrs Challoner's was in collecting Russian art.'

'Undoubtedly, though I consider myself rather more circumspect. Too – flamboyant, Russian art, for my own particular taste, shall we say? But I was happy to help her acquire many rather beautiful objects and, I might add, quite often instrumental in holding her back from being determined to get what she wanted at all costs.' He smiled a little. 'You must know how it is with auctions. She was inclined to be a little reckless, as my wife knows.'

Both of them smiled and Estrabon consulted his watch again. 'Now, if there is nothing else . . .?'

They repaired to the Rising Sun for a well-earned pint to review the meeting with Estrabon. *'I do not like thee, Dr Fell, the reason why, I cannot tell,'* said Gaines unexpectedly.

'Because he's a pompous ass, probably. Touch of the dago, what's more.'

'Plus a passionate nature to go with it?'

'Mrs Challoner, you mean?'

'There might well be a smouldering Latin behind that smile – something's there, for sure but just what, I don't know. Bit of an enigma all round, Mr Estrabon. One thing I would say, though – I'd bet next week's rent money he's too self-protective to mix business with pleasure. You noticed he was careful to provide an alibi for the time of the shooting.'

'He could,' Inskip said, 'have hired someone to do it.'

'But where's his motive? His association as far as we know with Mrs Challoner seems to have been mainly to do with salerooms. What about Mrs Estrabon?'

Inskip rolled his eyes.

'I know what you mean. While you're checking out Estrabon at the shooting club, find out if they have lady members. Some women do shoot, though I'll grant she looks a pretty unlikely candidate for that sort of thing. Besides, if what she says is true about being so intimate with Lydia, and I've no doubt it is, she has no reason to wish her dead. If she has, she'll have a cast-iron alibi as well. Like everybody else,' he added gloomily.

He took a sip of his pint and pondered. The elegant little book with its dainty gilt lock that had been Lydia's diary had not been very revealing. She hadn't been amongst those who compulsively wrote up the events of her day, even less had she confided secrets to it. It had in fact been an appointment diary rather than a journal, a few reminders and names against certain dates, though the more regularly occurring ones were indicated for the most part, irritatingly, with initials only; chief among these was 'F', presumably standing for Fanny.

'What about "S"?' Inskip asked. There had been several appointments with an 'S' noted, especially in the two or three weeks before she died.

'Hopefully, that will be revealed when we have Mrs Estrabon's list of Lydia's friends.'

The most interesting thing about the little book in fact was that the back half of it had been used as a private expenses account, where she had kept note of her personal shopping items and of bridge debts – sums owed and repaid – mostly between herself and 'F'. Fanny Estrabon again, presumably.

'And that's interesting,' Gaines said. 'Mrs Estrabon was right about Lydia not running up large debts, but that didn't apply to her.' There was a small sum to Fanny, still outstanding, but hers to Lydia, according to the little book, hadn't been repaid for some time. He'd looked at the total and whistled. Enough for her to want Lydia dead – to kill her herself? If she was already owing money she could hardly have paid someone else to do it – even if the idea of Mrs Estrabon knowing how to find a contract killer wasn't faintly ludicrous.

'And as far as Mrs Challoner accounting for her expenses, either she was naturally careful how she spent her money and kept tally of it, or Louis Challoner was tight-fisted with her allowance and demanded to see how she spent it.' He thought some more about the Challoners and the Estrabons. 'Why do I find all this lovesome foursome a bit too much? Have a poke around into it, Inskip. And into Estrabon's background. And while you're about it, his wife's might be interesting, too. See what the Challoners have to say. Don't forget that shooting club either.'

It was necessary to check Estrabon's statement that he had been lunching at the club but it was no surprise to find the staff confirming what he said. The club was a tight ship, run by an ex-army major of impeccable credentials. When he was satisfied Inskip was who he claimed to be, he was only too willing to be co-operative and gave the times of Estrabon's arrival and departure, the names of his fellow diners and even a list of what they'd had to eat – and drink.

It was in a gloomy mood that Inskip made his way once more to Egremont Gardens. He had been sent there several times during the last week to see what he could pick up and he suspected everyone living there was getting fed up of the police poking their noses in, and though it didn't bother him, he thought it likely to prove counter-productive with the sort of people they were dealing with. The Challoner family were unlikely to give away anything which might throw suspicion on Estrabon. Gaines might not like the man and Inskip himself hadn't been greatly impressed – but he seemed to be a favourite with them all.

He was a few streets away from his destination when he saw a woman stooping to adjust a shoe. He recognised the bouncing brown curls of the housemaid, Emma Pavell, and hurried to join her. 'Stroke of luck,' he said, 'just on my way to Egremont Gardens. I could walk you there. That's if you're going and not coming?'

She gave him a cool glance. 'Just coming back, as a matter of fact. I've been to see my mother.'

'Spare the time for a cup of tea?' he asked, indicating the teashop on the other side of the street. He liked what he'd seen of Emma but he hadn't really expected her to agree, and yet she did.

'Might as well. I haven't got long,' she said, 'but I wanted to see you anyway.' He would have liked to think she was taken with the idea of such a well-dressed fellow, but sadly, he thought not. She came from the same background as he did, where people normally avoided the police as far as possible. This must be serious. She was already crossing the road. He followed her inside and ordered tea. 'Toast? Scones?'

'Tea will do, thanks.' In spite of her brisk manner, Inskip saw she was nervous. Her hands, in crocheted, white cotton gloves, gripped a small, shabby handbag. Her polished buttoned boots pressed themselves tightly together. This robust young woman, with a good complexion and strapping figure, could have been a girl up from the country – a farmer's daughter, a milkmaid, rather than a product of the ghetto-like conditions in which he knew she'd been brought up . . . she ought to have been pale,

pinched, undernourished and undersized. But then Emma Pavell
had been in service since she was thirteen, working hard but
living in a healthy environment, eating nourishing meals. She had
good teeth, too, he'd noticed.

She was almost disconcertingly direct and to the point. 'I
wanted to tell you there's a woman called Rina Collingwood you
should keep your eye on. She's a suffragette and she organised
that demonstration in Hyde Park on the day Mrs Challoner was
killed.'

'Good Heavens! So you're one of those . . .' He was no longer
surprised that women from any walk of life should have joined
one of those witches' covens, but the look on her face warned him
to go no further.

She didn't look like a suffragette, but then, although some
of them were overtly aggressive, didn't bother to hide it and
invariably dressed in mannish clothes, most of them cultivated
a deliberately ordinary appearance in order not to attract notice
when they went about their unholy business. Others were so
outwardly feminine and charming it was nearly impossible
to associate them with having a thought in their heads beyond
the next new hat or the latest social event. He had learnt not
to trust any of them.

Wearing mourning for her employer was not compulsory
etiquette for such as Emma, and although she had on a black
skirt, in deference to the heatwave she was not wearing a jacket
and the high-necked muslin blouse tucked into it was a pale
flower-patterned lavender, possibly her best. Tendrils of damp hair
escaped from under her straw boater. She said impatiently, 'We're
not talking about me. Didn't you hear what I said?'

'You couldn't be saying that demonstration was arranged
specially so that Mrs Challoner could be shot?'

'I'm not saying that at all.'

'Go on, then.' He waited, now very interested.

'She had a grudge against Mrs Challoner.'

This was becoming bizarre. Were they going to have to revise
their opinions that the timing of the demonstration and the shot
which had killed Lydia Challoner might not be unconnected?
'This woman – what did you say her name was – Collingwood?'
Not such an unusual name, but he was sure he'd have remembered

if he'd seen it on the list of those few who, hampered by their long skirts, hadn't been able to run away fast enough.

'Yes. Rina Collingwood.' Emma looked down at the hands gripping the handbag. They looked red beneath their lacy covering, perhaps why she kept them on while she drank her tea. For the first time she seemed uneasy. 'I'm not one to go tale-telling, and I've cooked my goose if anybody finds I've been blabbing to you – there's no way those women'll let me work with them if they find out, but I can't rest. I draw the line at murder. Mrs Challoner was a lovely lady. She didn't deserve to be popped off like that.'

Inskip thought quickly. 'Do you mean this Miss Collingwood fired that fatal shot?'

'Rina Collingwood would do anything for the Cause,' she said shortly, 'but even she wouldn't go that far – I think. Bet your sweet life she'll have an alibi anyway – isn't that what you call it?'

'She certainly wasn't one of those women we picked up for running out in front of those horses that day.' But the shot had come from a distance – there were more people than Marcus Villiers to swear to that – so you couldn't put money on it that the fleeing figure presumed to have been the shooter couldn't have been a woman. 'You don't think she fired the shot – but she arranged the demonstration as cover for someone else? Why would she do that? What did she have against Mrs Challoner? How did she know her? We haven't found anything to suggest Mrs Challoner had anything to do with your movement.'

'That was the trouble – she didn't.' She was worrying at the finger-ends of her gloves, stretching them out of shape. 'Rina wrote to her asking for help with funds, never mind that Bridget had asked her not to.' Inskip felt a stab of surprise that the two young women should be on first name terms, but of course their sympathies obviously lay in the same direction . . . what these women saw as a crusade was a great leveller, bringing together women who would never otherwise have even met, never mind associated. 'Well, of course, she wrote back to say she wouldn't, and it put Rina's back up.'

'Because she refused to give money?'

'Well, it seems she had some plain-speaking things to say about the movement as well.'

'Did she indeed?'

'She could have a sharp tongue at times. But it's my opinion Rina Collingwood was against her for other reasons.' She picked up her teaspoon and put it back again. 'You see, Mrs Challoner was worried that what Bridget was doing would spoil her chances for Cambridge.'

'That's something you care about, too, Miss Pavell? Miss Devenish's future plans?'

For a moment she didn't say anything, unsuccessfully trying to smooth the lacy gloves back into position over her fingers. 'Yes, I do,' she said at last. 'And why shouldn't I? She's been very good to me – both of them have, Miss Bridget and Mrs Challoner. And she's a nasty piece of work, that Rina Collingwood.'

'It's a serious accusation.'

'I'm accusing nobody.' She stood up to go. 'I've said what I've got to say and I'm saying nothing more. Take it or leave it. But you haven't found anybody else, have you?'

He smiled. He rather liked this young woman. They spoke the same language. And she'd produced another bit of information to add to what they knew of Lydia Challoner. It might mean nothing, of course, what she had just told him. On the other hand, it could mean quite a lot.

Nineteen

Rather than the spacious and imposing offices Inskip had expected, the firm of Challoner and Estrabon ran its business from an unpromising building, high and narrow, situated in a side passage off the main road, a dingy thoroughfare scarcely wider than an alley, somewhere off Bishopsgate but not far from the Stock Market, in a district where financial institutions of all sorts abounded. Gaines had elected to go there rather than see Challoner at Egremont Gardens – and hoped not to encounter Estrabon while they were there.

The building occupied several floors. The ground floor was a hum of efficient activity: clerks bending over desks and behind them, visible through a half-glazed wall, a roomful of young women seated at typewriters. A young, pale-faced fellow showed them into Challoner's office upstairs. Any surprise he felt at seeing the two police officers he managed to hide and though slightly wary, he received them courteously, sending the young man downstairs again for coffee.

The interior of the offices was considerably more salubrious than the outside would have led one to believe, cleaner and tidier for one thing, and though its furnishings were old-fashioned, they were of a solid and comfortable nature: the big mahogany desk at which Challoner sat, no doubt his father's and grandfather's before him, was spacious and well polished, on three of the walls were prints of Whistler's 'Thames set' etchings, while the other wall was lined with files and folders stuffed into floor-to-ceiling shelves. Polished mahogany shelves matching the desk and the solid, heavy door with its shining brass door furniture. A thick Turkey carpet covered most of the floor, patterned in rich reds, greens and blues; a green-shaded lamp stood on his desk and a comfortable green-leather chair before it.

Though still haggard and dejected, Challoner, at home in these familiar surroundings, seemed slightly more pulled together than the man they had last interviewed and was more prepared, it seemed to Gaines, to be co-operative. The initial shock appeared to have worn off. He had pushed aside the papers he was working on to make room for the tray of coffee when it arrived, and said as he poured, 'I hope it's good news you have for me, gentlemen.' His sad-looking eyes looked even sadder when Gaines shook his head. 'So, how can I help you, then?'

'It's just that a few other questions have occurred to us, Mr Challoner, which need a little clarification.'

'More questions?' A frown of displeasure now. 'You kept me at the police station when I was in a distressed state and questioned me. For several hours. I don't have any more time to waste. I have a client to see in half an hour and papers to prepare before then.'

'I understand your time is valuable but we need more information if we are going to find out who killed your wife.'

'Then please be as quick as you can.' His fingers began tapping the leather desktop.

'I'll get straight to the point, sir. You will recall that Detective Sergeant Inskip and I were both present at your home when you opened your safe and discovered your pistol was missing.'

'Of course I recall. It was a shock not to find it there.'

'The pistol and what else?'

His foot jerked. 'I'm sorry? I don't believe I'm following you very well.'

'I'll try to be clearer. To be blunt, what I'm saying is, we don't believe you've been telling us the truth.'

For a moment, there was silence. 'I'll forget you said that, Inspector. I repeat – the pistol wasn't there. As you saw for yourselves.'

'When I said the truth, Mr Challoner, I meant the whole truth.' Challoner frowned again, reaching out for the loose pile of papers on his desk and making a show of squaring them together. 'On your own admission, no one else but yourself had access to the keys for the safe. No one except your wife, that is. You knew she could have taken your keys while you were asleep and opened the safe.'

'Why should she do that? You're assuming she needed a gun for some reason. But I had offered to buy her one. I thought she should carry one as a means of self-protection, and she flatly refused. I've told you this before. She was opposed to the use of firearms – for whatever reason.'

'All right. Leaving the gun aside, what else did you keep in the safe?'

He added more sugar to his coffee, stirred it round and round. 'As I said then, papers, deeds, insurance certificates and so on. And my wife's jewellery . . . not her everyday stuff, her trinkets, she kept all those in her bedroom. The sapphire necklace I gave her when Kitty was born, her pearls, the diamonds inherited from my mother, they were kept in the safe – where they still are, as far as I am aware.'

'And when you opened the safe in our presence, you didn't expect to see anything else?'

'No.'

'Mr Challoner, I still don't believe you are telling the truth.'

Challoner was a soft-living man. His life hitherto hadn't prepared him for this sort of situation and he was all too evidently uneasy in it, unable to deal with it without discomfort. He had blustered his way through when they had previously questioned him, perhaps even lied barefacedly, but he seemed to have exhausted his capability to do either. He was avoiding looking at them, and had fixed his gaze on the black and white etchings on the wall opposite, evidently finding Wapping Wharf, the warehouses and tumbledown tenement buildings of consuming interest. 'What do you want me to say?'

'You could start by telling us what else was in the safe.'

A heavy, black marble clock on the mantelpiece measured the seconds. Gaines leaned back, arms folded, prepared to wait. The room was stifling in the summer heat but the window was open only a crack at the top, through which came the sounds of everyday life being carried on outside: distant traffic, the shouts of a street hawker, the trundling of a barrow on cobbles. Challoner pulled out a handkerchief and mopped his brow but still didn't speak.

'Don't you *want* us to find out who killed your wife, Mr Challoner?'

At least that got home. 'What sort of question is that? What exactly do you mean by it?'

'I mean you can tell us whatever it is you are keeping from

us, and we can remain friends, or we can take the other way. What else was in the safe?'

Further seconds passed. 'I saw no need to mention it,' he admitted at last. 'It was something which could only have been of interest to my wife.'

'So there was something taken, then. Without your knowledge? Secretly, by your wife? Appropriating your keys to do so?'

'The icon belonged to her and she had a perfect right to remove it if she wished.'

'An *icon?*' Gaines looked as baffled as Inskip, who had only the vaguest idea what an icon was. 'A holy picture, like the one upstairs in Mrs Challoner's bedroom?'

'Just like it. The one you're referring to is only a copy. We kept the original locked up and had it copied, for safety's sake.' He leaned over the desk, looking down, pinching the bridge of his nose. 'The original was brought from Russia,' he said at last, 'and given to Lydia by her father. It was of great sentimental value to her.'

Gaines wondered how many people would have known the difference, copy or original, and why it had mattered. Few people could have seen the icon, since it hadn't been publicly displayed but tucked away in Lydia's bedroom. But after a moment he said, 'Can you think of why she should have taken it from the safe without telling you?'

'To sell, of course. She had – certain expenses, my wife. Clothes she'd paid a bit too much for, perhaps. Bridge debts.' He hesitated. 'Not that she was a *gambler,* not in that sense of the word. She liked a flutter on the cards, that was all. But she probably owed more money for other things than she wanted me to know about.'

'How valuable was this icon?'

'I don't know, precisely. These things are . . . it meant more to her than money.'

'Yet you believe she would have sold it?'

Challoner shrugged helplessly.

Unless she owed more than she had noted in those weekly personal accounts of hers in her diary, this didn't add up. 'All right, she took the icon without your knowing, even though you were bound to notice its absence sooner or later – but why take the pistol?'

'Look, I don't *know* why she took either. The icon was a family heirloom, from Russia. And the gun – I've told you, she hated them. *If* she was the one who took either . . .' His voice trailed off. Even he was finding it hard to maintain the pretence that anyone else could have opened the safe without his knowledge. He looked desperate, and there was something more behind it. Fear? 'Do you think I've slept since I found out, wondering why?'

'Where would she go to sell a valuable thing like that?'

'I have no idea. I'm an absolute philistine on art matters,' he admitted with a deprecating shrug, though the slight edge to his tone made him sound defensive about it. 'Why don't you ask my partner, Mr Estrabon? He's the one who knows about that sort of thing. He used to give my wife advice. I believe he was the one who advised us where to have it copied.'

'Your acquaintance with him goes back a long way, he tells us.'

'You've spoken to him? And his wife?' Gaines nodded. 'Yes, since schooldays.'

Could Estrabon have sold the icon for Lydia Challoner? Or even simply advised her where to sell it, in what must be a fairly specialised market? If so, he might possibly know why she'd been anxious to part with it.

Inskip was looking as though he wanted to ask a question. Gaines nodded. 'Did your wife happen to leave a will, sir?'

'*A will?*' Challoner was taken aback. 'She was a young woman, she didn't expect to die! I don't suppose making a will entered her head for one moment. More to the point, she had nothing to leave, except her jewellery, which of course is now Kitty's. As far as money went, she only had her monthly allowance. Anything more that she needed, I was happy to give her.' Seeming to have forgotten what he'd said a minute before about her not wanting him to know how much she had spent, he added, 'I gave her everything she ever wanted.'

'Including money for works of art that Mr Estrabon advised her about?' Gaines asked.

'Including that, naturally. I was pleased to do it.'

'What about the income from her writing?'

Challoner managed a wry smile. 'Pin money, Inspector. You'd be surprised.'

Gaines stood up. 'All right, Mr Challoner, we'll leave you, for now. Thank you for being honest with us. At least this is getting us somewhere.'

'It is?' He looked baffled. 'It seems to me things are getting more complicated than ever.'

'That's often the case when they start to unravel. That's when you have to start sorting the wheat from the chaff.'

Twenty

Marcus hadn't expected he would have to talk to the police yet again.

This morning, when they arrived at his sister's flat, two of them this time, the nattily dressed sergeant accompanied by the more soberly attired DCI Gaines, they arrived just as he was finishing his breakfast. They refused coffee and were taken into the drawing room. Marcus was bracing himself for more questions about the shooting but it wasn't about that Gaines began to speak, or not directly. 'Certain facts about this case have come to our notice, Mr Villiers, and it seems we shall have to talk further.'

Marcus was instantly on the alert. When he had asked to be relieved of that much-regretted commission laid upon him by the Home Secretary, letting it be known he had personal reasons for no longer being able to carry out such an assignment, no one had tried to persuade him otherwise and he'd assumed his involvement in the matter would be, if not entirely forgotten, then discreetly put aside. Then the unthinkable had happened: Lydia had been shot dead – while he was accompanying her. After that he had braced himself to face questions. There was, he realised, no use fooling himself that any suspicions hanging over Lydia and her possible connections with Russian anarchists would have been dropped simply because he, Marcus, had declined to follow them through. The Home Office would have continued to keep tabs on her one way or another. Communication between them and the Special Branch regarding any anarchist activities was no doubt immediate and therefore his own involvement would have been known to the police and even monitored almost from the start. They'd probably known about the man she had met at the Royal Academy, too, which meant these two Scotland Yard men also did, now.

'Well,' he said, 'have you come to tell me you know who shot Mrs Challoner?'

Gaines gave him a level glance, then shook his head. 'These

matters are rarely solved so quickly, I'm afraid. But we do have
reason to believe Mrs Challoner might possibly have connections
– however indirectly – with these Russian gangs that have been
causing us so much bother lately. We're here because we now
understand you can help us more than we first thought.' He
sounded patient but prepared to be implacable.

'Help us'. . . 'patriotism'. . . 'duty'. . . *where have I heard that
before?* Marcus asked himself. He was right, of course they must
know about Lydia's mysterious admirer. His own suspicions
surfaced. Was that how she had got herself murdered – by falling
in love with one who had persuaded her to get involved in matters
beyond her control? He had brought into the drawing room with
him the coffee he had been drinking when they arrived, and he
stretched a hand out for the cup, but it had already grown a
disgusting grey skin. He pushed it away. He was torn between
a strong desire to be open and help the police and his loyalty to
Kitty – besides a loyalty to Lydia's memory, not wanting to smirch
her name, for her own sake as well as Kitty's. 'How do you think
I can help? I'm as much at sea as you over the shooting.'

'Maybe we should leave that aside for the moment,' Gaines
said. 'The matter is growing more complicated. We've learnt that
a valuable item is missing from the Challoner home, which could
have some bearing. In any case, it rather alters the investigation
from when we first began it.'

Did that mean they *didn't* know, then, about her supposed
connection with subversive activities? Or just that they were not
pursuing that line for the moment? Marcus waited, feeling that
whatever he said was going to be the wrong thing. The valuable
item Gaines was referring to was unlikely to be anything else but
the missing icon Kitty had told him about and he was relieved
its disappearance had come to light: she'd now be absolved from
the need to disobey her father and tell the police – unless the
reason they knew was because she'd already done so, he thought,
his stomach lurching uneasily at the idea she might have been
bamboozled into it by these two. He didn't think she would have
gone to them voluntarily, after promising Louis she would keep
to herself what he had told her. They must have found out about
it some other way.

'What do you know about icons, Mr Villiers?' Gaines asked.

'Icons? Less than nothing,' Marcus answered guardedly. 'Why?'

'It's an icon we're talking about. A valuable item that should have been in Mr Challoner's safe, but like the gun that was also kept there, it seems to have mysteriously disappeared. Some of these icons aren't much to look at – to people like me, with an uneducated eye, that is – but apparently they can be much sought after. They can change hands for considerable sums, and this one was no exception.' He kept his eyes on Marcus.

He suspects that I know about it being missing, Marcus thought, but he's keeping his suspicion to himself, for some reason. Could it be that Kitty *had* told these detectives she'd discussed its disappearance with him? He didn't think so – much less that she'd told them about the other things she was worried over – the cross and that damned drawing. It hadn't been until she told him about the other half of the wolf being in that box of her mother's that he'd started to feel any unease about the half that had been sent to him. *Sent to him.* He had been thinking about that a lot and the more he thought about what it might mean, the less he liked it. 'Do you really think it was connected with Mrs Challoner being killed – the icon, I mean?'

'Who knows? It was her own property and her husband seems to think she took it from the safe herself.'

So that was it – Louis Challoner had decided to come clean. 'If it belonged to her then surely she was entitled to remove it – if that's what she did.'

'It certainly looks like that's what must have happened – there's nothing to suggest the safe was broken into, and only she had access to Mr Challoner's key. It might have made things easier for us if he'd seen fit to tell us this right at the first, but people don't, I'm afraid.' He looked Marcus straight in the eye. 'Understandable, perhaps, that he wouldn't want it to be thought he didn't trust his wife. But what did she do with it? The thing is, you see, we haven't been able to find it – and so far, we've come across no trace of it being sold.'

Did they think he, Marcus, had anything to do with it? That was so far-fetched he didn't feel a reply was called for. Gaines let the silence continue then he said, 'Look, Mr Villiers, let's not beat about the bush. We're fully aware that some time ago you were detailed by certain people to keep an eye on Mrs Challoner.'

Keep an eye on her! That was rich. 'Then you must also know I failed in my duty.'

'That's as maybe. In all the time you knew her, you never saw anything which led you to believe she was in touch with the radical politics emanating from Russia?'

'Mrs Challoner was not a political animal. She was a woman very much concerned with the rights of the individual, particularly those exiled from what she considered her homeland. But she was not actively involved with any of them.' He hoped they believed him. He hoped fervently it was true.

Inskip slid his hand into his inside breast pocket and withdrew a folded newspaper – so slim it hadn't marred the contours of his tightly tailored jacket – and opened it. *Britannia Voice.* Merely a four-page spread. 'Ever seen this publication before, Mr Villiers?'

'I've heard of it, but never read it.'

'A left-wing paper, edited by Jonathan Devenish, Mrs Challoner's nephew.'

'Yes, I'm aware of that.'

'During the course of your acquaintance with Mrs Challoner, did she ever say anything about contributing to the paper?'

'No. And I have to say I find the suggestion rather offensive. Your investigations into Mrs Challoner must be a long way off the mark if you think she'd anything to do with this sort of stuff.'

'No offence meant, Mr Villiers. But we'll leave you to think it over.'

'You can keep the paper and have a read of it,' the sergeant said as Gaines stood up. 'You might find the contents interesting.'

When they'd gone, Marcus sat and thought. What had they really wanted, or expected from him? He thought perhaps they hadn't known themselves, that it had just been a fishing trip. They certainly didn't seem to be progressing very far towards the nub of the problem – finding out who had killed Lydia.

He opened the newspaper they'd left with him and read all of it, all four pages, everything written on the fuzzily printed, poor quality paper. He read the advertisements as well as the articles with blaring headlines: one urging a support of the dockers' strike by other workers; one reporting on talks about another proposed strike by railway workers; an article about the redistribution of wealth; details of a soup kitchen which had been set up in a chapel to feed children, the elderly and the destitute. A good deal of space had also been given to an obituary of the great writer Leo Tolstoy. He had died last November to universal sorrow from those who had revered and admired him for his pacifist and anarchist beliefs, the renunciation of his wealth and position, and his support of the movement to free the peasants in Russia. There was a grainy memorial photograph of the bearded writer, copies of which were for sale. Running alongside were articles on the several experimental communities which had sprung up in Britain, founded on the same principles of simple communal living he had expounded.

Marcus diligently read through everything and refolded the paper. It had been something of an eye-opener. More, it had left him with a certain respect for Jon Devenish. For some time he studied the front page, the Gothic font proclaiming it to be the *Britannia Voice* and underneath it, its logo. A few minutes later, he put on his hat and left.

Twenty-One

Although the dreaded ordeal of the funeral was at last over, something that had to be endured as best you could and then put away, they were still in London. Bridget had protested that they must stay there until the coronation, only three weeks away now, before going down to Southfields and Aunt Ursula, unable to sustain arguments to the contrary, had eventually given in. 'Very well. Goodness knows, we are all in need of some sort of diversion.' Probably the truth was in part that she would have been quite sorry to miss all the pomp and ceremony herself.

Meanwhile, the heatwave continued. Inside the house, the atmosphere was stifling. Too much had happened too quickly, leaving a vacuum, as if the shock had sucked up all the air. An unnerving, almost abnormal silence hung over a house where people slept, ate and worked, people who normally made a domesticated stir while going about their everyday business. Voices and footsteps were now hushed. No noisily closed doors, no one apart from the servants appearing to have anything urgent to do, except for Hester Drax, still busy on her clacking machine as if her life depended on it. No Mama, and her quick way of moving through the rooms, nothing of her laughter, her occasional stormy outbursts, sending the servants scurrying. Now, it seemed as though her absence was a presence in itself. Her clothes, all her possessions, were still exactly as she had left them. No one, not even Ursula, had as yet been able to face getting rid of them.

It was as if time was hanging in suspension, waiting. For what? The police seemed no nearer finding the person who had so wantonly killed her.

Into this hiatus Marcus came. They had seemingly told him he would find her here in the square garden. The hot weather had finished off the lilacs – their season had been too short, and now the blossoms were withered and brown, their scent only a memory. Kitty was sitting on a seat in a tree-shaded spot at the intersection of two paths, mindlessly tracing lines on the gravel with the toe of her shoe. She was too hot, even though she was wearing a thin muslin blouse tucked into her black skirt, and a hideous, black straw hat, its only virtue an extra-wide brim, that had once belonged to Aunt Ursula. She wished she had been wearing anything but that when she saw Marcus striding down the path.

'Is your father at home, Kitty?'

'He's at the office. He seems to feel better, occupied there.' Which was true enough, and she envied him the opportunity, though in such a short space he had turned into an old man, as if some wicked fairy had waved a wand over him. His hair, already receding, surely had more grey in it. His skin was the colour and texture of putty, slightly damp. Kitty could not get through to him. He patted her hand and spoke to her but he did not see her. Indeed he didn't seem to see, or feel, anything. He seemed to have locked the door on his emotions.

'Then I can't ask him if I may take you out for a drive in my motor,' Marcus said. 'You need some air, a change of scene. It's my guess you haven't been far from the house for days.'

'Aunt Ursula makes me, and sometimes Bridget, when she decides to spare the time, take a walk each day. She's thinking of buying me a little dog and then I can't back out of it.' That daily exercise stint, shortening her stride to her aunt's, did nothing for Kitty, but maybe Ursula was right to insist. *You mustn't let yourself mope, Kitty. That sort of thing won't do.* It was a daily trial, although inactivity was worse, with nothing to do but think. It was too hot to play tennis. Dulcinea, her little pony, stayed where she was, except when she was ridden by one of the lads at the livery stable, to exercise her. Kitty didn't think she would ever be able to face riding her again, or at least not here in London, and certainly not in the Row. The once-despised activities that had previously helped to fill her days, trivial though they'd been – going shopping or taking lunch out with Mama, making calls, the occasional treat of visiting an art gallery – had left her with little time on her hands, and she would have welcomed them now. Meeting her friends, playing tennis or taking tea with them was out of the question. They would all be chattering about their coming-out dances, their clothes, the young fellows they hoped to meet . . . studiously avoiding the topic of Kitty's mother – or worse, smothering her with sympathy. She would be nothing but an embarrassment.

She thought Marcus had been expecting a refusal from her. He'd expected to need her father's permission for Kitty to accompany him of course, but when she said she simply needed to tell Aunt Ursula where she was going and to change her hat, he only asked what was wrong with the one she was wearing. She rolled her eyes and he said if she must change it, then she must bring a scarf to tie the new one on – he already had in the motor an alpaca dust-coat he had borrowed from his sister. Suddenly, as she ran up the stairs for a better hat, shaken from her apathy, she felt more alive than she had in weeks, and in the mirror she noticed that even the obligatory black silk jacket she put on to cover her blouse failed to drain the trace of colour from her cheeks.

'Shall we go down into Kent?' Marcus said when she rejoined him. It was more a statement than a question. 'We can be at Loddhurst in a couple of hours or so and have lunch with my father.'

Loddhurst was, Kitty knew, the Villiers family home to where his father, Sir Aiden, who had worked at the Foreign Office, had now retired. She had heard Aunt Ursula speak of him, and had the impression of a rather formidable person. She wasn't sure whether she would be capable of keeping up a conversation with such an experienced, polished man of the world, especially when she thought of the part he'd played in that matter of Marcus and Mr Churchill. Marcus, she suspected, felt he had been manipulated on that occasion, and had been hurt by it, though a visit to his father seemed to indicate he wasn't still holding that against him.

He drove fast and seemed preoccupied until they had left London behind. A proper conversation would have been difficult anyway, over the noise of the motor and the hair-raising negotiations through the traffic that surrounded them, not to mention the necessity of holding on to the slippery leather seat. It hadn't rained since the thunderstorm that Sunday night and the dust flew up in clouds. The motor had no roof. All the same, it was exhilarating, sitting there, rushing through the warm breeze with everything flying past. They only had to stop once for oil and petrol.

'I should like you to see the improvements my father is making at Loddhurst,' Marcus said at last, the noise of the engine subsiding somewhat as he drove slowly up to the house. 'Every generation has to make its mark on the property but he's never had the opportunity before, serving abroad. He's making up for lost time now. Electricity, bathrooms, telephone . . . no one is going to be able to say we're behind the times.'

It was smaller than she'd expected, less grand than she'd feared. A low-gabled huddle of grey Kentish ragstone, partly creeper-covered and with warm, red-tiled roofs, sitting prettily in the fold of a small hill. Once a priory, it had, Marcus informed her, a long and complex history: a nun walled in, dissolution, rebuilding, knights killed in battle, honours received. Destruction by Henry VIII had left only part of it habitable and much of that had fallen into ruin over the centuries. Marcus' great-grandfather, and later his grandfather, had done much to restore what remained into a more comfortable place to live. The garden was Sir Aiden's current project, and his greatest love. 'I'm afraid you'll be dragooned into being shown around. I telephoned while you were getting your hat, and he's expecting us.'

They drove up to an ancient oak front door, silvered with age, and climbed out. The heat enveloped them after the draughts caused by rushing through the air at speed in an open motor car. Kitty took off the ankle-length, enveloping coat that had saved her from much of the road dust and kept her from shivering, even on such a day, untied the scarf and adjusted her hat. Marcus took a step towards her, pulling out the folded, white handkerchief from his breast pocket. 'Forgive me, but – you have a little oil speck. I'm afraid that does happen sometimes. Rather more often than sometimes, actually.' Carefully, he dabbed at her cheek, but when he had finished he didn't step away.

How long they stood like that she didn't know.

The gravel crunched behind them. 'Marcus, my dear boy!'

For some reason, she hadn't expected them to look so alike. But even without the neat, Imperial beard he wore, like that of the new king's, it was easy to see the resemblance between father and son, down to the direct look and the dark colouring, though Sir Aiden was a smoother, more elegant version of Marcus, the grey sprinkling his hair adding distinction. He had a firm handclasp and a warm smile disconcertingly like the smile Marcus rarely used.

A woman had followed him around the corner, and was introduced as Madame Bouvier. She was a short, dark Frenchwoman of about his own age, with a commanding bust and small, elegant feet and ankles. Her hands were slim, white and be-ringed; she laid one of them on Sir Aiden's arm in a familiar manner, and kissed Marcus and Kitty on both cheeks. Marcus was evidently surprised to see her and although she greeted him effusively, Kitty had a distinct impression he was not altogether pleased to encounter her here.

It was the first time Madame had visited Loddhurst, Kitty gathered as they sat down to a light but very French-inspired lunch, but she was clearly impressed by what she had seen of the improvements being made, and was in fact already suggesting more. Sir Aiden smilingly went along with her chatter. He himself was an easy conversationalist and the meal passed without any of the awkwardness Kitty had feared. She found him not at all alarming after all, and Mme Bouvier very agreeable. There was a Dover sole and they ate cheese before the dessert – a delicious lemon soufflé – then champagne was brought. Sir Aiden spoke to the manservant, and when he had left them, rose to his feet, glass in hand. 'I – *we* – have a little surprise for you. I am extremely happy to tell you that Estelle and I are to be married.' He was looking directly at Marcus as he spoke.

If it was a surprise to Marcus, he gave no sign, save for a slight pause before he responded. Perhaps he had known, or suspected, this was likely to happen, and was not pleased, though there did not seem to be any reason why these two people should not have a chance of happiness together. There was no wedding ring amongst the many on Madame Bouvier's fingers, so Kitty presumed she was a widow. But Marcus then raised his glass, offered his congratulations and kissed her hand. 'Welcome to the best pianist I know into our family.'

'Ah, we will make a diplomat of you yet, Marcus! So gallant to a mere amateur!' She turned to Kitty. 'I have known Marcus since he was a young boy in St Petersburg, you know. Where my late husband was an attaché.'

Barely missing a beat, her future husband suggested, smiling, 'Perhaps you could play something for Miss Kitty, later, my dear.'

'Another time, perhaps. Today, this afternoon, is for outdoors.' She smiled and turned the conversation to arrangements for the wedding, although few would be necessary, since it was to take place in France, a private ceremony without fuss, after which they were to honeymoon in Italy before returning here.

'You intend to make Loddhurst your permanent home then, Father?' Marcus asked.

'To be sure.'

'And you won't regret leaving France, Madame?'

'I have already sold my own house in Paris. I have no family, so what is to keep me there?'

'And Loddhurst needs a woman, Marcus.'

'Of course. I hope you will be very happy here.' His face relaxed; his mouth turned up at the corners. A smile. There, he *could* smile when he wanted to.

When they rose from the table, Madame announced that she would take her usual afternoon nap for an hour, and while Marcus went up to his old room to collect some books to take back to London with him, Kitty was taken off to make the predicted tour of the gardens. Sir Aiden carefully checked his watch as they set off. Kitty smiled. Madame looked like the sort of lady who, when she said an hour, meant sixty minutes, no more and no less.

The time passed interestingly, inspecting the extensive altera-tions to the garden he was proposing as well as those already made to the house. Madame was exceedingly fond of roses and the rose garden was to be renewed, taking inspiration from the *roseraie* at the Parc de Bagatelle in Paris. There was a cracked, dried-up fountain which he meant to have replaced, a gazebo that would be repaired and repainted. More than anything, Kitty was fascinated to see the remains of the old cloisters where once nuns had walked, and which a gang of workmen was even now busy turning into what he said would later be an orangery. 'Restoring Loddhurst has become my hobby horse, you might say my passion.' He smiled. 'But not one I expect everyone to share – come, it's too hot to linger out here for long.' He escorted her to where a group of comfortable chairs was ranged in the shade of a great old apple tree, so old, gnarled and misshapen that one of its branches had to be propped up. 'They'll bring lemonade out presently.'

Kitty leaned back against the cushions of her chair. Between the thick leaves of the tree, she could see whole clusters of the tiny, green knobs that would eventually become fruit. 'Ribston Pippin,' Sir Aiden said, 'not one of our Kentish apples but it does well here. It's a pity you weren't here to see the blossom. Ah, there you are, Marcus. You must bring Kitty down when the fruit's ripe – they're funny, lopsided things, these Ribstons, but very sweet.'

Marcus threw himself down into a chair that looked as comfortable as Kitty's. The men began talking but the wine at lunch was making her too relaxed to follow. She gazed at the sky through the leafy canopy, then into the distance where she thought she saw a group of deer under the dappled shade of trees, but they were too far off to be sure. Construction noises could be heard in the background. Bees droned, but there was no birdsong; the heat seemed too much for them, as well.

When she woke, Marcus and his father had moved away. They were standing by the old defunct fountain, still talking earnestly. She saw them shake hands, then after a moment his father took a step forward. They embraced in a manly way. For a moment she felt a pang, almost of jealousy. How long since Papa had given her a hug? But she was pleased to think she must have imagined those tensions over the champagne toast.

The promised lemonade arrived at the same time as Madame, on the dot of the hour, and the rest of the afternoon passed pleasantly until it was time for them to leave.

On the way home, Marcus hardly spoke. She guessed his mind was on his father's forthcoming marriage. But how could you talk when the motor was making that racket?

The thought must have passed itself to him because a few minutes later he drew the motor into the side of a deserted road. The engine died; the silence was thick around them. The late afternoon sun shone on the metalwork of the motor, reflecting the heat and sending a blinding glare from the silver of the winged Mercury mascot on the bonnet. Kitty shielded her eyes at first but then turned towards Marcus. 'I so enjoyed seeing Loddhurst, meeting your father – and Mme Bouvier.'

'I wanted you to meet him. I hoped you would get on.'

'We did, I liked him very much.'

'He wasn't a diplomat for nothing. But he can be a little – intimidating – at times.'

'Oh, but I found him charming!'

'That's because he likes you, too.' He paused. 'I wanted you to meet him but I had another reason for asking you to come to Loddhurst, too. Excuse would be a better word. I hoped we could find some time to talk – alone. There always seem to be too many people around, and there are things you need to know – though I was afraid your aunt would insist on coming too.'

She would have done, Kitty was certain – if she had been told, but she had not. She flushed at her own temerity. Ursula had been resting in her room when Marcus arrived and Kitty had merely left a note saying where she had gone. By the time she'd read it, Kitty would have been on the way to Loddhurst, alone with a young man she sensed Ursula didn't entirely trust. She put away the thought of the severe scolding she would have to face when she got home.

Suddenly, she remembered she had to tell Marcus that the police now knew about the missing icon. 'Papa told them himself. He must have decided it was the right thing to do, after all.'

'Yes, they told me they knew and I was afraid it was you they might have coerced into telling.'

'I would never have done that!' she exclaimed, indignant that he should believe she would. After a moment she said, 'So you've seen the police again?'

'Yes, they came to see me. It was quite odd. I'm not sure what they wanted exactly, but they left me with a copy of *Britannia Voice*. Afterwards, I went to their office and saw your cousin, Jon.'

Whitechapel had seethed in the heat. He had decided it would be more prudent to walk, rather than use his motor car, given the locality he was heading for. Walking would also give him time to work out some of the thoughts that were buzzing around like angry bees disturbed in a hive.

It had been a wise decision not to bring his car, he reflected, as the fashionable West End gave way to cobbled alleys and ramshackle slums running between tall tenement blocks and rows of shops, and his nose was assaulted by what seemed like a thousand different smells, none of them pleasant. He picked his way through the crowds, earning himself not a few stares. Yiddish grandmothers gossiping with Russian babushkas wearing scarves tied under their chins. Coffee stalls and traders of all nationalities with their goods spilling on to the street. Drinkers crowding outside the legion of public houses. Crossing the road, he skirted a pile of manure left by the patiently breathing, sway-backed old nag harnessed in the shafts of a cart that was inconveniently parked on a corner, while its driver snored drunkenly on the seat.

He finally located what he took to be the offices of the *Voice,* ran up the uncarpeted stairs and knocked on the peeling door.

Jon was working as hard as he could, given how much the circumstances of his aunt's murder had disturbed, not to say angered him, so much more than he was prepared to admit. He could hardly bear to think he would never see Lydia again – a sparkling glance from under a tilted hat brim, quick to laughter – and tears. A joy to be with when she was pleased with life, a hand to be held when the shades of melancholy had her in their darkness. Everyone had liked, if not actually loved her, men and women both.

He wasn't sleeping too well and he had a semi-permanent head-ache; it was stifling in the office of the *Voice* and the rich smells issuing from the piemaker's ovens downstairs were overpowering. He mopped the sweat from his brow and thought that what he needed was a month in the country, at Southfields. Time to reconsolidate. A bath – oh, luxury! – whenever he wanted it. Tea on the lawn on summer days like this; in winter the deep chairs in the library where he could read for hours, legs stretched to the fire – lit and replenished by the footman – a glass at his elbow if he rang for it. His mother's excellent cook. Bacon and egg breakfasts and roast dinners – oh yes. Food had never been a top priority with Jon, but you couldn't live on pies forever.

Marcus Villiers was probably the last person he either expected or wanted to see at that moment, but when Nolly opened the door to him, he took his feet off the desk, and reluctantly went forward to shake his hand.

Marcus blinked as he entered the overflowing room.

'Would you like some lemonade, Mr Villiers?'

'I would indeed.' His clothing, light and summer-weight though it was, was sticking to him and felt unsuitable for the day or the place. Jon was in shirtsleeves, and Nolly wore a muslin blouse, but they both looked as hot as he felt. How did they manage to get any work done in these conditions?

'Well,' said Jon, when the girl had disappeared into a room next door, 'what brings you here? Rather slumming it, aren't you, old boy?'

Marcus pretended not to notice the tone. He thought Jon looked tired, as though the world was on his shoulders; at the same time something suggested he was just about ready for a fight, didn't matter with whom, and that wasn't what Marcus was here for. 'I happened to see a copy of your paper, and I thought it would be interesting to see how it was made up.'

Jon raised unconvinced eyebrows. 'Well, take a look,' he said after a minute, throwing his arm out in a wide gesture, indicating the confusion of papers spread around. 'It grows, bit by bit, as you can see — I'm not talking about the circulation, of course.' He laughed shortly. 'Copy accumulates until we have enough to put together, usually about once a fortnight.'

Nolly reappeared with three glasses. 'You mustn't mind him. He's been like a bear with a sore head recently.'

The lemonade was lukewarm, but Marcus drank thirstily. 'I've been a bit the same way myself. We've all been knocked sideways by what's happened.'

Jon gave him a sharp glance but then nodded in a way that seemed grudgingly to admit a shared distress.

Marcus gave the young woman — 'Oh, Nolly, please,' she'd said when they were introduced — a curious glance, wondering what sort of position she occupied here. She seemed to be allowed to make free of what were probably Jon's living quarters and though he had no experience of lady typists, he didn't think they would normally speak to their employers as she had done.

At Cambridge Jon Devenish had had a reputation as a firebrand. A brilliant young fellow who had muffed his chances of a first class degree — as Marcus himself had done, though by a different route. While Devenish had been honing his political awareness Marcus had simply been messing around (at which he could and did blush for shame now, when he allowed himself to do so). But the young man who had appeared at Egremont Gardens after the shooting had been a very different proposition to the one he remembered from Cambridge, and despite the would-be inflammatory nature of some of those articles Marcus had just read in the *Voice* he was inclined to believe the firebrand had cooled down somewhat. All the same, the police obviously had their eye on the paper – and on Jon Devenish? Could he possibly know more about his aunt's killing than any of his family suspected?

'What are you really here for, Villiers?'

He realised he had been wool-gathering under pretext of looking round the office, in a way that wouldn't have fooled anyone.

'If you're short of copy, maybe . . .' He had expected this question from Devenish in one form or another and had his answer ready, but it sounded rather lame.

'You?' The sardonic look said it had sounded that way to Devenish, too.

'You'd be surprised. I'm no radical but I've knocked about the world, lived in repressed countries when I was younger—'

'In an embassy enclave. Shielded from the reality.'

'But not entirely unaware, my friend.' Marcus was stung. Their glances met, and locked.

'I appreciate the effort you've made to visit us, but if that's why you've come . . .'

Devenish was being bloody patronising and Marcus didn't want this to end in a row. He hadn't intended it to turn out the way it had. Maybe he'd been too impulsive. Maybe he ought to have thought out his moves better. 'Thank you for sparing the time to talk to me,' he said dryly. He stood up, ready to leave. His eyes fell on a copy of the *Voice* on the desk, the real reason he'd made this ill-considered trip. He pointed to the logo. 'Did you design it?'

'What, me?' All of a sudden, Devenish dropped the underlying belligerence and laughed. 'The extent of my artistic abilities doesn't stretch further than drawing the back view of a cat.' He held out his hand. 'I appreciate the offer to contribute. I won't forget.'

Marcus took the hand. 'Thanks. Who did design it, then? The logo?'

Jon shrugged. 'You'd better ask Lukin. The owner, Aleksandr Lukin. Why do you ask?'

'Oh, just out of interest. It's very striking, isn't it?'

'If you grasp the meaning.' A wolf with bared teeth, set within a circle that might or might not have been a snake, and behind it a rising sun. Jon shrugged. 'Read as you will.'

'Well,' Kitty said when Marcus had finished recounting his visit, 'it doesn't really matter who designed it, does it? The question is, who sent it to you – and to Mama, and why. Do you think it was this man Lukin?'

'I don't know,' said Marcus, 'but I intend to find out.'

Twenty-Two

The house was in an uproar when they returned. At least what passed for uproar at Egremont Gardens. Louis Challoner had been sent for from his office and had come home immediately. The police were there. They had formed a habit of turning up at the house at unexpected times, which was disconcerting – though perhaps this was the intention – but this time, they had been summoned. The gun, the one Louis said had been stolen from the safe, had been found.

It had turned up underneath a big, enormously heavy piece of furniture that stood in the hall, a tall five-drawer chest that was supported on flat bun feet, leaving just enough space beneath for a small gun to have been slid right to the back. Young Thomas and the kitchen boy had pulled the chest aside for one of the housemaids, Agnes, who was getting on and not as spry as she had been, to clean the underneath thoroughly with dustpan and brush. It was a chore that might have been left undone for months, or even years, in a less well-run household. This time it had revealed more than dust or spiders. 'You see!' Challoner said excitedly, his recent lethargy seeming to have dispersed in minutes. 'You see, I told you!'

'You don't think you could have dropped it accidentally, and it got kicked underneath, sir?'

Louis didn't bother to answer. He shot the sergeant a withering glance but his momentary elation subsided. He must have known he was not yet in the clear. Although he seemed to think that finding the gun went some way to exonerating him from the suspicion of not telling the truth about it being missing from the safe; whether he or someone else had put it where it had been found was still open to question. But if he had first hidden it there as a temporary hiding place, intending to remove it at some time, he would hardly have left it until it was found accidentally. Perhaps it had even been put there by Lydia Challoner herself, so that it had lain undiscovered until now. If, on the other hand, some other person had stolen it, and found it necessary to hide it, why choose there? There were more intelligent ways of ridding oneself of a gun. Unless it was someone who knew the routines of the house and knew the chest would be moved at some point, and that finding the gun would throw doubts on Louis's credibility.

None of these theories could be considered as more than a remote possibility, and not only because the gun was free of dust. Maybe the housemaid who had found it had dusted it in an excess of zeal. Even so, to Gaines its discovery was a bonus; it meant the chance of things moving forward. A chink appearing in someone's armour.

This gun was after all not the murder weapon, and though he was convinced it must have played in a part in the mystery of Lydia Challoner's murder, he hadn't previously deemed it necessary to make a search of the house. Nor for the icon, either, when Louis had finally admitted to that being missing. The gun was small and the icon, too, was only the same size as its copy – roughly twelve inches by about ten, at a guess – which would make it easy to keep either of them well hidden in a house of this size . . . in the unlikely event that neither had been got rid of immediately. Besides, such a step was not to be taken lightly; people were likely to feel affronted and complain about rights of privacy when their personal space was invaded, especially when they were likely to have friends in high places to whom they could complain.

When the footman opened the front door to Kitty and Marcus, the sight of the big old chest of drawers dragged into the centre of the hall brought her to a standstill. Her eyes widened further when she saw Gaines and his sergeant, back once more. 'What's happened?'

'Oh, Kitty, what do you think, your father's gun has turned up, thanks to Mrs Thorpe!' cried her aunt, who had been hovering in the background. 'If she wasn't such an admirably efficient housekeeper, it might never have been found.'

Kitty was alarmed and relieved both at once. Alarmed at the discovery of the gun but relieved that it had for the moment absolved her from her aunt's scolding at risking her good name, of being thought *fast* in allowing Marcus to drive her out. Alone!

Gaines said, 'Is there somewhere we can all talk, Mr Challoner? You as well, Mr Villiers.'

'There's the book room.'

'I think my daughter's working in there, but I'll ask her to leave for a while,' Ursula offered. 'Or you *could* use the sun room.'

'That'll do nicely,' Gaines answered. 'No need to disturb her, Lady Devenish – and we needn't trouble you any more, either. You've already been very helpful.'

'Oh. Very well.' She took the virtual dismissal without rancour and it was her brother who led them to what she had called the sun room. It was a misnomer: a ground floor room at the back of the house that had perhaps once been intended as such but was barely used because it didn't really get that much sun at all, though it was stuffy and hot today. It was furnished with creaking wicker furniture and a solitary but flourishing palm in a hideous and over-decorated jardinière. A brick wall with shrubs beneath did not entirely succeed in its attempts at screening the tiny courtyard outside from the kitchen yard where a line of tea towels hung to dry. Kitty threw open the French window, then Gaines and Inskip sat together on one side of the small centre table, while the other three – Kitty, her father and Marcus – were each motioned to take a side. It looked alarmingly like a scenario for interrogation. Perhaps it was.

Gaines chose not to say anything immediately, seeming deep in thought, doodling on the pad in front of him. At last he looked up. 'This has been a distressing time for you all. I am sorry for it. And for the fact that we haven't yet caught the person responsible for shooting Mrs Challoner.' He paused. 'But I say frankly, we haven't been helped in this because you haven't been open with us. Any of you.'

No one replied. He let the silence continue until in the end Challoner said stiffly, 'And what precisely do you mean by that, Inspector?'

'I mean that we might be much further on if you, for instance, had told us right away about that valuable item that was taken from your safe, sir. Each day it's missing reduces the chances of finding it.' There was a new edge to his voice, as if he'd had enough. 'Have we now been informed of all the facts, or is there anything else you wish to tell us?'

Louis lifted his shoulders in a shrug.

Gaines then turned to Marcus but before he could speak Marcus forestalled him. After exchanging glances with Kitty, he had reached for his wallet, and he now drew out the two halves of the wolf drawing and spread them on the table, matching the torn edges. Gaines frowned over them while Inskip leaned over to look closer. 'Do you recognise that, Inspector?'

'I know what it is – a wolf, obviously – but not what it means. Why has it been torn in two?'

'I came across one half,' Kitty began. 'And—'

'And the other half was sent to me,' Marcus finished. 'I've no idea by whom.'

'Explain, if you please.'

'I'm not sure I can.'

How many readers actually *looked* at a newspaper's logo, especially when the headlines immediately beneath it were large and strident? And even if they had, how many of *Britannia Voice's* readers would have recognised this one for what it was? Or known what it signified? The words *seryy volk,* the snarling wolf, a snake and a rising sun might have been seen by anyone living under Tsarist oppression as symbols of hope and retaliation against tyranny, but the very name of the paper represented an appeal towards the workers of Britain.

Gaines said, pointing to the words, 'Have you any idea what it might mean?'

'*Seryy volk* is Russian for grey wolf,' Kitty supplied.

'You speak Russian, Miss Challoner?'

'No. Just a few words I've picked up here and there.'

'Hmm. Well, perhaps a logo like that isn't so surprising. The paper is after all Russian owned. So this part of the drawing was sent to you, Mr Villiers?' Marcus related how Kitty had found the one half in the box belonging to her mother, and the other had been sent to him, without any other message, on the same day that Lydia had died. 'Addressed directly to you? Do you have the envelope?'

'No, I threw it away. It wouldn't have told you anything. It was addressed in block capitals.' Gaines lifted an eyebrow but made no further comment, absently moving his pencil across his pad. 'It was pure chance that I connected the two. I'd never seen the

Voice until you gave me that copy but I read it through with interest – wondering just why you'd left it with me.'

'It's a radical newspaper. You must be aware of the connections this case is likely to have and you were on good terms with Mrs Challoner. It's possible—'

'Now look here!' This was evidently too much for Louis. 'I don't like the inferences you are making. You're implying my wife had connections with that socialist rag.'

'Reluctant as I am to say it, sir, I'm afraid there may be some truth in that.'

Seconds passed. Then Louis scraped back his chair and without another word, left the room. Gaines watched but made no attempt stop him. Kitty half rose to follow, until Marcus laid a hand on her sleeve. Meeting his glance, she sat down again and closed her eyes, willing herself to keep calm.

When the door had shut behind Louis, Gaines waited a moment, then went on as if nothing had happened. 'So Mrs Challoner had one half of this drawing, Mr Villiers . . . who do you think sent the other half to you? Mrs Challoner herself, for some reason? You're sure it wasn't delivered that day before you went riding with her and you failed to notice it?'

'No,' Marcus answered shortly. 'Other people were in the house. Someone would have seen it had it been delivered earlier. And if I may say so, it's ludicrous to suggest Lydia sent it. Apart from anything else, I could have no idea what it meant.'

Beside him, Kitty had given a little start.

'Miss Challoner?'

She blinked. Just for a moment, a memory had come – and gone, magic lantern pictures behind her closed lids of that terrible day. 'Oh, nothing,' she said.

'Well,' he continued, 'if we assume it was Mrs Challoner herself who put the one half of the wolf into that box of hers, who sent the other half to you? Someone who, it seems to me,' he said after a moment, looking hard at Marcus, 'might have wanted to direct you to the *Britannia Voice*.'

'Other than you, of course,' Marcus returned sharply. 'Surely that was what you meant when you left a copy with me?'

Gaines did not rise to this. His pencil continued to make complicated patterns on the paper, as if they would help him to think. Marcus waited for an answer while Kitty tried without success to recapture that flash of memory which had come and gone again in a moment. Inskip leaned back and stared at the ceiling. All at once, he sat bolt upright, his wicker chair creaking its protest. 'That thing you're drawing, sir.' He pointed to Gaines' pad. 'I've seen something like that recently, only I can't think where.'

Gaines looked down, surprised himself to see what he had subconsciously been scribbling. 'Very likely you have, considering where you live. It's a Russian cross – more or less, I'm no artist – and I don't suppose it's the only one in existence.' Something struck him. 'Didn't you tell me, Miss Challoner, that something like this was missing, the day you showed me your mother's bedroom?'

'Yes, I did, but it's probably just been put in some safe place. Although it wasn't valuable it meant a lot to her. I'm sure it will turn up if we make a thorough search. Does it matter?'

'Probably not. But small, unexplained things have a habit of turning out to matter a great deal, sometimes. It's a Russian crucifix, meant to be worn on a chain, am I right?'

'Yes, it's known as a three-barred cross – one shorter crossbar above the one where the arms are stretched, and a diagonal one by the feet.' She held out her hand, palm upwards, and sketched a cross on it. 'About that size . . . no, less than that.' She had a small hand and the sketch had only reached the tip of her little finger.

'All the same, that's large to wear, even as a piece of devotional jewellery.'

'That's why Mama rarely wore it. It was too heavy, too – masculine, I suppose.' Inskip was still staring at Gaines' sketch, scratching the side of his nose. 'But look, it can't be important, can it? I told you, it's not at all valuable.' She had a sudden inspiration. 'Why don't you ask Miss Drax about it? She knew where Mama kept everything.'

'We were told Miss Drax was out when we arrived.'

'I'll go and see if she's back,' Inskip said, springing up with some alacrity and leaving the room.

'So,' Gaines said, judiciously steepling his hands. 'We have a mysterious drawing, a missing cross – and anything else?'

'Well . . .' began Marcus. He looked across the table and met

Kitty's pleading eyes. 'Well, all this is very distressing for Miss Challoner. Also, it's getting rather late and she's had a very tiring day,' he said, as if she were some swooning Victorian heroine. 'Don't you think she may be excused?'

At that moment Inskip came back to say Miss Drax had still not returned, and in some excitement. 'But sir, it's come to me where I've seen that cross before – or one like it. A fellow I met on the staircase at the *Britannia Voice* was wearing it round his neck – I'm pretty sure he was the owner of the paper – Aleksandr Lukin, his name is.'

After dinner, Hester Drax still hadn't put in an appearance. Maybe she'd gone straight to her room without seeing anyone. Kitty went to look for her. She wasn't there, nor was she anywhere else in the house, and it soon became evident she had no intention of returning. As well as her bedroom, her little office was stripped bare of all her personal possessions. She'd emptied her waste basket, covered her typewriter. The only thing she had left was the manuscript she'd been working on, tidily packed into a brown paper parcel, tied with string, addressed to Marie Bartholemew's publishers and left on her desk.

'But she was owed a week's wages!' said Ursula.

Kitty frowned. 'Yes, that is odd, because from what she said to me, she could ill afford to waste money.'

'Where did she come from? Where was her home, I mean? She might have gone back there,' Bridget said.

'Somewhere up north. Leicester, or somewhere, I think. But she told me she had a brother in a private institution near here. She worked to pay the fees. I don't think she would leave him.'

'*Near* here – that could mean anywhere,' Bridget said. 'Do you think the servants might have an idea? I'll ask Emma.' Having been working undisturbed when the gun had been found, she had missed all the excitement and was keen not to miss any more.

'Emma? No.' Her mother shook her head. 'Mrs Thorpe is much more likely to know. She's been housekeeper here ever since Louis bought this house, when they were first married – and I believe Miss Drax was here almost from the first, too.'

'Miss Drax kept herself to herself. She did not mix below stairs,' Mrs Thorpe said stiffly when asked. A sternly proper woman, unmarried, the 'Mrs' being a courtesy title, she was very much aware of her position. 'I know nothing of her personal life and I doubt very much if any of the staff know, either.'

'How did she come to be working here? How did Mrs Challoner find her?'

'Through the agency, I would imagine. The one we always use. The one just around the corner.'

If she was surprised by the sight of two very young ladies who didn't fit into the category of either would-be employer or employee arriving at her agency the following morning, Mrs Olive Jameson didn't show it but smilingly asked them to sit down and waited for them to state their business. The Jameson Domestic and Secretarial Agency had turned out to be a discreet undertaking occupying a room on the first floor of a building, over a dentists' surgery. The stairs were carpeted; the door at the top bore a shining brass bell push and a notice giving the name and the times of opening. Mrs Jameson was equally discreet in her person, wearing a neat blouse and skirt and her hair drawn tidily up into a bun. A motherly, middle-aged lady with a comfortable figure, she gave off an air of reassurance and quiet competence.

There was only one desk in the office, behind which she sat, so presumably she conducted her business herself without the need of secretarial help. She looked like the sort of person who would remember the details of every client she had ever dealt with. And indeed, when she learnt who they were and that Mrs Thorpe, who engaged staff for the Challoner household, had sent them, she nodded gravely before venturing to say how sorry she was to hear the sad news about Mrs Challoner.

'Thank you. You're very kind,' said Kitty.

At the mention of Miss Drax's name, however, she drew back a little. 'You must realise I am not at liberty to give out personal details.'

'You remember her, though?' Bridget said.

'Yes, indeed. A trustworthy person. I understand she'd been with your mother, Miss Challoner, ever since I first introduced them. But there is nothing more I can tell you.' Her look said she was not going to be pushed into anything.

'She's in need of another position now, though. We thought you'd be the person she'd think of coming to,' Bridget said. Mrs Jameson pursed her lips. 'She did, didn't she?'

Something told Kitty the assumption was correct – but if they were going to get the answer they wanted, persistence was going to be needed, and for that reason she was glad Bridget was with her. Aunt Ursula didn't know they were here – in fact, Kitty had wanted to come alone, or better, with Marcus, until Bridget had persuaded her that firstly, these things were better dealt with by women and secondly that an unsophisticated young woman such as Kitty, on her own, was unlikely to get the answers she wanted. Bridget, on the other hand, was experienced enough to know how to deal with anyone likely to be difficult at the agency. 'We very much need to get in touch with her, Mrs Jameson,' pressed that young woman of the world.

Mrs Jameson stiffened. 'Has she done something wrong?'

Kitty said hastily, 'Oh, please, don't think that! It's just that she left without any warning – and there's money owing to her, which I am sure she could do with. I promise you, we only need to speak to her. It's very important. Just give us her address and we won't mention your name.'

'Miss Challoner, I can't do that! I have never violated my clients' privacy in all the time I've been running my agency, and that's been nearly twenty-five years.'

The girls exchanged glances. Mrs Jameson looked as unmoving as the Rock of Gibraltar. Kitty stood up, unwilling to admit defeat but uncertain what else they could do. 'I understand your position, Mrs Jameson.'

Bridget looked prepared to argue further, but even she could see they had failed in what they had come to do. She went to the door, followed by Kitty, but as they reached the bottom of the stairs, Kitty looked back and saw the woman standing at the top. By the time Kitty had run back up she was closing her office door again. Kitty pushed it open with the flat of her hand. 'Mrs Jameson—'

She already stood behind her desk. Their glances met, Kitty's pleading, the older woman's uncertain. 'You say you have money for her?' she said at last. 'Well, then, I can't tell you where she is living but – oh, goodness knows if I'm doing right – I can tell you that she is due to come and see me this afternoon at four.'

'Well,' said Bridget, when Kitty rejoined her, 'what had she to say?'

Kitty answered truthfully, 'She still wouldn't tell me where she lived.'

Twenty-Three

She came out of the agency at about quarter past the hour. Kitty had been afraid that Mrs Jameson, who must have guessed they would try to intercept Miss Drax, might have changed her mind and warned her not to keep her appointment, but it seemed she had not. From the table in the wide window of the teashop just further along the street from the agency (the same little café Inskip and Emma had visited, had she known) Kitty saw her trailing along, in her dreary, grey costume, the picture of dejection. Once, the ribbon on her hat had been fresh and neat but its bow was frayed a little now, and the curved hat-brim had lost its resilience and sagged to match her shoulders.

This time, Kitty had come alone. Rightly or wrongly, she felt that when Hester had confessed to writing the books they had established some sort of rapport, and that Bridget's presence would inhibit her from anything further she might be persuaded to say. She stepped out of the doorway just as Hester reached it. The woman's colour fled as she felt a hand on her sleeve and when she saw it was Kitty she pulled herself angrily away.

'Please don't be alarmed, Miss Drax. I have something for you. Will you come and have a cup of tea with me?'

'Go away, Kitty. Don't get mixed up in this, you don't know what you're doing.'

Kitty stayed where she was. Hester still resisted, not unexpectedly, but in the end she gave in either to Kitty's entreaties or a desire not to arouse any further the curiosity of those in the teashop who were observing the encounter with interest through the window.

Kitty led the way back to the table she'd occupied before, and ordered more tea and cakes. Hester took the cup gratefully and chose a maid of honour from the pastries when they were offered but left it on her plate, untouched. Kitty passed an envelope across the table. 'My papa has sent it. It's what you have earned for all the work you've put in.' Since Hester had so conscientiously finished the manuscript before leaving, she had managed to persuade Louis to add a little more; rather a triumph in view of his opinion of Hester Drax.

'Your father sent this?' Her mouth twisted. She pushed the envelope back.

'Oh, do take it, please.'

A deep flush of embarrassment washed over her face and then receded, leaving her pale as milk. She gave the envelope a further push but then abruptly changed her mind, snatched it up and tucked it into her large bag, her fingers shaking slightly. 'I can't afford to be high-minded,' she said bitterly. 'Goodness knows when I shall get another position like the one I had with your mother.'

'You might not need one.' Kitty took the parcelled-up manuscript from her bag and pushed that across the table, too.

Miss Drax drew back. 'I couldn't . . . I couldn't possibly.'

'We all want you to have it and to acknowledge it as yours – all of us, Papa included. It's your work.' Learning who had really written it had caused something of a sensation in the family.

The book sat there while the elderly waitress cleared the vacated table next to them. Hester took off her spectacles, rubbed the crease between her brows, and nervously put them back again. 'Why did you leave without telling anyone?' Kitty asked.

'Don't ask me that. It's something I can't tell you, or anyone.' Kitty sensed something more than embarrassment now. Her eyes, unprotected by the thick glasses, had been full of pain – and more. If it hadn't been too melodramatic, she would have called it fear. She was not doing this out of cussedness, but because she felt she must. For reasons Kitty could not begin to fathom. She pitied her.

'The police are going to find out, sooner or later, that Mama didn't write those books, and they're not going to stop until they find out why she had to pretend she did. Don't you think,' she asked carefully, wondering how she dare say this to someone whom she had always found a little forbidding, 'that you'd do better to tell them yourself?'

'Or if I don't, you will?'

'No,' Kitty said evenly, trying to recapture the feeling of pity, 'no, I won't do that.'

'I told you why it mustn't be made public.'

'Not really, you didn't. Or not the whole reason. She did it partly to help you, yes, I believe that, but there was something more, wasn't there?'

Hester drained her cup and held it out for more. She began to eat the maid of honour, swallowing hard after each forkful, as though it tasted of sawdust. Finally, she gave up the attempt. 'I told you – I promised her I wouldn't.' She sounded desperate.

Promises to the dead. Kitty didn't believe her mother would have wanted that. She took a deep breath and said, 'Inspector Gaines thinks she was writing articles for my cousin Jon's paper.'

'For *Britannia Voice?* She never wrote articles, for that or any other newspaper.' There was no reason to disbelieve this. From what had previously passed between them about Lydia's writing ability, Kitty thought it must almost certainly be true.

'Then why? What was all the secrecy about?'

'Don't ask me, Kitty, I can't tell you. It's not my secret to tell.'

'I don't believe Mama would have wished to hold you to that in the circumstances.'

Hester stared down at the remains of crumbled cake on her plate, then began to thrust her hands into her gloves. She pushed her chair back and stood up. 'I've done something incredibly foolish and I can't take it back, though I desperately wish I could. But I'm not going to make it worse by incriminating someone else. Please don't try to get in touch any more, Kitty.'

She turned to go. 'You've forgotten your parcel.'

She looked at it, hesitated. 'No, I . . .' Then she picked it up, thrust it out of sight into her large bag and said in a rush, 'Speak to your father, Kitty. Ask him.'

By the time Kitty had fumbled for money to pay for their tea and hurried out of the door, Hester had disappeared. She realised she hadn't even asked her, as she'd intended, about the cross which Gaines seemed to think important.

Kitty was alone the next morning, Louis having left for the office, when the letter arrived, hand-delivered by an urchin no doubt glad to earn a few coppers. The envelope was addressed to her but the letter began abruptly without salutation and was signed H.D. It was as terse and matter of fact as Hester Drax herself.

> I am sorry for the way I left you yesterday. I have since had time to think and I see I have been mistaken. You have been kind to me and I now think I owe you the truth – or as much of it as I know myself.
>
> Some time ago, your mother was introduced to a man by your cousin, Jon Devenish . . .

Kitty shut her eyes. So Jon was involved after all. And this man . . . Perhaps Miss Drax had been right in the first place, maybe she was better remaining in ignorance of these things. She ought to burn this without reading it further. But she knew she couldn't. After a restless night, during which she had veered between knowing she must confront her father this morning, and terror at what she might discover if she did, she'd tried to convince herself that Hester had simply been speaking out of spite, that Papa couldn't possibly have been keeping to himself something which might help the police to discover why Mama had been killed. But then she thought, of course he must know something, how else to account for the way he'd been acting since she died?

Read. Read it, know the worst.

> The man was a Russian. I never knew what his real name was but he used to sign himself 'Seryy Volk', which seemed to amuse her.

Remembering the drawings, the logo and the words under it, Kitty felt a leap of something like fear. Go on!

> I am sure you are aware of the extensive smuggling of illegal newspapers and books to Russia – the sort of subversive literature which hopes to pass on the new ideologies and latest political thought current in the West. But books and newspapers written in English are no good to those who cannot read the language. Your cousin Jon persuaded your mother to become

one of those who are willing to translate these books into Russian, after which they are printed on onionskin paper and sent by ship, disguised as Bibles or hidden in the false bottoms of travellers' suitcases. I am convinced that although doing this would have satisfied a longing to help in the patriotic struggles, all the cloak and dagger intrigue appealed to her nearly as much. I did not like it. I was afraid she would be stepping into a world she knew nothing about, mixing with people who are relentless in their aims, to whom human life is cheap. She would be out of her depth.

And in the end, she was forced to admit that the task of translating a whole book would be beyond her capabilities. She did, however, see that translating short, political articles by Russian agitators into English would be a much easier matter, and when your cousin asked her to do this for his paper, she agreed. She was of course fluent in Russian but such work is not done without effort, not to say time, spent on it. Moreover, it was necessary to keep secret what she was doing. You know by now that she had discovered my ambitions to be a novelist, and how she invented the idea of Marie Bartholemew. It seemed best not to try to hide from you all as a family that she had become an authoress under an assumed name, and I was glad she did not reveal my part in all that. Now, it served as a cover for what she was really doing. Did your father suspect? I have wondered since if he guessed something of the truth and was afraid she might be putting herself at risk. Why else did he try to persuade her to carry a small pistol? But she just laughed at that. She always believed herself invincible.

Despite this, I think all would have continued to go well had it not been for that man – that Grey Wolf I mentioned earlier. They had met when she was delivering one of her translated articles to the *Voice*. I did not care for this man I had never seen: I thought he had a malevolent influence over her. Whatever he told her to do, she did without question. She gave him presents, that silver cross with the black amber which

had been her mother's, and I think money, too, on
occasions. He was not just another beau, as she liked
people to think Marcus Villiers was. She even extended
her efforts and translated tracts written by British sympathisers for smuggling into Russia. She was infatuated;
her face lit up whenever his name cropped up. But the
Grey Wolf began to grow hungry – hungry for money,
that is, for funds to send back to Russia – or so he said.

Your father and I have not always seen eye to eye –
he thought writing novels was a foolish pursuit which
I encouraged – but I must admit that he was always
generous to her, even to the extent of covering her
gambling debts. Which were small fry compared with
what that man eventually wanted from her – nothing
less than the icon which had come down through her
family, to be sold and the money sent to the freedom
fighters in Russia. I could not believe she was serious
in agreeing to this. There is a world of difference between
translating articles and sacrificing precious family heir-
looms, but she would have none of it. 'Don't you see,
the harder the sacrifice, the more worthwhile it is!'

It was only then I learnt that the icon hanging in
the holy corner in her bedroom was simply a copy and
the real one – the one she intended to give away – was
in your father's safe. And no, it would not do, she
insisted, to give Grey Wolf the copy, even though it is
a work of art in its own right, and must be valuable.
'He has a right to the real thing,' she insisted. 'In any
case, it's mine to do with as I wish.'

I could only hope your father would prevent this,
but she told him nothing of her decision. She knew
only too well what he would say to her parting with
something as precious and valuable as that. Instead, she
thought up a wild scheme of simply taking it and hoping
it would look like a robbery, an idea I told her was too
much even for Marie Bartholemew! 'I don't want to
quarrel with Louis over what I want to do with it,' she
said. 'He sleeps like a log and will never know.'

I begged her to think again, but she wouldn't listen.

When I think of her now, I could weep. She was almost
like a child, planning this mad escapade. And yet, there
was something different about her that night, something
hard and determined that I didn't recognise and made
me even more uneasy. Especially when she took the
gun as well as the icon. To add verisimilitude, she said
with a very odd smile. It all went as easily as she had
predicted, after which she carried them both to her
room. The icon was given to the Grey Wolf, but she
hid the gun in her firebird box.

A week later, she was dead.

It was all Kitty could do to force herself to read on.

That terrible day, when the police came. Everyone
asking why, and who – when all the time I knew. I
knew it was what I had feared would come from asso-
ciating with that fiend she called Grey Wolf. I knew
it instinctively but what proof had I? I did not even
know his real name, who he was. She had once
mentioned someone called Sasha who might or might
not have been him. All I knew was that she had been
drawn into all this by Jon Devenish introducing them.
I did not believe then, and I do not now, that he had
anything to do with her being killed, but the whole
affair had started with that visit to the *Voice*.

I told you when I saw you yesterday that I had done
something incredibly foolish. That afternoon, when we
learnt that she had been murdered, I suddenly remembered the gun. I left you all in the drawing room and
went up to her room with the intention of hiding it
before the police found it. It seemed important it should
not be known to have been in her possession. As I
took it out of the box an idea as wild as any Lydia
herself had ever had came to me. Underneath the gun
I noticed a sketch, presumably drawn either by Lydia
or Grey Wolf himself, of the wolf that appears on the
front page of the *Voice*. I didn't stop to examine my
motives or think through what I was doing. I simply

tore it across, left one half in the box and put the other in an envelope which I addressed to Marcus Villiers. Before I could change my mind, I went out immediately and put it through his door.

Why him? There is a great deal more to Marcus Villiers, I have always thought, than appears on the surface and I had long suspected his motives in acting as lapdog to Lydia were not quite what they seemed to be. I hoped he would be intrigued by the torn drawing and sooner or later I knew he would connect it with your cousin's newspaper. If not, there was the other half in the firebird box which would lead someone else in the same direction.

How naive! You will have realised by now that I was right, Kitty, when I said I had no imagination. Otherwise, I would have seen that my actions might be less likely to throw suspicion on to this Grey Wolf than on to Jon Devenish, who I am convinced, for all his faults, cannot be guilty of such a crime against Lydia. Even now, I cannot believe what possessed me. But there is nothing I can do about it, not now.

I cannot bring myself to go to the police but you may show them this letter.

P.S. When I left Egremont Gardens for good, I could not think of anything else to do with the gun but push it under the big, five-drawer chest of drawers. It should still be there.

Kitty pushed away her cold tea after she had finished reading. Despite her disclaimers, she wondered if Miss Drax was as unoriginal in thought as she made out. The crazy idea of delivering half of a drawing to set Marcus thinking had worked, in a weird sort of way. And she herself could now recall what had escaped her yesterday: while waiting for her father to return from being questioned by the police that day, she'd been staring out over the square and had seen the hurrying figure of Miss Drax leaving the house and wondered where she was going. Now she knew that she had been on her way to deliver the drawing to Marcus. She thought of the unknown life her mother had been pursuing, she thought of that man, Grey Wolf, the copy icon in the *krasny ugol* and its powerful radiance, and wondered just what the original must have been like, and what it must have cost her mother to part with it. And where it was now. Already exchanged for money by Grey Wolf, no doubt.

The household telephone lived in small, glass-doored space under the stairs. Kitty closed the door behind her and put through a telephone call to Marcus. She was informed that he was out and had left no indication as to when he would be back. For a moment she sat wondering what to do, then she went upstairs and made a careful copy of the letter. She collected her hat and gloves, checked she had enough money in her purse, and left the house. She hadn't told anyone where she was going. Rules that had before seemed immutable didn't seem to matter any more.

Twenty-Four

The tight feeling was back in Kitty's chest, and she sipped valiantly at the strong, sweet tea she had been given, almost wishing she hadn't accepted the offer, however well meant it had been. They had found a cup and saucer too, rather than a mug, though it was thick and white and as unlike the rose-garlanded bone china she had drunk her breakfast tea from as this place was from Egremont Gardens. Gaines had clearly been startled when she arrived alone and he'd done his best to put her at her ease. He must have wondered why she had decided to come to Scotland Yard rather than send for him, but the last thing she'd wanted was for the police to come to the house, with all the explanations to her family that would have meant. Explanations which might not be necessary if there was some big mistake, some innocent explanation for what Miss Drax had written. But that she knew was wishful thinking; it was beyond the bounds of credibility.

Inskip seemed to be thinking the same. She was by now looking on the sergeant more favourably than she had done previously. He'd reacted to the information she'd brought with more enthusiasm than Gaines, quickly cottoning on to the implications while Gaines remained apparently unimpressed. But suddenly Gaines roused himself from his cogitations and thanked her for coming. 'This is useful information, Miss Challoner. We shall act on it, you may be sure, and we'll let you know the outcome.'

Kitty hesitated. 'She – my mother – wasn't doing anything actually against the law, was she?'

'From our point of view, no. As far as the Russians are concerned – smuggling subversive literature into the country, I'm not so sure.'

'I see.' That didn't feel like reassurance. 'But Miss Drax is right about one thing, you know. My cousin, Mr Devenish, would never have deliberately involved her in anything – in anything that was likely to endanger her life.'

'Probably not.'

Kitty played with the button on her glove. She'd known she ought not to have stopped Marcus when he'd been about to tell the police about the man Mama had been meeting, however much against the grain it went. Miss Drax's letter had changed all that. However unpalatable the facts were, however hard it was to swallow, saving Mama's reputation didn't seem so vital an issue now as finding out who had killed her. She told Gaines everything, about the rendezvous at Burlington House which Marcus had witnessed, her own glimpse of the man in the garden. When she'd finished it was as if something disagreeable which she'd swallowed had become dislodged and she could breathe easily again.

'Thank you, Miss Challoner,' Gaines said. He made no reproaches for withholding information, as he had before, but held out his hand and smiled, as if he knew what it had cost her. 'We shall do our best.'

She was escorted to the door by a bashful young constable who whistled up a cab for her.

She reached home and found that no one had missed her. And her father was not at home.

'The question is,' said Gaines, 'what does it all mean?'

'Well, look at that mark,' Inskip said, pointing to the smudge in the corner of the wolf drawing on the desk between them.

'That squiggle?'

'It could be an "S", you know. Like those in Lydia's diary . . . S for Sasha, short for Aleksandr – and Aleksandr Lukin's the owner of the *Voice*. The man I saw wearing that cross.' Inskip, growing excited, waved the copy letter Kitty had left. 'Sasha – Miss Drax's Grey Wolf.'

'Yes, yes, of course it could,' Gaines replied, annoyingly unimpressed. 'So it seems that Lydia *apparently* gave the real icon to someone known as Grey Wolf, or Sasha – who isn't necessarily Aleksandr Lukin. How many Sashas are there in and around London just now?'

'Oh, come on, sir'!' Inskip stared in disbelief. They should have been making straight for the offices of the *Britannia Voice* right now, to get out of Jon Devenish where they could find this Lukin and knock the truth out of him. 'Sorry, sir, but—'

'Hold your horses, Inskip,' Gaines said irritably. 'We can't bring him in on supposition, and that's all we have so far – a cross *similar* to Mrs Challoner's missing one, a possible "S" which may or may not mean Sasha, short for Aleksandr, and a drawing a child could have done.' He fell silent, lost in thought, doodling again as if it helped his thought processes. 'Lydia Challoner *gave* away the icon,' he said at last. 'Yet she's never struck me, from what we've learnt of her, as being enough of a fanatic to do that.'

'They were lovers.'

'So it would seem.'

'And she cared a lot about all this business with Russia.'

'Enough to give away a family heirloom? One she prized above everything, according to her daughter?'

When he'd seen the icon, even though it was apparently a skilful copy, he hadn't thought it beautiful. Compelling, yes, but beauty was in the eye of the beholder, or so they said. In itself the copy must have been worth something – so how far had Lydia Challoner's loyalties extended – and to whom – for her to be willing to give away the far more valuable original? He said suddenly, 'Estrabon would know. Know its value, where it might have been sold, for how much.'

'Estrabon?' Inskip made a dubious face. Like all good detectives, he had his own ways of getting information. Gaines hadn't enquired too closely how Inskip had acquired the backstairs gossip that Estrabon apparently had a bit of a reputation with the ladies – which in Inskip's opinion wasn't surprising, with a wife like his. Gaines had put him down as too careful and calculated to indulge himself with extra-marital affairs, but you never knew. When it came down to that, nobody was immune.

Meanwhile, like the rest of them, this Lukin had an alibi. He and Jon Devenish had been together just before the murder. Gaines rubbed his hand across his face. There was every chance they might be left with that miserable option of a contract killing – the worst of all worlds, because unless they actually found the man who'd pulled the trigger and he was persuaded to confess who'd hired him, they were unlikely ever to know who the real culprit was. 'Maybe we need to look at the suffragettes again, after all,' Inskip suggested gloomily.

This didn't seem to raise the DCI's spirits. 'We're dealing with facts, not improbable fantasy.'

'I know how it sounds. But they do keep cropping up, don't they?'

'They crop up everywhere,' he said wearily, 'and they will, till they get the bloomin' vote. Wear us down, they will. Nothing as persistent as a woman when she's determined to have her way.' Something in his voice said he spoke from experience. 'All right, if you think there's anything in it, get out there and find this Rina Collingwood.'

'She's not on any of our lists and we can't get her for what she might have done. We've no basis for questioning her, always supposing we've any hope of finding her.' Which Gaines knew as well as he. If she'd decided to drop out of circulation, there was no knowing where she could be. Losing herself in London, or anywhere else in the country for that matter, would be as easy as falling off a log, when women all over England were beginning to give their support – to those convalescing after the ordeal of prison and forcible feeding, or to those still on the run from authority after the crimes they'd committed – and all simply in the name of female franchise. Inskip just couldn't understand the hysteria that was gripping the women of this country.

'Well, I don't think Emma Pavell was talking out of spite,' he ended. 'I think she was genuinely worried about Bridget Devenish.'

'With good reason, probably,' Gaines muttered. 'Clever as a box of monkeys, that one. And you know what they say – intellectually bright but lacking in the common sense department.'

And if she was under the influence of this Collingwood woman she wasn't likely to volunteer information on her whereabouts. It would simply waste more time, following up what at best could be called a woman's intuition, at worst spite. Though Inskip could have sworn Emma Pavell wasn't the sort to bear a grudge.

Unlike Gaines, he didn't have a wife and family to go home to and, late in the day, he settled down to get his daily report into some sort of order. The written word didn't come easily to him but Renshaw was sure to be demanding it at any time. He typed with two fingers and a well-used eraser. Scratched his head. Puzzled over the sometimes incomprehensible hieroglyphics that stood for notes in his notebook which were never as good as his memory . . .

A shadow fell on the desk. 'I've just had a session with Renshaw,' said Gaines. He looked tired. Renshaw, probably, giving him a hard time. 'He agrees we should talk to Lukin. Stir your stumps, Sergeant.'

'Now?'

'That's the general idea. The *Voice* offices. Devenish lives on the premises, doesn't he? He'll know where we can find him.'

'Right.' Inskip was already halfway to the door. 'Armed?' he chanced, without much hope. Despite a noisily growing representation for officers of the law to be routinely armed, following all the publicity those police murders had generated, they could still only carry arms by special dispensation. The more moderate men in the Force were in agreement with this, knowing what arming the police could lead to. But some were in agreement with the press and members of the public. Not Gaines.

'This isn't a bloody raid, Sergeant.' Gaines rarely swore and Inskip bit back the retort that it hadn't been a raid at Houndsditch, either, the police had simply been called in to investigate a suspicious noise. They hadn't expected guns to be pulled on them, that three of them would end up dead. 'We're merely going to question someone who might give us a lead,' Gaines said more mildly. 'We're not out to intimidate.'

'Think that matters to a Bolshie? He'll have a gun out as soon as look at us.'

'Assuming he's not entirely innocent. Which we've no reason to assume.'

True enough, they couldn't enter with all guns blazing but Inskip felt they could be walking into it. Trapped like rats in a cage if Lukin wasn't the innocent Gaines was trying to believe in, especially if he had any of his associates with him.

They left, on the way picking up another man to go with them, the only person still left in the office, an inexperienced young DC by the name of Watts, but keen as mustard and evidently not giving a damn that he was being thrown in at the deep end.

Approaching the piemaker's shop above which the *Voice* offices were situated, Gaines confessed himself curious to speak to the newspaper's editor, this young fellow, Devenish, as yet only a name to him. There was no time, however, for that. Devenish was eating his supper but after a slight hesitation, when Inskip told him who they were looking for, said they were fortunate, Mr Lukin was on the premises at that very moment. Upstairs, in the attic room above the offices which was rented by a group of his Russian friends. Giving him no time to ask further questions, Gaines told him to stay where he was. Inskip was already halfway out of the door and Gaines went after him, motioning young Watts to follow.

An intimation that things might not go as Gaines hoped came as they were filing quietly up the next leg of the narrow stairs and the door at the top opened. Someone was coming down the steps. Inskip was going up first and his gut wrenched. One of their colleagues murdered in Houndsditch had been killed by a gun fired from the top of a staircase. In a rush, he shouldered the man aside, spun him round and forced him back up the stairs, through the still-open door. He was too surprised even to make a sound.

There were three other men in the room, one leaning against the wall, smoking and paring his nails, another sitting on the floor with his knees up and his back to the wall, strumming on a balalaika, an undersized lad of about seventeen, with a mop of curls and eyes too big for his malnourished face. The nail-parer made up for him: he was fat as a barrel of lard and his breath wheezed as he levered himself from the wall and stood upright. The knife he'd been using on his nails looked sharp but he didn't even protest as Gaines stepped forward and took it from him. Neither he nor the balalaika player, nor the individual Inskip still had in an arm-lock seemed much of a threat. The big man seated at a large square table did not appear to be armed, either. He had not moved a muscle.

The attic room was insufficiently lit by a window in the roof and a couple of guttering candles fixed by their own wax to the table; there was an iron bedstead with a thin straw mattress and no bedding, several rickety chairs and a liberal sprinkling of cigarette butts and empty bottles strewing the floor. The air was thick with tobacco and alcohol fumes and an air of ineffectuality emanating from the occupants like ectoplasm. As a band of revolutionaries, they were less than frightening. They swore they were engaged in nothing more culpable than practising for a concert they were to take part in at one of their clubs, and nothing looked more likely. 'Names then. You first,' Gaines said to the boy.

He scrambled to his feet, shaking his head and looking terrified. 'No English.'

The man Inskip was still holding found his voice. 'He is Yuri Petroff, and he' – indicating the fat nail-parer – 'is Gregor Mishkin.'

'And who are you?'

'My name is Ilya Yacubov. They do not speak English.'

Perhaps not, but they all appeared to understand it well enough. 'And your friend here is Aleksandr Lukin,' Inskip said, addressing the man at the table. 'We've met before, I believe.'

'You are the owner of the newspaper downstairs?' Gaines asked him.

'No.'

'You're *not* Lukin?'

'That is my name, Aleksandr Nikolaivitch Lukin – but I am sorry to disappoint you. I regret I am not the owner. I am merely an émigré from Russia.' His English was fluent but with a strong Russian accent. He had a wide, Slavic face with high cheekbones, thin lips and a strong jaw. But it was his eyes that dominated, so pale a blue as to be almost colourless.

'Who does own the paper then?'

Lukin inclined his head and mentioned a name not even Inskip recognised, with all his comprehensive memory for anyone in his area who had ever come remotely under suspicion: Maxim Dimitrov. But these people used so many aliases they themselves often forgot who they were supposed to be at any one time.

'Where can we find him?'

Lukin shrugged and smiled, revealing strong white teeth. 'Paris, St Petersburg, Switzerland, who knows? He has not been in London for three months.'

'Don't admit anything Sasha.' Yacubov's command of English seemed as good as Lukin's.

Gaines threw him a glance. 'Take them downstairs, Sergeant. Tell Mr Devenish I'll be down to talk to them later. You come back here and you, Constable, stay with them.'

Inskip and Watts hustled the three down the stairs and in a moment or two Inskip returned.

Gaines drew up one of the chairs to the table, as did Inskip. 'What do you want with me?' asked Lukin.

'We are investigating the murder of Mrs Lydia Challoner, and we have reason to believe you may be able to help us.'

Lukin raised his eyebrows.

Gaines began with the questions that were routine at the beginning of any interview and it was soon established that Aleksandr Lukin was going to keep up the assertion that he was not the wealthy entrepreneur who had put money into starting up the paper. He was, he said, thirty-seven years old, and had left Russia years ago, after completing his studies at university. Like so many of his contemporaries he had led a footloose existence around Europe, searching for a better life and scraping together what he could to earn a living, until he had met this man, Maxim Dimitrov, who had offered him money to set up the *Britannia Voice* here in London. He was flattered. He had in his younger days been involved in student politics, and though he didn't say so Gaines felt that was almost certainly why he had left Russia, that he had been actively involved and thus become *persona non grata* in his own country. He had leapt at the chance offered to him, he said, because Britain had always been his ultimate goal. He shrugged when asked why. 'Why not? So tolerant of foreigners, so laissez-faire. And yet . . . so willing to let them – and your own people – work like slaves and live like animals.'

Gaines was not insulted. This was standard revolutionary jargon, parroted regularly at every street corner in the East End. In fact, if it came down to it, he wondered where Lukin would stand. He couldn't see him manning the barricades. And yet – was he the sort of dangerous fanatic to shoot Lydia? Yes, those eyes, cold as a Siberian winter, said he could be merciless if need be, and it needed no stretch of the imagination to believe him capable of using a pistol, aiming to kill – even though from a distance maybe. But still . . . He had a disconcerting air of having something up his sleeve.

'You were acquainted with Mrs Challoner.'

'Of course. She was the aunt of my editor.' 'My editor' said with a proprietary air. 'A charming lady.'

'You were having an affair with her.'

For a moment, Lukin stared, then threw back his head and gave a great laugh. He broke off suddenly. 'It would suit you to think that, but you would be wrong.'

'You were seen together. You received a packet from her.'

He was all at once alert. 'Seen? Where?' Gaines looked blandly at him. Suddenly he smiled and held up a finger. 'Aha. The art gallery. I told her it was too public a place to be seen with me.'

'If you weren't having an affair why didn't you wish to be seen together?'

'She was a married lady. People get the wrong ideas,' he answered carelessly. 'Especially as the packet she gave me was a present.' He touched the heavy silver cross which he was still wearing around his neck to hold his necktie in place much as a tiepin would have done.

'It wasn't the only present she gave you. An icon, for instance? Does that ring any bells?' Lukin didn't answer. 'She gave – or sent – an icon to you, to raise money to send back to Russia.'

After a moment, he said, 'She promised, but one thing you must know.' He paused. 'Promises are one thing. It never reached me.'

Silence.

'Did you kill her because of that?'

The reaction was startling, to say the least. 'Kill her? Why should I do that, policeman? You ask why I wanted to come to England? I came to find her. I loved her, yes. Because Lydia Nikolovna Kasparov was my sister.'

Twenty-Five

'*Ask your father,*' Hester Drax had said – but when the letter had come she hadn't waited until Louis came home. That had been a mistake, and Kitty had spent most of yesterday and half of the previous night regretting it. She knew she would have to face him now, to confess she'd already shown the letter to the police, though she wouldn't say that was partly because she was beginning to be a little scared of his unpredictable reactions to any mention of Lydia. She desperately needed some moral support. After a moment, she went again into the little telephone room under the stairs and asked for Marcus's number, and this time when the operator put her through, the manservant who answered said he was at home and asked her to wait until he was found.

The two minutes were nearly up when she eventually heard his voice. There wasn't enough time to explain anything. 'Please, can you meet me in the square garden?' she asked urgently. 'I have to talk to Papa, but first I must see you. Such a lot seems to have happened.'

'I'll come round immediately.'

Would Papa be less responsive with Marcus present? Perhaps, but that seemed to matter less than just knowing he would be there.

Later, feeling like a delinquent child, she explained to Louis how she'd gone to find Miss Drax, then repeated their conversation and finally told how she'd received the letter. Marcus propped himself on the arm of a chair, arms folded, saying nothing but listening intently. Louis took the letter and scanned it briefly, nodded and then refolded it.

'The police have already been in touch and want to see me.' He tapped the letter sadly. 'Did you not feel you could come to me first about this, Kitty?'

He had every right to be angry. It wasn't anger, though: he

was hurt, deeply. She felt herself shrink. 'If I've done wrong . . .' she began hesitantly.

'You've done nothing wrong at all, Kitty,' intervened Marcus.

'I'm sorry, sir but—'

Louis looked from one to the other and shook his head. 'There's no need for apologies from either of you. You're not alone in being at fault, Kitty. It should have been I who spoke to you of this, not that woman. And she should not have interfered. I always knew she was trouble.'

'Then it's true, what she says about . . . the . . . the man she calls Grey Wolf.'

'Substantially.' She couldn't understand why he didn't sound more bitter about Mama and this man Miss Drax hated so much. 'Yes, it's true, Kitten.' This time the pet name didn't irritate her. Something of the Papa she remembered seemed to have returned. He had aged irrevocably since her mother's death; for too long he'd moved like someone in a trance but now, in some inexplicable way something, perhaps something in that letter, seemed to have shocked him back into some semblance of life. She was encouraged to say, 'You knew Mama had taken the icon as well, didn't you, and why? Before you read the letter?'

He didn't answer immediately. 'I suspected she had,' he said at last, 'but I was wrong about the reason. There are things about your mother I would have preferred you not to know, Kitty, but since they're now here in black and white . . .' He again tapped the folded pages. 'Sit down, child. You too, Marcus. The police are on their way so I haven't much time and I need to explain before they arrive. I suspect they will have contacted Aleksandr Lukin by now.'

'Lukin, sir?'

'Yes, Marcus. Before they come, I need to tell you both about Aleksandr Lukin . . .'

Aleksandr Lukin, a murderer? Gaines weighed up the possibility. He'd spent over an hour yesterday with the man, until the questioning reached stalemate. For all that, they were little further forward. Men had been known to kill their sisters, even their half-sisters, as Lukin had claimed she was, and for even less motive – but the mere fact that she hadn't kept her promise to send him the icon – could that possibly have been compelling enough? And if she hadn't sent it to him, where was it now?

Lukin had a history that might well have led him to murder. Gaines had elicited from him that he was the illegitimate son of Nikolai Kasparov and the woman Nikolai had taken up with after the death of his wife, left behind with her when Nikolai had fled Russia with his daughter, Lydia. Lukin's mother had died and he had spent most of his adult life trying to trace his father, only to discover, at last, that he too was dead. But the daughter – 'My sister!' – was very much alive, and living in England.

'Rich, too,' remarked Inskip sourly. And who knew what other issues there were as well: jealousy, revenge?

'God knows,' Gaines said. The man had seemed to be genuinely fond of Lydia, genuinely upset that she had been murdered, but of all the killers Gaines had dealt with claiming to be innocent of murdering someone close to them, he couldn't think of one who hadn't tried this on.

There was no clear evidence against him. Another with an unshakeable alibi – if Jon Devenish was to be believed when he said that Lukin had been with him at the time of the shooting. But . . . nothing simpler than for Lukin to have known where to find a man with a gun to do the shooting for him.

Questions remained unanswered. How deeply was he committed to the cause of Russian freedom? Or had that been a cover up for his own ends? Was the story of being Nikolai Kasparov's son credible? More to the point, why had Lydia so easily accepted it?

Meanwhile, here was Inskip to remind him that they were bound for Egremont Gardens and another meeting with Louis Challoner. He groaned. Having a conversation with Challoner was as unpleasant as squeezing a half-blown-up balloon. It neither burst nor deflated properly. It just stayed limp and sad, like his handshake.

When they arrived, the young footman showed them into the drawing room at the front of the house; Mr Challoner sent his apologies, he would be with them very shortly. After a few minutes the door opened but it was Bridget Devenish who stepped into the room. 'Oh, I'm sorry. I heard voices and I thought . . .' She backed away.

'Don't go, Miss Devenish. I'd like a word or two with you,' Gaines said, waving her to a seat.

She looked a little wary, but sat down. Very composed, very straight in her chair, a good-looking young woman with smooth, dark hair and intelligent eyes.

'What can you tell us about a letter your aunt received from Miss Rina Collingwood?' Gaines asked, straight to the point. Inskip felt a small jolt of satisfaction that the DCI hadn't entirely dismissed what Emma Pavell had said after all.

He wasn't pressing for an answer and it was some time before she gave it. 'It was a mistake,' she said coolly at last, but for all that she was neither as nonchalant nor as much at ease as she tried to appear. Her hands, clasped too tightly together, gave her away. She was still quite young, after all. 'Rina – Miss Collingwood, is a member of the W.S.P.U. and she works extremely hard for it. Funds are something they're always looking for and she was under the impression my aunt would be willing to contribute.'

'Really? It doesn't seem to have been a secret that Mrs Challoner wasn't in sympathy with the movement.'

She tucked back a stray tendril of hair and licked her lips. Distinctly uneasy now. Wondering how much to say. 'I suppose – well, I suppose she thought Aunt Lydia might have second thoughts about it, the appeal coming from Mrs Estrabon's sister.'

The silence seemed to go on for a long time.

'Miss Collingwood was Mrs Estrabon's sister?'

'Yes.'

'Why should that make her any more inclined to give money?'

'Well.' Bridget was beginning to sound a little desperate. 'I suppose Fanny knew a lot about Aunt Lydia and how she might be persuaded . . .'

'She knew of something she could hold over her,' suggested Gaines softly.

Bridget turned scarlet. At that moment, Louis Challoner came into the room. Bridget, with a muttered excuse, seized the opportunity and fled.

Gaines had arranged to see Louis Challoner because he felt obliged to discuss Miss Drax's letter with him, not least because of her doubts as to Louis's unawareness of Lydia's activities, which echoed his own. What sort of man was he, not to have known his wife was dabbling in potentially dangerous waters? He'd indulged her in the matter of her supposed novel writing, even so far as keeping it a secret from the outside world, but had he really never asked how she had suddenly found such talent? And had he really not known about Lukin and the relationship to his wife? He'd sounded dumbfounded when Gaines had earlier relayed the information over the telephone, though he'd quickly recovered. These were pressing questions, but now in view of that encounter with Bridget Devenish another, perhaps not unimportant one had cropped up. Deal with that, but first . . .

Louis was inviting them into his study.

When they were seated, he said, 'Mr Challoner, what do you know about a letter your wife received some time ago? From a Miss Collingwood?'

His face closed. He hadn't expected that. For some time he sat with his eyes lowered, but at last he began to speak . Yes, he knew the letter the inspector was referring to . . .

It had been good of Mrs Estrabon to call, though in fact she had been the last person anyone at Egremont Gardens wished to see. With her brittle social chatter, she had an ability to amuse by passing on the wicked pieces of gossip she always managed to pick up, though surely even she would have realised that sort of thing would hardly be appropriate at this time. In particular Louis had been disinclined to play the host to a woman he had never liked and now detested. Hearing her voice, he had retreated into the study that had become his refuge, leaving the visitor to Kitty and her aunt.

She had come oozing kindness and sympathy (and in deepest black) and it would have been churlish of them to refuse to see her. The obligatory half-hour calling time could not have been comfortable for them but Mrs Estrabon had finally refused more tea and drew on her gloves, preparatory to leaving. 'I must see dear Louis once more for a moment before I go,' she'd murmured. 'No, no, please don't bother. I'm familiar enough with the way to his study.'

The reminder that she had always been a frequent visitor to this house, that she had been Lydia's friend, had been enough for Ursula, apologetic afterwards, to allow her to go and find Louis herself.

He had looked up when the door opened and when he saw who it was drew back like a caged animal. She held up a hand. 'Don't worry,

I won't disturb you for long, Louis. Paul told me you were at home today for a meeting with your lawyers.'

'Lydia's affairs,' he managed. 'What do you want, Fanny?'

'Now, why should you think I want anything?'

'I cannot imagine you came here for the pleasure of seeing me.' She smiled and sat down.

'If it's money you're after, the source has gone.'

There was a small silence while she considered. 'Ah, yes, I thought that was what had happened. You opened that letter. How very ungentlemanly! Paul would not dream of opening my correspondence. I should like it back, please.'

'You would like it back? Well, you're too late. You don't think I would keep such scurrilous stuff?' He regarded her with loathing. 'It's long been consigned to the flames. I can't be blackmailed as you tried to do with Lydia – your best friend.'

'A fact that did not prevent her having an affair with my husband. Which you were willing to condone . . . because we all know, don't we, that Paul is the driving force in the firm? Without him, there would be no firm.'

'Well, Lydia is no longer here to threaten, and since I already know everything, your threats mean nothing. Now, go.'

She settled herself more comfortably and crossed her dainty ankles. A small smile played around her lips. 'I've never before thought you obtuse, Louis, but you're not being very perceptive now, are you? What I know puts you in an even worse position than before. If I go to the police.'

The image of the fashionably dressed, agreeably smiling woman had vanished. He thought she looked like a small, desiccated crow in her black garments, her eyes predatory and her hands, as they tightened on the arms of her chair, like claws.

'It doesn't matter what you do,' he said. 'My life is over anyway, now that she's gone.'

'The letter, sir?' Gaines prompted. Louis seemed to have forgotten where he was.

He blinked. Yes. Yes, of course. It had arrived some time ago, and he fancied it had upset his wife when she'd opened it at breakfast though she'd said it was nothing important. Later when he'd caught her reading it again, she'd tried to conceal it in her handbag, so he'd later searched for the bag and found it still there. 'I'd no compunction in reading something which had upset her so much, especially when I found the sender was Fanny Estrabon's sister. I'd never met that young woman, but the apple never falls far from the tree, does it? And Fanny . . . she was always a bad influence on Lydia and now I knew she'd been spying on her, too. It was she who'd passed on the slanderous details to her sister.'

'Go on, sir.'

'It was a blackmail letter, demanding funds for those suffragettes. Otherwise she threatened to make public an affair my wife had supposedly had with my partner, Paul Estrabon, Fanny's husband. I did not believe that and yet – God forgive me – I confronted Lydia and demanded to know if there was any truth in it. I should never have done that, never doubted her.' His voice shook. Lydia, he went on when he was able, had admitted she had perhaps flirted with Paul, they'd carried on a little dalliance, maybe not entirely platonic. She had been unwise, it had given rise to gossip. But there was nothing more to it.

Had he believed it? Had he shut his eyes to that as to so much else about his wife? 'Do you have the letter?'

'It's long since been consigned to the flames – my precise words to Fanny Estrabon when she tried to use the letter and switch the pressure on to me. Money for herself, of course – the suffra-gette's cause is the last thing to appeal to Fanny. Lydia could no longer be blackmailed over the affair, but it gave me a motive, don't you see, for shooting my wife. Or so she said.'

A silence fell while they digested this. 'I've been frank with you, Inspector, but I hope you'll not let this go any further. I do not want my daughter to know of this.'

'As you wish – if it doesn't interfere with the enquiry, I must add,' Gaines said. After a moment or two, he went on, 'In her letter Miss Drax states that Mrs Challoner gave the icon to Alexander Lukin but he swears not. Have you any idea what might have happened to it, sir? Such as where it might have been sold?'

'I've told you, I'm a Philistine in these matters.'

Of course, it was Estrabon who had been Lydia's unofficial adviser – but who could mention Paul Estrabon's name now?

Gaines stood up to leave. He had spent enough time here and had another plan now. It was sometimes necessary to sup with the devil.

★　★　★

It was after they'd parted company that Inskip, left more or less to his own devices, saw this as a chance to follow through a train of thought started by those few minutes with Bridget Devenish.

The young woman Jon Devenish called Nolly wasn't the sort you forgot easily, and when she'd served him coffee in the offices of the *Voice* it hadn't taken him long to remember where he'd seen her before, but he hadn't thought any more about it until now. Bridget Devenish, in that brief encounter, hadn't given much away but Miss Brent-Paxton might be easier.

He hadn't expected to find her alone, and had been thinking up excuses as to how this might be accomplished, but Jon Devenish was in fact not there when he reached the *Britannia* offices. This seemed like a hopeful sign.

'I've been remembering where we met before, Miss,' were his opening words.

She lost colour but didn't pretend not to understand. 'Yes, well. I hope you're not going to tell Jon – Mr Devenish. He knows what I do, but only that I help behind the scenes, a sort of dogsbody. He knows I'm not one of the brave ones.'

Wasn't it brave to have been prepared to throw a brick through the windows of Leman Street police station at the time he was still working there? Foolhardy, more like. Misguided from the first. She'd been one of three women brought up before the magistrates for the misdemeanour, but since they'd been intercepted before she'd had a chance to throw hers – though not before she'd had the presence of mind to drop it – she'd been let off with a caution, while the other two had each received a six-week prison sentence.

'I've never done anything like that before or since.'

He was inclined to believe her but that wasn't going to let her off the hook, so he merely got on with what he'd come here for. 'I'm interested in anything you can tell me about the demonstration in Hyde Park on the day Mrs Challoner was killed.'

If anything, she went a little paler. 'I don't know anything about that . . . and Jon's due back at three, so . . .'

It had only been a guess that she would know – there were dozens if not more of these women's groups all over London, after all, and who knew which one had planned that particular demonstration? 'Does the name Rina Collingwood mean anything to you?'

He saw it did, the way her eyes flickered, but her chin went up. She might consider herself only a dosgbody but she had the same stubbornness as the rest. They didn't give in easily, these women. 'Look, we know—' know was stretching the truth but he went on '—we know she was involved in that disturbance in Hyde Park the day Mrs Challoner was killed. Were you there?'

After a moment, she said, 'It was only a little demonstration.'

'Not so little that it didn't confuse the scene and stop the killer being apprehended.'

She said, glancing nervously at the clock, 'Jon will be back any time.' But it was nowhere near three o'clock yet. The unreliable timepiece was at least forty-five minutes fast.

'Then perhaps you'd better tell me where I can find Rina Collingwood before he gets here.'

She gazed directly at him. Those eyes – you couldn't blame Jon Devenish. 'I thought you punished blackmailers. I didn't think you did blackmail yourself, but it's no good. I don't know, I really don't know anything about her private life. No one seems to, and nobody's seen her for weeks.'

This time, he believed her, but he gave it one last try. 'Have you any knowledge of any dealings she might have had with Mr Lukin – your boss?'

'Certainly not!' But she frowned and looked puzzled. It didn't seem as if Devenish had told her much, if anything, about that raid on the upstairs room.

'I need Lukin's address.'

The way she coloured up he saw there was no love lost there. 'I believe he lodges with a family somewhere just around the corner,' she said with a shrug.

'But I won't find him there, will I?'

Her glance sharpened. 'Sometimes he sleeps upstairs. I think – I think he might have slept there last night.'

'Yes,' murmured Paul Estrabon. 'Your assumptions are correct, Inspector. Lydia did indeed bring the icon to me, to sell for her.'

He and Gaines were sitting in the smoking room of Estrabon's club. Glasses of brandy on the table, coffee, and a fat cigar between Estrabon's elegant fingers breathing rich smoke. Leather chairs, masculine, deeply comfortable.

Estrabon swirled the brandy round in his glass and sipped, but Gaines' brandy remained untouched, save for the first small sip. He hadn't yet had his own lunch and drinking on an empty stomach was never a good idea. Plus a conviction he had that you needed to keep a clear head when dealing with Paul Estrabon. He stayed with the coffee.

'So it's true what Lukin said, that she changed her mind and didn't send it to him after all. He must have been furious.'

'Possibly, but not because he didn't receive it.' Estrabon stretched out his long legs and smiled. 'I packed it up myself and had it sent around by special messenger.'

In the far corner two men, expansive after lunch, uproariously shared a joke, a momentary aberration quickly silenced by the overall hallowed hush of the room and the presence of several post-prandial sleepers.

'Did you know Lukin claims to have been her brother?'

'Lydia always believed what she wanted to believe.' He shrugged. 'But who knows?'

Not at ease in these gentleman's club surroundings, and certainly not with a man he didn't trust, Gaines didn't want to go into that. The sooner this was over, the better. 'So why should Lukin lie about not receiving the icon?'

'Because I suspect he never has received it.' A small smile played around the edges of his mouth. He flicked ash from his cigar and inhaled deeply on it. 'Or not the one he was expecting . . . you don't look too surprised.'

Gaines, thinking fast, found he wasn't, or not too much. 'I've always asked myself why Lydia Challoner was willing to give away something that meant so much to her. The one in her bedroom isn't the copy, is it? It's the original.'

'I should be extremely surprised if it was not. I myself had it copied for her by someone who knew the correct way to age it and so on, but it wouldn't deceive anyone who knows – and there are many who do. There's a market out there, not only Orthodox believers, but those who collect examples of traditional art and culture, and are willing to pay for it.'

Gaines thought about it while he finished his coffee.

'Your wife has a sister, Rina Collingwood,' he said suddenly at last, and had the satisfaction of seeing the smiling mask slip, the face harden. 'Is there any chance you might know where I can find her?'

'Hardly. The less I know about my sister-in-law and her activities, the better.' He didn't ask why the police should want to know – for the obvious reason that he knew of her suffragette activities, Gaines assumed. He wondered whether to stir the pot by mentioning Fanny and the letter but there was no point to it now. He stood up.

'One last word, Mr Estrabon.' One parting shot. 'Did you kill Lydia Challoner?'

'No.'

'Did you arrange to have her killed?'

'No!' The raw syllable matched the raw pain on his face. And Gaines saw that for all his faults it seemed entirely possible that he had loved Lydia Challoner. But within a few seconds, the mask had been assumed again. 'Is there anything else I can get you before you go, Inspector?'

'No thank you, Mr Estrabon. I think I know where we are going with this now.'

Twenty-Six

From the street they saw the office and Jon Devenish's living room were in darkness, but a light was burning in that upstairs room. Gaines led the way quietly up the stairs. He held his hand on the knob, turning it silently, and pushed. The door gave inwards and Gaines found himself looking down the barrel of a gun. There was complete silence while he and Lukin stared eye to eye.

'Put the gun down, Lukin,' Gaines said. 'We're only here to question you. Put it down.'

And he did. At least he lowered his hand, though he left the gun dangling from it. A Mauser 'broomhandle'. The two policemen moved forward and Lukin's hand tightened its grip as he backed away and threw himself on to a chair. They stood facing him across the heavy table which still bore the remnants of a meal. 'I did not believe British police burst into a room when they only have questions. Why don't you sit down?'

'Depends what the questions are, Lukin,' said Inskip. They remained standing.

He was in shirtsleeves and braces, unshaven and his hair in mad disarray. A rumpled, grey blanket had been thrown on to the bare mattress, another served as a pillow as if he'd been sprawled on it minutes before, but it hadn't prevented a lightning reaction to reach for his gun and a swift move to the door. 'Sleeping rough?' Inskip asked, his eye on the weapon.

'For now. I am leaving London, leaving England. The *Voice* is closing.'

He spoke carefully, enunciating each word; his eyes glittered – though if the bottle standing on the floor beside the bed was the first he'd broached, he hadn't drunk much.

'What have you done with the icon?' Gaines asked.

'The icon I did not receive?' He laughed.

'No, the copy that was sent to you – a facsimile of the real thing, but not worthless, by any means.'

Lukin's expression underwent a change. He must have known it was useless to protest but his face became ugly with a sudden rage. 'It was a fake!' He added something in Russian that sounded like a curse. 'That icon – the genuine one – was an heirloom of my family. It belonged to me by rights.' It was an echo of Lydia's words, but she had not, in the end, entrusted it to him. 'It was the only thing I was ever likely to have from my family, to treasure until I die.'

'Oh dear me, no. Fine words, Lukin, but you wanted it to sell, to send funds to Russia.' Gaines shifted, and the pistol was raised a fraction. 'Fine words, from someone so concerned about his family heirloom. Why did you kill Lydia Challoner? She was your sister.'

His face was expressionless, his eyes, those curious light eyes, were empty. 'What is a sister? Someone you have grown up with, shared a mother and father with, not a stranger who had lived a pampered life in a foreign land, never known want.' He was wrong there, thought Gaines. Lydia's early years with her father could scarcely have been a picnic. 'She was nothing to me. Nothing. I was too late to kill my father, God rot his soul – he left my mother to die of starvation, in poverty and misery such as you cannot begin to imagine here in your safe little world – and he should have paid for it—'

'So Lydia paid the price instead.'

'If she had not tried to cheat me she would still be alive.'

Inskip drew in a breath and Gaines ventured a warning glance at him. Tread softly. Lukin was not releasing his grip on the gun. 'It was risky, shooting her in a public place like that,' he said carefully. 'You were lucky those women chose to demonstrate at that particular time and divert attention from you.'

His head came up at the suggestion that luck, rather than his own cunning had anything to do with it. 'I *chose* that time. I chose it because it was ideal – those women causing a disturbance just when Lydia would be riding there with that – that young puppy who followed her around.'

'And how did you know what those women planned?'

He laughed, without humour. 'There is not much that goes on in that office downstairs – with either of them – that I do not know about. The walls and floors are thin. And that one – the office girl – is not so discreet when she is having conversations, even when I am there. It was not difficult to put two and two together.'

Such a statement would be impossible to prove – and perhaps it was even true. The cracks in the floorboards up here were big enough to drive a horse and cart through.

Afterwards, Inskip blamed himself for what happened, but it was all done so quickly there was in fact no chance to stop it. He had merely shifted his feet but without warning, Lukin had stood up, grasping the edges of the heavy table and tipping it forward so that it fell full against both men and sent them staggering amidst dirty plates and glasses. They saw his arm raised, there was the crack of a pistol shot, the smell of cordite filling the room, blood flying. And Lukin's body slumped to the ground, dead.

After that, it was all over quickly. Within ten minutes of the removal of the body, the copy icon was found under the straw mattress, along with another pistol and ammunition. He had been an expert marksman who, according to a later statement by the woman in whose house he had lodged, practised by shooting rats in her back yard. Forensic examination proved that the bullet which had killed Lydia had come from the same pistol he had used to kill himself. Gaines hadn't expected that. But it turned out he had a history of violence and was wanted by the Russian secret police. Expecting nothing less of the British police than to act in the same way as the Ochrana did, he would think himself better off dead, Inskip said, and probably was. Several years ago, he had escaped from them and lain low, and since then lived on the Continent, where he was supposed to have met his benefactor. There was every possibility that this Maxim Dimitrov was a fiction, but if so, how Lukin had obtained funds to finance the paper would remain a mystery, though not why: he had used the *Voice* to recruit Jon Devenish, and through him get to know Lydia.

'Why did Devenish lie about Lukin being with him that Sunday?' Gaines asked. 'Because he was careful of his position as editor, I suppose.'

'No,' said Inskip. 'It was that office clock, about as useful as a bent screwdriver. It gains ten minutes a day, minimum, and Devenish never so much as notices. If it was as fast as when I saw it last, Lukin could have left him an hour before he said.'

Epilogue

London still wilted in the heat – would it hold out for the coronation? – but before that came a special coronation procession staged by the suffragettes. About forty thousand women were expected to take part. Special excursion trains had been put on to bring people to the capital for the event and Ursula had managed to get seats on the stands that were already in place for the coronation.

The secret was out about the white dress with the green and purple sash. Bridget had realised that was probably the one day when she wouldn't be able to find any excuse to slip away unnoticed, but she was determined to have what she called a last fling. 'But don't worry, the whole point of the demonstration,' she assured her mother, 'is that it's to be entirely peaceful, to show people we're not the harridans they think we are. Just women with a serious and justifiable cause.'

The march, held in the evening, was a huge success. A river of colour four miles long, winding from Trafalgar Square via Pall Mall and Piccadilly to Kensington, to climax in a rally at the Albert Hall, where those lucky enough to get tickets were to hear Mrs Pankhurst's triumphal speech. Splendid embroidered banners were carried high; there were floats with tableaux, national costumes, choirs from Wales, pipes from Scotland, harps from Ireland and seven hundred women, dressed plainly and totally in white, who had suffered imprisonment for their beliefs. No doubt somewhere among these last was Rina Collingwood with her proud coronet of black hair, no longer of interest to the police – at present.

Ursula was sitting with friends but Kitty had shocked her aunt by deciding to walk alongside Bridget and Jon's friend, Nolly – and several other unlikely women Kitty recognised, whom she would never have dreamt could be supporters of women's rights. Jon himself marched behind, a banner-carrier in the band of men keen to show they supported the women's movement. He might have lost his job, but not his principles. By the time they set off, Kitty half-expected to see Miss Drax, encouraged by finding independence: she had sent the book to the publishers, they had liked it and were to meet the hitherto anonymous Marie Bartholemew next week.

The procession moved along decorously with good-humoured well-wishers lining the route. There were relatively few jeers and catcalls among the cheers and none of the expected disturbances. Those who were against them had shown their disapproval by their absence. By half past eight it was all over, with the crowds streaming towards the tube and the day trippers making their way back to the various stations where the excursion trains would take them home, the trams and omnibuses lurching along, their passengers packed like sardines. Nowhere was a taxi-cab to be found.

Marcus was waiting for Kitty as the marchers dispersed. He had declined to be among the marching men, not giving his reasons. He was not easily persuadable, even for a righteous cause. He took her arm and kept it pressed to his side as they walked, her hand tightly in his lest they should get separated as they made their way through the thinning crowds. 'Your father wasn't with your aunt, then?'

'He's at home with his stamp collection.'

Louis was still wrapped up in himself. He hadn't yet found a way to fill the gap left in his life, but Kitty was convinced there was more on his mind than Lydia's murder, and that it concerned Paul Estrabon. Challoner and Estrabon had ceased to exist, as such. Louis's sudden retirement hadn't been explained to her, but she wasn't sure she wanted to know the reason. Whatever had happened was now in the past, where it should remain. Lydia had not been able to forget the past – and look where it had led. 'He's talking of going to Australia, my father,' she told Marcus now, 'to work with my uncle, Barnabus.' The thought of Louis working on a sheep farm struck them simultaneously as utterly absurd, and they were still laughing when, neither caring nor noticing which way they had been going, they found they had walked as far as the Embankment.

After the crowds, the cheering and the music which had surrounded them for the last few hours, it was quiet and peaceful here where the noises of London, the city that was never silent or asleep, were distant. In the gathering dusk, the lamps gave off a hazy, lemony glow. They paused and Marcus propped himself against a lamp-post pillar and watched Kitty leaning on the balustrade, looking at the pinpricks of light showing on the opposite bank and in the still-moving river traffic.

'Do you dream, Marcus?' she asked suddenly.

She looked so young, vulnerable, yet oddly mature in an expensively simple, high-necked blouse under a chic jacket, her hair under her fashionable hat elaborately arranged by Emma Pavell this morning. 'Yes, I do,' he said gently.

'I've been having such dreams lately, like the ones I told you about – the wolf, and the unicorn, and, and . . . I wish—' She stopped. 'No, wishes are liars. They hold out too much hope. That's what Mama always said.'

'Then I hope she was wrong. I think she was. We sometimes wish for too much – but not always.' He slid a box from his pocket, small and square, and gave it to her.

It winked on its black velvet, a tiny, golden feather, a brooch so finely wrought its fronds seemed to move in the lamplight. Lydia's ghost walked with them all, and Kitty felt her presence now as she looked up and saw the tension in his dark-browed face turned towards her. And then, unexpectedly, he smiled.

No, she didn't think Marcus was wishing for too much.